CHARLES BROCKDEN BROWN (1771-1810) was born to a Quaker merchant family in Philadelphia. As a teenager he studied to become a lawyer, but developed literary ambitions after joining a group of New York-based writers and intellectuals. Brown and his friends engaged with the progressive British politics of the time and as Brown's writing activity increased, influence from across the Atlantic became reciprocal; Mary Shelley was said to have been influenced by his work while writing her masterpiece *Frankenstein*.

Brown is often claimed as the father of the American novel as well as the progenitor of a distinctly American style of Gothic fiction, as revealed in his four primary novels *Wieland, Ormond, Edgar Huntly,* and *Arthur Mervyn.* After writing his last novel in 1801, Brown continued to publish essays, political pamphlets and magazine articles on a range of reformist subjects (women's rights, salvery and abolitionism) and edited his own literary journal before dying of tuberculosis at the age of 39.

CHARLES BROCKDEN BROWN.

C. B. Brown

Memoirs of Stephen Calvert

A Novel

CHARLES BROCKDEN BROWN

Edited by Charles Harrigan

DARLE PRESS

Published by
DARLEY PRESS,
Delaware, USA

Originally published in serialized form 1799-1800

First Darley Press Edition ©2021
ISBN 978-1-955741-05-7
Cat # DP002

A NOTE ON THE TEXT:
The copytext has been brought into conformity
with modern standards of punctuation,
capitalization and spelling, except in the author's
forbearance of quotation marks around the
narrator's speech, which has been retained.

Cover Art:
Portrait of the Artist, 1800 by John Vanderlyn
The Metropolitan Museum of Art, NY

Book design and formatting by Edgar's Ghost
Printed in The United States of America

WWW.DARLEYPRESS.COM

MEMOIRS OF STEPHEN CALVERT

Yes, my friend, I admit the justice of your claim. There is but one mode of appeasing your wonder at my present condition, and that is, the relation of the events of my life. This will amply justify my choice of an abode in these mountainous and unvisited recesses, and explain, why I thus anxiously shut out from my retreat the footsteps and society of men.

My present scene is without perils or vicissitudes. I cultivate my field of maize, I ramble on the bank of the lake,* I fish in a canoe made by my own hands, I eat the product of my own labour, I hewed the logs of which my dwelling is built, I conform all my measures to a certain standard of simplicity and order, and am rewarded by the uninterrupted enjoyment of health and tranquility. I make no use of my rifle but to exterminate panthers and wolves. What my own hands do not supply me, I purchase from Canadian traders, and my poverty secures me, for the most part, from the visits of the Red-men.

For this solitude and labour, I was induced to change my habits of corruption and idleness, by a just estimate of benefits and evils. I tried the world,

---

* Michigan

and found it too abundant in temptation and calamity for me safely to remain in it. Some men, gifted with extraordinary endowments, or fortified by an auspicious education, may preserve their integrity in every scene, but, as to me, experience has taught me that I can be safe only by withdrawing from temptation, and can escape from guilt and remorse, only by interposing deserts between me and the haunts of mankind.

It was a taste not wholly incongenial with mine that led your steps hither. You are delighted with the aspect of rude nature. You reflect on the destiny for which this extensive wilderness is reserved. Scarcely half a century will elapse, before this desolation will give place to farms and villages, and commerce will be busy on the banks of the Ohio, and in the islands of this lake. You are willing to contemplate one stage in this memorable progress, and to view this region, covered as it now is, with marshes and woods. To these views I am indebted for this visit, and wish you would prolong it sufficiently to discover all the advantages of my condition.

Cast your eye over this wide expanse. That waving and bluish line which almost blends itself with air, is a chain of rocky summits, ninety miles distant from the spot where we stand. They range along the opposite shore of the lake. Your eyes, unaccustomed to the scrutiny of distant objects, are, perhaps, unable to discover a darker spot which breaks the uniformity of this line. That is a lofty isle, about half way across, which contains six hundred acres of fertile ground. The banks are steep, and only accessible at one spot. This entrance was detected by me, by a rare fortune, and would probably escape the notice of any other. Here, if you please, you may take up your abode, and be in no danger of molestation or intrusion. Exuberant verdure, spouting rivulets, hickory and poplar shades, commodiously and sparingly distributed, preclude the necessity of any laborious preparation. No animal larger than squirrels and rabbits, can be found in it. There will, therefore, be no foes, either of human or beastial kind, with which you will be under the necessity of waging war. I will enable you to go thither, and assist you in making a plantation, and erecting a house.

But this scheme, desirable as it is, more experience of the evils of society may be necessary to induce you to adopt. Return, therefore, to the world, and, when tired of its monotony, and disgusted with its iniquities, remember the recluse of Michigan, and take refuge on this peaceful shore. Perhaps, this is a choice which can be recommended only by calamities similar to those which I have endured. There would be cruelty in wishing you a fate like mine, and yet, if your course should terminate in the same manner, and misfortune should instruct you in the benefits of this seclusion, this wish might, perhaps, be reconciled to benevolence.

There is, indeed, little danger that the story of any other human being will resemble mine. My fate is marked by uncommon hues: neither imagination nor memory can supply you with a parallel. Of this, however, you will be more qualified to judge after my tale has been told, I have brought you hither for the purpose of relating it: now, therefore, lend me a patient ear.

My ancestry were English. If I had not long since dismissed the folly of annexing dignity to birth, I might lay claim to some respect on this account, since I can number, in the founders of my line, some of those who aided the achievements of Rollo in France, and Bohemond in Syria. A younger branch of my family owes the dignity of baronet to the profusion of James the First, and the English usurpations in Ireland. He, that first acquired the dignity, was Stephen Porter. This man, like the rest of the gentlemen of that age, conceived that all merit was comprised in the profession of arms. He early enlisted in the Palatine wars, and relinquished the service of Gustavus, only to take part in the contest between Charles the first and his parliament.

When this contest was terminated, he retired to an ample patrimony which he possessed in Lancashire. Here, a life which had so often been exposed to pikes and bullets was destroyed by a stag, whose despair prompted him to turn upon his hunters. His estate passed to his son, whose character was, in many respects, the reverse of that of his parent. He was indolent, vindictive, irascible, and carried the pride of birth to a ridiculous excess.

In his marriage choice he was governed by no considerations but those of family and property. His wife, however, chanced to possess many excellent qualities. These did not secure to her the affections of her husband. Some slight opposition to his will changed his indifference to hatred, and compelled her to live apart from him. No time, and no concessions on her part, could abate his animosity. He vowed never to admit her to his presence, and when a friend, by means unsuspected by him, had brought about an interview, he not only spurned her from him as she kneeled at his feet, but challenged the officious agent, who expiated the offence by his death.

His separation from his wife was preceded by the birth of two sons. These were torn from the arms of their mother, and consigned to the care of hirelings. No solicitations could obtain from him permission that the mother should be indulged, even for a moment, with the sight of her offspring. This inflexible severity soon put a period to the life of this unfortunate lady.

The sons were educated at a foreign seminary, in the religious faith of their father, which was that of Rome. One of them was the heir of the estate, and the other was intended, by the father, for the military service of Austria or Spain. In proportion as the younger advanced in age, and exercised his judgment, he found reason to disapprove of these parental schemes. He had been exposed, while in Flanders, to the arguments of a Protestant divine, who had nearly won over his belief. His return to England interposed to prevent or suspend his renunciation of his ancient faith, but his attachment to his country, and his love of the peaceful occupations of learning, made him irreconcilably averse to military service among foreigners. He knew, however, his father's inflexibility, his lofty notions of prerogative, and his impatience of contradiction. These reflections were a source of considerable inquietude.

The brothers arrived in London. The elder was a thoughtless and generous youth, who was willing that his conduct and opinions should be moulded by convenience. He, therefore, readily complied with the will of his father, who had taken care, in his absence, to select for him a bride, and who had called him home for the purpose of fulfilling the contract. The younger, whose name was Stephen, was fraught with different sentiments and principles. He felt insuperable reluctance to pursue the path which was chalked out for him, while his obedience was enjoined by the most powerful considerations. With regard to property he was wholly dependant on his father, and his education had unfitted him for any servile or lucrative occupation. He was summoned, at the same time with his brother, to the paternal residence in Lancashire. He would willingly have dispensed with the interview, the purpose of which he knew to be the final settlement of plans for his future life, but this was not possible. He prepared himself, therefore, for his journey, but eagerly sought and profited by any excuse that tended to delay.

At Chester he permitted a trifling impediment to detain him for some weeks. At the end of this time, an accident enabled him to perform a friendly office for a family who resided in the environs. The master of it, who was an exile from France, had been pursued by the vengeance of an hereditary enemy to his retreat. Assassins had been hired to destroy him, and, being apprised of his motions, they had posted themselves so as to encounter him on his return from the city to his own habitation. The timely interference of my father (for it is to this man that I am indebted for my being) rescued him from the power of the ruffians, and conducted him to his family, but not until he had received wounds which shortly put a period to his life. This incident gave birth to intercourse and friendship between my father and the wife and daughter of the deceased. On making suitable inquiries as to their name and condition, he discovered the following particulars.

The Calverts were a noble family of Provence. Their domain consisted of obscure and elevated valleys, embosomed among those Alps which border upon Italy. They early became converts to the reformation, and the head of their family was renowned among the defenders of Rochelle. Persecution and war had nearly extirpated their race, and the only survivors were brothers of the name of Felix and Gaspard. These, on the revocation of the edict of Nantz, were driven into exile. The eldest retired first into Flanders, and, twenty years afterwards, emigrated to America. He purchased and cultivated ground on the bank of Delaware, just below its conflux with Schuylkill, where his antique and humble dwelling is still to be discovered.

The younger, who possessed some property, in consequence of marriage, passed into England, and took up his abode in the neighbourhood of Chester. Here he led an obscure and indigent life till the institution of French regiments, under king William. He then obtained a command in the army, and signalised himself in Flanders, Thence he went to Ireland, and died of his wounds received at the siege of Limerick.

His daughter accompanied her father in all his perils. On his death she accepted the protection of a young officer of her own country. Wedlock succeeded, and they returned to her ancient abode, near Chester. Their union was productive of one child, to whose improvement and felicity their cares were limited.

This was he whose life was now sacrificed to private revenge, and, by whose death, his wife and daughter were deprived of their protector. My father easily invented excuses for postponing his departure from this city, and for devoting most of his hours to the society of his new friends. The lady was a woman endowed with peculiar advantages of education, a zealous adherent to her faith, and eager to impart its benefits to others. My father's belief had already been undermined, and the exhortations of this eloquent apostle accomplished its destruction. Perhaps his facility of conviction might be partly-owing to the charms of the young lady, of whom he speedily became enamoured, and of whose favour he could entertain no hope as long as he adhered to what she deemed an idolatrous and detestable religion.

His condition was now changed, and his embarrassments greatly multiplied. A change of religion, the marriage of an outcast indigent, of obscure birth, and an heretic, were, in the eyes of his father, the deepest crimes that it was possible for him to commit. He would punish it by inexorable wrath, by rejecting all claims to pecuniary assistance, and, perhaps, by the infliction of some greater evil. Sir Stephen was powerful and subtle, and would not scruple any means of vengeance om an occasion like this. If the son flattered himself that his personal safety would be unaffected, he could not hope but that the helpless objects of his passion would incur the bitterest persecution. Means, at least, would be employed to raise an insuperable bar between them. His imagination contemplated no greater evil than this, and, in order to prevent it, he secretly embraced the protestant religion, and prevailed upon the lady to consent to a private marriage. For the present, this marriage was solicitously concealed. He trusted that some propitious event would occur, putting an end to the necessity of secrecy. For the present, a separation took place, and my father arrived, at length, at Sir Stephen's residence.

The intercourse between them proceeded for some time without any occurrence to ruffle its tranquility. By judicious forbearance and a circumspect demeanour, Sir Stephen was prevented from imbibing any suspicion of the genuine condition and creed of his son. The future was occasionally mentioned, and the plan of foreign service alluded to, as something about which no hesitation or question could arise. No measures to effect this plan were immediately suggested. A delay which Sir Stephen hinted to arise from a project of a more momentous and general nature, which had lately started into birth, and, in which, the efforts of Stephen would be wanted.

Stephen had a perfect reliance on the justice and fidelity of his brother, and therefore, with regard to him, made no secret either of his change of religion or his marriage. Both of these were heartily disapproved by Henry, but one could not be recalled and the other was irreparable by any strength which he could apply to the task, he exerted himself to make the evil flowing from them as light as possible. He laboured to penetrate into the designs of his father, and insensibly to sway his thoughts conformably to the wishes of Stephen.

In no long time, proposals were formally made to Sir Stephen, for marriage between his second son and a daughter of the earl of Lucan, who had been king James's general in Ireland, and who had attained great wealth and honours in Spain. No alliance could more flatter the pride, bigotry, and avarice of this man. It coincided with his fondest schemes of military promotion, and as the young lady was maid of honour to the Spanish queen, the road would thus be opened to the most illustrious elevation.

Stephen was seasonably apprized, by his brother, of these proposals. He had reason to regard himself as remarkably unfortunate. Every new event seemed to conspire against him. He watched it in anxious expectation of a summons to his father's presence, in which, this inauspicious union would be proposed to him.

This summons, however, was delayed. Week after week passed, and no intimation was received. It seemed impossible that an offer like this should be rejected, or that the indecorum of a slow or difficult acceptance would be practised, it was not less incredible that sir Stephen should not hasten to impart the tidings of his good fortune to his son. The brothers, at length, began to doubt the truth of this intelligence, but a new and closer inquiry removed their doubts. Some interviews had taken place between Stephen and the lady, during some months' residence of the former at Madrid. At that time nothing existed to render this union undesirable, and the lady had been pursued by Stephen, with a juvenile and incautious enthusiasm. Now, however, these crude feelings were supplanted by a rational attachment, and conscience, as well as love, regarded this alliance with horror.

In the midst of this perplexity, a message was delivered to my father, commanding him into sir Stephen's presence. The purpose of this interview was easily divined. Obedience, however, was inevitable, and the interview took place. It was accompanied by much appearance of mystery. Solitude and a solemn hour was selected. Avenues were shut, and care taken that no listener should be posted near. These precautions being employed, sir Stephen began, by communicating to his son the proposals which had been offered and accepted on his behalf. He reminded my father of his former devotion to the lady, noticed the purity of her religion, the illustriousness of her rank, the high station which she occupied at the court of Spain, and inferred that Providence could not have ordained an event more auspicious than this. He easily anticipated the desires of his son, and experienced all the sympathy of a parent in his happiness, but he appealed to my father whether this were not a blessing which, in reality, outstripped his merits. He was young, and had hitherto made no sacrifice to duty, or exerted his talents in any cause of national utility. Though much might be expected from his birth and education, yet, perhaps, it would be unreasonable to expect his consent to postpone this union on any consideration thatc ould be proposed. Perhaps, indeed, in labouring to avoid the favourable prepossessions of a parent, he had passed into the opposite extreme, and underrated the zeal of his son in the cause of his country and of God. He should rejoice to discover that this was the case, and would therefore propose to him a scheme, for the sake of which he might postpone his marriage, because the disinterestedness of this conduct would enhance his title to the happiness that awaited him.

He then proceeded to unfold a plan of insurrection in favour of Charles Stewart, which had long been meditated by the English Catholics, and which the present was believed to be a suitable opportunity for carrying into effect. Caution bwas the soul of this enterprise, and men of long experience, deep views and unconquerable perseverance, had been selected for this purpose. The concealment of all preliminary measures was indispensableto its success, but sir Stephen so little suspected the change that had taken place in the opinion of his son, that he deemed it superfluous to enjoin secrecy.

Such is the imperfection of every scheme founded on imposture. Sir Stephen's character was well known. His devotion to the persecuted family and faith of the Stewarts, his wariness and penetration had raised him to the station of leader in this plot, yet, such is the deceitfulness of appearances, that this man, unknowing to himself, was now disclosing a scheme of rebellion and massacre to one whose principles compelled him to abhor the project, and who would probably conceive it his duty tocounteract it by all his efforts.

He did not enter, in this first interview, into a minute detail of particulars. He mentioned no names, and vaguely alluded to the means which had been suggested. Enough, however, was unfolded to show the horror and extent of this treason. All lenient and dubious measures were rejected. The long triumph of heresy and usurpation required a rigorous and unrelenting hand. The sanctity and greatness of the cause would be disgraced by narrow schemes and effeminate scruples. The spirit of Charles the ninth, and of Guy Faux were applauded asmodels of true heroism, and success was to be rendered certain by a blow, which should exterminate, at a moment, every adversary. The king, his ministers, and three hundred of those whose opulence, and talents, and birth, rendered them obnoxious, was to perish in the hour in which an invading army was to land in Scotland.

The agents of this destruction were to be sublimed above all selfish considerations. They were to devote their lives to this cause, and the same poniard which dispatched the victim, each assassin was immediately to turn against his own breast. Stephen was even allowed to suspect that the part most illustrious and arduous in this drama was reserved for him, and that his claim to execute vengeance on the reigning prince would be readily admitted.

The interview ended with an admonition to deliberate on this proposal with calmness. The preference of public to private good, the magnanimity of sacrificing love and life to the altar of the true God, and in the service of the rightful prince, were artfully insisted upon, but, if this effort were too great, he might fill an inferior part, and perform essential services without relinquishing these blessings. The possession of his mistress would merely be postponed, and his personal safety be, in a slight degree, endangered. He would assign no period to the deliberation of his son, but wait patiently till Stephen, having formed his determinations, should himself demand an interview.

The sensations with which my father parted from this conference may be more easily conceived than described. Concurrence in either of these schemes was impossible, yet what would be the consequence of refusing to concur? The real impediments must be disclosed, for no others will be deemed sufficient. What shall screen him from the rage of his imperious father? He will not be permitted to retire from the interview, in which his real situation shall be disclosed, with life. Sir Stephen acknowledged no bounds to paternal prerogatives. The life which he gave, he believed to be forfeited by disobedience, and conceived himself authorised to take it away. But now, in addition to the crimes of disobedience and apostacy, the secret of this plot resided with him, and, to prevent a discovery, his death would be inevitably exacted.

For a time my father was absorbed in fears for his own safety, but, at length, his thoughts were turned to the nature of that conspiracy which had thus been proved to exist. Was his duty limited to mere forbearance? Should he stand an idle spectator, while his religion and his country were destroyed? Was he not bound to communicate his knowledge of this plot, and exert himself in its suppression?

As his father's honour and life were involved in this disclosure, no wonder that this suggestion was a plenteous source of anxiety. He fled into solitude to avoid all witnesses to his perturbation. His purposes perpetually fluctuated. When he thought upon the extent of that ruin which was threatened, he felt himself disposed to prevent it, even by the ignominious execution of his father: but when he recollected his imperfect knowledge of the scheme, and its connection with invasion, which a thousand accidents might frustrate, he was again restored to irresolution and reluctance.

Meanwhile, some decision daily became more urgent. Some delay to concur in his scheme would be forgiven, and was expectedby his father, but to protract his silence would excite suspicion. He felt irreconcilable repugnance to an interviewin which his true condition should be disclosed, and yet was at a loss by what other means to account for his aversion to the plot.

At length it occurred to him, that he might withdraw himself beyond the knowledge and the vengeance of his father. He might decline a second interview, and immure himself in some remote and inaccessible corner, and live with his wife and mother, beyond the circle of sir Stephen's operations and researches. His father might not only be kept in ignorance of his place of abode, his marriage, and his change of religion, but might be taught to believe that he was dead.

This scheme was highly advantageous , but the obstacles to its execution were not few. No part of the British Islands would be sufficiently secure. In Holland, he would be easily detected. Difficulty of subsistence would attend him everywhere. Some provision must be made for his immediate support in a foreign country. The means of secret and unsuspected flight were neither obvious nor easy. My mother was pregnant, and the usual period had nearly elapsed. Until her delivery should have taken place, her removal was nearly impossible.

His visits to his family, who still occupied their ancient abode, had hitherto been frequent, but clandestine. Now thedisturbance of his mind made him visit them more rarely. He had too much regard for the health of his wife to unfold to her the dangers of his situation, and to exclude from his countenance every token of the anguish of his mind, was an undertaking that surpassed his strength.

To forbear his visits entirely was, for similar reasons, improper. At one of these interviews the name of one who dwelt in their neighbourhood was introduced into conversation. It appeared that he was one of those known by the appellation of Quakers, that his religious scruples had subjected him to numerous vexations, from a continuance of which he was now preparing to escape, by emigration to the English colonies in America.

This incident suggested a train of ideas to my father, which terminated in a resolution to follow his example. Pennsylvania was remote, unvisited: subsistence was easily procured: and hither it was less likely he should be pursued by paternal vengeance than to any other asylum. He might easily embark in London , and as he was personally known to few in that city, the interval previous to embarkation might be passed there with more security than elsewhere.

His marriage was an event known only to the parties themselves, his mother-in-law, and the clergyman who performed the ceremony, and who was now a chaplain to the regiment in garrison at Gibraltar. My mother was contented to endure the loss of reputation, because the seclusion in which she lived exposed her to few of the inconveniences that flow from it. Her personal condition could not escape the notice of all, and was a source of some obloquy, but this she even preferred to the publication of the truth. The knowledge of my father's visits would never have generated a suspicion that he was herhusband. The world would merely have inferred the existence of an illicit connection, but even this inference was precluded by the secrecy which all parties observed.

In due time this lady became the mother of twins. A feeble constitution hindered her from nursing both her children. One of them, therefore, was entrusted to the charge of a French woman, whose mother had been the companion of the flight of the deceased madame de Calvert from Provence, and who had lately married an honest and thrifty farmer in the neighbouring district, by name Thurston.

This woman had been eminent for her affection and fidelity to the Calverts, but it had not been deemed prudent by my mother to entrust her with the secret of the marriage. She was willing to sink in the good opinion of her servant, rather than to incur the least hazard of being betrayed. Alice cheerfully assumed the province assigned her, and divided with the stranger the tenderness due to her own child.

This obstacle being now removed, my father began to think seriously of the execution of his project. A second interview with sir Stephen had not yet taken place. This delay was owing to a severe indisposition by which the former had been seized. No more fortunate or seasonable occurrence could have happened, but the respite which it afforded was short. His recovery was speedily effected, and certain tokens had appeared, which showed that the procrastinations of my father had excited some suspicion. The necessity of removal became hourly more urgent, but the want of money rendered it impossible.

Since his return to his father's house, the annual pittance formerly allowed to him had been withdrawn. Sir Stephen was far from being of a covetous temper, and his fortune was ample, but the scheme on which he had embarked his personal safety absorbed likewise all his revenue, and he whom the world considered as incessantly hoarding his income, and daily becoming more rich, distributed his wealth with so lavish an hand, as sometimes to reduce himself to absolute though temporary need.

In this strait my father bethought himself of relying on the friendship of his brother. He did not think proper to disclose to him the whole truth, but stated, as reasons for changing his abode, the impossibility of otherwise concealing his condition from sir Stephen, and the indignation with which he should probably be overwhelmed when the truth should come to beknown.

These motives were deemed insufficient by Henry, but finding my father proof against all his remonstrances, he readily consented to aid him in the execution of his scheme. Henry had been enriched, and thus rendered independent of his father, by his marriage. He offered to divide his possessions with his brother, but Stephen was satisfied with a small sum at present, and with an annual remittance, until he should be able to provide for his own subsistence.

Philip Thurston had conceived the design of improving his fortune by emigration to America. His little property, however, could not be disposed of time enough for him to accompany my father. My mother's health disabled her from affording nour-ishment to more than one child. A substitute might, perhaps, have been found for Alice, but this woman had contracted a mother's fondness for the babe which she nursed, and her fidelity was liable to no doubt. She entreated to be still allowed the care of the infant, and as her husband prepared to embark for the same port in America, in a few months, it was thought that no inconvenience would arise from leaving the infant in her charge. The separation would be brief, and this arrangement enabled them to keep Alice and her husband in their former ignorance as to that connection which subsisted between my father and the Calverts.

Suitable preparations being made, my father secretly embarked at London with his wife, her mother and her son, in a shipbound to Philadelphia. Here they safely arrived, and, taking an obscure house, they hoped to enjoy the remnant of their days in tranquility. My father assumed his wife's name, and permitted the world to consider him as one of the victims of the blind and destructive policy of the French government in recalling its concessions to the Protestants.

Meanwhile, it will be supposed, that some impatience was felt for the arrival of the son who had been left in the care of Alice Thurston. Henry was apprised of the existence of this child, and of the views which had been adopted with regard to it. He had promised to bestow some attention on its welfare, and not to withdraw from it his guardianship until it was safely embarked. A punctual correspondence was maintained by the brothers.

The sudden disappearance of his son excited no small alarm in sir Stephen. For a time he was willing to ascribe it to some casual and unimportant cause. At length his anxiety prompted him to set inquiries on foot. Stephen had appeared as usual at breakfast and dinner, but in the evening he was no where to be found. He had left behind him neither verbal nor written intimations of his absence. The servants and tenants were unable to remove his uncertainty. Henry, when interrogated respecting his brother's destiny, pretended the same ignorance. More exact inquiries and extensive searches were made, butwere no less ineffectual. Weeks and months rolled away, and produced no tidings of the fugitive.

As no conjecture was less probable than the true, time produced no cessation of the father's inquiries and doubts. At length he was compelled to acquiesce in the belief that the son had perished by some unwitnessed and untoward accident. This event was fatal to his fondest hopes, and he deplored it as the most signal calamity that could befal him.

Thurston found no difficulty in the disposal of his property, and was taking measures for entering on the meditated voyage, when he was attacked by a fever which, in a few days, put an end to his life. This event incapacitated Alice for prosecuting her design. The Calverts used to be her counsellors in every difficulty, and she knew no other on whose sympathy or succour she could place dependance. Henry was speedily informed of this disaster. He saw that Alice, encumbered with two infants, and resigned to her own guidance, would be exposed to numerous embarrassments and dangers. Hence originated a scheme which he made haste to impart to his brother, and which he recommended with uncommon zeal. He proposed that Alice and the child should continue in England, under his protection, and that as soon as his nephew should grow beyond the necessity of her care, he should be taken under his own protection, and treated as his child.

The letter, containing this proposal, was received by the vessel in which my father impatiently expected the arrival of Alice and her charge. Deep and almost insupportable, especially to my mother, was this disappointment of their hopes. She was by no means inclined to adopt this proposal, but she yielded to my father's councils and wishes, and my brother was transferred to the family of Henry.

Time would, of course, reconcile my mother to separation from her offspring, especially as the charge was so auspicious. Their fears, however, were quickly roused by the failure of a letter from my uncle, and by the receipt of an incoherent epistle from Alice, who, to their unspeakable astonishment and grief, informed them, first, of the death of Henry Porter, and, secondly, of the loss of my brother Felix. She related that the two children had been left alone for a few minutes, at the door of her cottage, in the dusk of evening, and that, on her return to the spot, Felix was missing. Her random and limited inquiries had led to no discovery.

The influence of such tidings may be easily conceived. As to the fate of their infant son, there was room only for the gloomiest predictions. Such instances were not uncommon. Beggars, and the vilest of mankind, were accustomed to make prize of helpless innocence, and train up the unfortunate subject of their theft to their own detestable profession. This lot was infinitely more deplorable than death. All the hope that remains to the parents in such cases, is, that negligence and cruelty may put a speedy end to the life of the unfortunate victim.

It is not certain that my mother would have long survived to sustain the anguish of these thoughts. A new occurrence diversified, and in some degree, alleviated their grief. If Henry Porter were dead, his father would, of course, become the guardian of his child and of his property. Letters had passed between the brothers, in which the secret of his flight, his marriage, and his conversion, were copiously related or intelligently alluded to. It was possible, that these letters, in obedience to the writer's injunctions, were destroyed, but it was likewise possible, that they had been preserved, and therefore had fallen into the hands of Sir Stephen. What use he would make of them, to what excesses his anger and his bigotry would transport him, were subjects of fearful conjecture.

In no long time, a letter was received, in which my father's apprehensions were confirmed. Sir Stephen was the writer. The sudden death of his eldest son had made him master of his cabinet, and all that my father desired to be concealed was known. The first burst of indignation in the mind of Sir Stephen was followed by impulses of terror, lest the unwary disclosure of his plot should have tended to defeat it. Rage yielded to policy. Alice was robbed of her charge, and my father was informed that the son was kept as a sort of pledge of his fidelity. Maledictions and invectives were heaped upon the fugitive, the rights of kindred were disclaimed, but my father was flattered with impunity, provided he maintained an inflexible silence on certain topics.

This epistle assured my parents of the personal safety of their offspring, but they naturally inferred from it, the incurable perversion of his principles. He would be tainted in an obnoxious faith, and, perhaps, kept in ignorance of his birth. To them, therefore, he was lost, and his destiny, though some-what better than that for which they had before imagined him reserved, was more to be lamented than his death. Their affection was now concentred in me, on whom they bestowed the name of my brother. My original appellation was Stephen, but henceforth I was called Felix.

The death of his brother deprived my father of the established means of his subsistence. It was necessary to discover some new method of supply-ing his wants. Several expedients were tried, but he at length decided in favour of the legal profession. To fit him for this pursuit, time and money must be previously consumed, and he reconciled himself to this necessity by the lucrative employment of his pen. A practical knowledge of conveyancing was easily gained, and by this he procured the means of subsistence till he was qualified for the bar.

Meanwhile, my father could not but reflect on that criminal project in which he had been invited to concur. He was haunted by fears, that his duty to his country enjoined upon him a different proceeding from that which he had adopted. At one time, he painted to himself the scenes of confiscation and proscription which would ensue the success of this plot, and was almost prompted to abjure his silence, and hasten to disclose the knowledge he possessed. Then he revolved the numberless incidents which might occur to frustrate it, to hinder the conspirators from prosecuting their design, or detect it before its execution. This scheme was to coincide with a project of invasion, but France was the only power from which an attack could be dreaded, and the sceptical and pacific character of the regent duke of Orleans was well known. It seemed as if the jacobite enthusiasm had nearly vanished, and that the adherents of the exile family must at length have discovered the desperateness of their cause.

Peace of mind was incompatible with these thoughts. My father's anxieties could not escape the watchful tenderness of his wife. It was easy for him to assign a plausible cause for appearances very different from the true one, and his dissimulation succeeded for a time. He knew not the consequences of disclosure, even to his bosom friend. My mother fostered a magnanimous spirit, and was an enthusiast in religion. What use she might conceive it her duty to make of her knowledge could not be foreseen. He recollected the penalty that had been menaced, if he should violate his faith, and these reflections fortified him in concealment.

But the impossibility of destroying the connection between thought and speech was eminently illustrated in my father's case. My mother was a jealous and perpetual observer. The negligent and yielding moment was skilfully employed, and the secret was extorted.

My mother had no ties of habit or affection to restrain her from compliance with the dictates of duty. She permitted her actions to be controlled by her husband, and forbore to make any other use of the knowledge she had acquired, than to exhort my father to unveil and defeat this plot. She proposed nothing less than that he should entrust the protection and subsistence of his family to Providence, and immediately embark for England, where he should hasten to communicate the particulars of this conspiracy to government.

Her remonstrances were earnest and incessant, and might, probably, have finally conquered his aversion, had not the next packet brought tidings which precluded the necessity of his interference.

Intimations of this plot had been conveyed to the ministers, and sir Stephen Porter was marked out as the principal agent. Messengers were secretly dispatched to arrest him.

One hour before the messengers arrived at the end of their journey, sir Stephen was engaged at dinner, with a numerous company. In the midst of their festivity, a person entered the hall, and whispered something in the ear of the host, and instantly retired. A pause of uneasiness and abstraction ensued. Sir Stephen, at length, rose from the table, and retired, under pretence of some unexpected and urgent business. Shortly after, the messengers arrived, but their victim had profited by this interval, to assume the disguise of a clown, and effect his escape. On the most diligent search, no papers, throwing any light on these transactions, could be discovered: either they had been burnt, or buried, or secreted, or, which was least probable, had been carried away by the suspected person.

These are the only facts relative to this plot which were made public. No further discovery, nor any other consequence, is generally supposed to have been produced. To this detection, however, it is probable that my father was indebted for an early and untimely grave. He could not but rejoice at the defeat of so destructive a project, especially as the personal safety of his father had not been affected, but he that imparted this information to the government had probably stipulated for concealment. The conspirators, therefore, would remain ignorant of their betrayer: but were there not reasons to believe that sir Stephen's suspicions would fall upon his son? Vengeance, cruel and implacable, would probably be excited in his bosom. This vengeance would fall on his defenceless child, and might extend to himself. This imagination could not fashion to itself the species of injury that was to flow from this source, but this uncertainty, by precluding him from the means of defence, only aggravated his terrors.

My mother partook of these anxieties. Time had some tendency to lighten them, but this effect was not allowed to be produced. One evening, four months after the receipt of this intelligence, a letter was found by my father in the entry of his house. It was couched in the following terms:

Sir,

You need not be informed of your offences: you know that they surpass those of the greatest criminals whose guilt has been recorded. You have rebelled against your God, you have been a traitor to your rightful prince, and, finally, you have done all that in you lay, to bring your father to the scaffold. What punishment do you think you deserve? Tremble! Vengeance, though so long delayed, is now preparing to crush you!

This epistle was written in an unknown hand, and was without superscription or signature. Its purport was fully comprehended. He was conceived to be the betrayer of this fatal project, and the dreaded vengeance was at length to be inflicted. No condition is more deplorable than that in which my father was now placed. When we know that danger impends over us, but are unable to assign to it a distinct shape, there is no respite to our fears.

What measures of safety were adapted to his situation he knew not , or at what hour, and in what spot the toils were to close upon him. Whether his life would be taken, or his reputation destroyed, or his means of subsistence annihilated, whether he should be assailed in his own person or in that of his wife, or whether both were to perish by a common fate, were questions not to be solved.

My father's mind was distinguished by some degree of imbecility. He allowed this incident to affect his happiness in a greater degree than a reasonable estimate of danger would justify. It was scarcely ever absent from his thought, and when present, it filled him with disquiet and suspicion. Solitude enhanced his fears, and the aspect of a stranger was regarded with a shuddering he bwas scarcely able to conceal. He was careful to bar up all avenues to his house. Not only the windows, but he shutters of his chamber, were closed. His dreams terrified him into wakefulness, and he was startled by the slightest sound, the cause of which was, in any degree, ambiguous.

My mother was endowed with a masculine and daring spirit. She was far from being devoid of apprehension, but her mind escaped more easily from it, and she was more inclined to extenuate the danger. My father conformed himself to many of her precepts, but her efforts to encourage and console him on this occasion were resisted with an obstinacy that almost allowed room to suspect that terror had confused his intellect.

Among other precautions which he used, was that of never venturing abroad at night. To this resolution he inflexibly adhered for some time, but, at length, there occurred an event which induced him to forego it.

A man of large fortune, who resided a mile beyond Schuykill, was seized with a mortal disease. His death was predicted to be near, and, in this extremity, my father, who had received from him many friendly offices, was summoned from the city to draw up his will. This summons was received at eight o'clock in the evening, and his immediate attendance was required. There were many motives to enforce compliance with this summons. It was probable, that in the disposal of his estate, this person would not forget my father, whom he had always distinguished by marks of peculiar regard. He had requested my father's attendance, on this occasion, as a favour, and, to refuse without assigning any plausible reason, might be expected to give offence. The scruples of the dying man were fastidious on this head, and his refusal might, at least, occasion a delay which perhaps might hinder the will from being made. In that case the sick man's property would be given, by the law, to one in whose hands it would merely be an instrument of viceand oppression, whereas, a testamentary act would probably transfer it to those whose personal merits and wants gave the man unquestionable title.

Notwithstanding these reasons for going, my father would have declined the task, had not my mother's remonstrance interposed. With much reluctance, and a bosom filled with dreary forebodings, he set out upon his journey. The messenger who brought the summons accompanied him, and contracted, in some degree, to his security. It was resolved that he should postpone his return till the next day.

Her husband having gone, my mother composed herself in rest as usual. The succeeding day was stormy and inclement. My father did not appear. The state of the atmosphere would naturally account for his detenbrion, but my mother's mind was not free from uneasiness. The question could not fail to occur, would not her husband quiet those alarms which he knew that his absence would excite, by dispatching a messenger to acquaint her with the cause of it? The patient might indeed be dead, and the sorrow and confusion consequent on such an event, might exclude all other thoughts.

The succeeding night she passed in like manner alone, but not without a great increase of uneasiness. On the second day, at noon, her suspense became too painful to be longer endured, and a man and horse was dispatched to procure some tidings of his situation. The messenger speedily returned with a letter from the lady who superintended the family of Mr. Thompson, informing her, that her husband, having performed the business for which he came, had immediately left the house on his return to the city, that he had been earnestly solicited to postpone his departure till the next day, but had persisted in his resolution to go immediately. He had set out on foot, though an horse had been offered him.

On returning, as on going, it was requisite to cross the ferry. Enquiry being made, it was found that he had not applied for a passage at the river. What then had become of him? Diligent searches were made, but none of them were effectual. Six weeks passed away and no tidings of his destiny were received. At the end of that period a dead body was discovered concealed among the reeds, at low water, on the left shore of League-Island. The remnant of clothes which still adhered to him, served to ascertain this to be the body of my father.

No marks of violence being discoverable, it was

unavoidable to conclude that he had been drowned. It was difficult to conceive that chance had occasioned this event. My mother had some reason to believe it to be the result of a malignant stratagem, and the accomplishment of that vengeance that had been threatened. Her fancy teemed with distressful images. In her dreams she beheld him set upon by ruffians, his speech inhumanly stifled, and his body cast into the river. By this means their cunning would best avoid not only detection, but suspicion.

Sometimes, she admitted a doubt whether he had not been the author of his own destruction. His resolution, suddenly conceived, to return to the city alone, on foot, and at midnight, was opposite to the usual tenor of his conduct, and so apparently unnecessary, was remembered. He had often expressed his impatience of existence, linked as it was with incessant and excruciating fears. His profession was obnoxious to all his indolent and literary habits, and he had placed considerable dependance on the generosity of Thompson. A trifling legacy, however, was all that was bequeathed to him. These causes might have concurred to sink him to despair, and prompt him to this act of self-violence.

This event deprived my mother not only of a protector and friend, but of the means of subsistence. I was three years of age at this time, and was therefore helpless and wholly dependant on her care. Her mother had died shortly after their arrival in America, and the pittance which that lady enjoyed in right of her husband, ceased to be paid. My father's profession supplied merely his daily wants. His friends were numerous, but my mother's exigencies were of the most urgent and momentous kind, and such as common friendship could hardly be expected to obviate.

In this desolate state she was not deserted by her fortitude. She deliberated calmly on the best means of supplying her wants. She possessed considerable accomplishments, and was encouraged to institute a sort of boarding school for a small number of female pupils. This scheme was conducted with remarkable skill and success. Her character and situation being known, her terms, though more expensive than was common, were eagerly accepted. The best families in the province contended with each other for the benefits of her tuition. She limited herself to six girls, and three being selected at a very early age, and being wholly consigned to her care, she contracted for them all the fondness, while she exercised the authority of a parent.

When I had attained my sixth year, I was sent to a public school, which a Scottish adventurer had established at the town of Woodbury, in New Jersey. The plan of this establishment was comprehensive, and all the learning, which indeed was small, which it was thought proper for me to acquire, was acquired in ten years under this man's direction.

During this period my mother had discharged every obligation to her pupils. She had dissolved her family and retired to an habitation near Burlington, which the generosity of a deceased friend, and the profits of preceptress-ship had enabled her to purchase. On leaving Woodbury, I retired to her house. The management of domestic concerns were divided between us. My chief employment consisted in the cultivation of the garden which appended to the mansion, and which supplied us with the greater part of our annual provision. Health, and pleasure, and agricultural improvement, were blended in this pursuit, and these few acres afforded a perpetual theatre for contemplation and experiment. The intervals were spent in the recreations of poetry and music, and in the society of my mother, the excellence of whose character became the more conspicuous, the more closely and constantly it was inspected.

For some years there was nothing to disturb my repose. I was molested by no gloomy anticipations of the future. The property which I should inherit from my mother would suffice for the abundant supply of all my wants, and I felt no desire to augment it. In this immoveable calm there was no temptation to lead aside, or passion to bewilder my steps.

The first incident that called away my thoughts from this scene, was connected with the fate of my family in Europe. Sir Stephen Porter, refusing to obey a summons to return and subject his conduct to legal examination, was attainted. His estate was confiscated, but restored,   by the bounty of the prince, to his grandson Henry. This person, to whom I stood in the relation of cousin, now entered into his majority, and into the possession of his estate. He became early apprised of the fortunes of his uncle, and was influenced, by a sense of justice, to assist his aunt and his cousin to the utmost of his power. He had been solicitously trained in the Romish religion, but had formally abjured it. This served as an additional incitement to repair the evils which my father had incurred, in consequence of a similar deportment. It was not till after long and painful searches, and the intervention of some propitious chance, that he traced us to our retreat on the banks of Delaware. A correspondence then commenced between my mother and him, in which he persuaded her to resume her ancient country, and to accept of a liberal provision.

Her estimate of happiness was too correct to permit her to accept his offers. Finding her invincible, he addressed himself to me in the same terms, and solicited me to come and partake with him in all the goods which fortune had bestowed upon him.

My youthful and untutored imagination was delighted with the pictures which he drew, and I was sufficiently inclined to adopt his proposals, but

I could not hesitate to sacrifice these crude visions to the desires of my mother, and to prefer being her companion and consoler to any other office. I could not forget, however, that her feeble constitution, and the course of nature, must put a speedy end to her life, and then there would exist no impediment to the adoption of this scheme.

My cousin had made strenuous exertions to ascertain the destiny of my lost brother. Alice, his nurse, had been extricated by him from hardship and poverty, and sent to America. She was now become my mother's sole and faithful domestic, but all his efforts to recover the lost Felix were unavailing. On this topic I was chiefly prone to indulge a romantic disposition. My recluse, literary and bookish education, tended to imbue me with the refinements of sentiment and the heroism of friendship. I was without compeers and associates, and those sympathies which are always ardent at my age wasted themselves on visionary objects. I consoled myself with the belief that my brother was still alive, and that a meeting would one day take place between us. For want of experience I imagined that there was something peculiarly sacred and tender in the bond of brotherhood, and that this tie was unspeakably enhanced by the circumstance of being ushered into being together, of being coeval in age, and alike in constitution and figure: these resemblances being supposed by me to exist, in those cases, in an eminent degree.

The sensations that flowed from these ideas were not always pleasurable. I was conscious that eternal and insuperable obstacles to our meeting might very possibly exist, and this persuasion was a fertile source of regret. I believed that the chance of separation was increased by the remoteness and seclusion of my present residence, and would be diminished by crossing the Atlantic. This belief was no inconsiderable recommendation to the scheme proposed by my cousin. This scheme, however, was utterly impracticable till the death of my mother. Till this event should take place I expected and desired to remain in my present abode, but my expectations were frustrated from a quarter whence it was least likely to come.

I have mentioned that one of the Calverts, whom the bigotry of Louis the fourteenth drove into exile, had, after many years residence in Flanders, emigrated to America. He brought with him money sufficient for the purchase of what, in Europe, would be deemed a spacious domain. Here he devoted himself to agriculture, and the gradual increase of population augmented the value of his estate, till he became respectable among his neighbours for opulence.

He was succeeded in the possession of this ground by a Frenchman, remotely allied to him, and of the same name, to whom he had married his daughter. This person, whose name was Ambrose Calvert, had insinuated himself, by a long train of hypocrisy, into the good opinion of the last possessor. His habits of dissimulation, in some degree, continued after his accession to the property. He was as punctual as ever in the forms of religious worship, was as strictly observant of the Sabbath, excluded as austerely all mirth from his features, and levities from his deport-ment. In these respects he was uniform to the end of life, but in other particulars he conceived himself, by the death of the elder Calvert, delivered from all restraint, and at liberty to obey the genuine impulse of his temper.

This temper was the cause of suffering to those only who were subjected to his power. In his inter-course with his neighbours and with the world, his brow was smooth, his accents tempered into sweet-ness, and his whole deportment a model of urbanity and graciousness. He was just, and even generous, in his dealings with others, and was always more prone to yield up than to persist in his claims. Little would a casual observer suspect that this man was the slave of ferocious and immitigable passions, that he was a domestic tyrant, and exercised the sternest cruelty in the government of his family and slaves.

His fields were cultivated by Africans. To these he did not allot disproportionate tasks, or condemn them to the use of poor, scanty, or unwholesome food, or deny them necessary, or even decent cloth-ing. His disposition was remote from avarice, but it was savage and capricious. He inflicted on them the most excruciating punishments for the most trifling offences. He made little or no discrimination in the choice of objects of his wrath. No tenderness of age or sex, no degree of fidelity or diligence, exempted from suffering, the unfortunate beings who were placed under his yoke. His imagination created crimes when they were wanting, and that was an unexpiable offence at one time, which, at another, was laudable or indifferent. When in a sullen mood, merely to smile in his presence was guilt, and incurred inhuman chastisement.

His wife was of a soft and compassionate temper. Many of the servants were of the same age, born and reared under the same roof, and regarded with somewhat of sisterly and maternal emotions. Her father's government had been full of lenity and prudence, and nothing had occurred, previous to his death, which indicated a contrary disposition in her husband.

When, therefore, he dropped the mask, the reverse was the more disastrous and astonishing. The tears, the shrieks, and the deep traces of the lash, in those who had formerly been treated with nearly as much forbearance and affection as herself, were sources of horror and grief not to be endured. To be a silent and passive spectator was impossible, but his cruelty was only exasperated by intercession and remonstrance. By persisting in these, his affection appeared gradually to be withdrawn from her, and she sunk, by rapid degrees, from the condition of an equal into that of a slave.

Her education and temper were of that kind which made contempt and indignity more insupportable to her than stripes and blows. The former, however, were only introductory to the latter, and her untimely death bore witness to the acuteness of her sufferings. Even at this distance I cannot trust myself with the task of describing his enormities. When I think of them, abhorrence and rancour arise in my heart, from which I endeavour to escape by diverting my attention to other objects.

One daughter, Louisa, was the fruit of this union. Her mother died soon after her birth. Her education, during her early years, was nearly the product of chance. Her grandfather, who had not been destitute of literary propensities, left behind him some books, to which, in the abundance of her leisure, she betook herself in search of amusement. From these she gleaned crude and numerous ideas, which time, and more judicious instruction, finally converted into useful and admirable knowledge.

She was not exempted from parental tyranny. If these had been limited to stern commands, loud rebukes, and intervals of sullen silence, it would, by habit, have been rendered, perhaps, endurable, and these, it should seem, were sufficient antidotes to content: but these were bounds by which his passion was not accustomed to be circumscribed. I shudder tothink of the excesses of which this unhappy girl was the victim. How deeply it is to be regretted, that the happiness of one being should be swayed by the perverseness of another! From the first dawning of reflection till the age of fifteen, pain and fear were almost the perpetual companions of Louisa Calvert. The solace of society, the blessings of liberty, were denied to her. All the affections of her heart were chilled andcurbed. No vigilance nor caution could give her any security against mistreatment. If a known path, however dark, intricate, and rugged, had been assigned to her, and her safety was made wholly to depend upon her adherence to it, her lot would have been less deplorable, but the caprice of her father was wholly irregular. He seemed to act by the instigations of a demon and to be impelled by pure, unadulterated malice.

In her fifteenth year her condition underwent a change. Her father made occasional journies to the city, which was ten miles from his place of residence. Hither, late in autumn, his engagements chanced to call him. He proposed to return on the evening of the same day. The evening elapsed however, without producing any token of his approach. His daughter was, by this delay, thrown into a state of considerable perplexity. Whether she should await his arrival, or retire to her chamber, leaving a female servant to attend his coming, was a question on which much depended, but which she was unable to decide.

The mood in which Calvert might return, might make him condemn her retirement as disrepectful, or her watchfulness as officious, and his absurd rage would vent itself in blows and contumelies. After some fruitless deliberation, she concluded to go to bed.

There is an energy in the human mind which enables it to conquer every inquietude, or a flexibility that reconciles itself to every constraint. Louisa was gifted with that temper which is not easily bereaved of cheerfulness. Her condition was well known, and no one acquainted with it could refrain from expressing their wonder at the fortitude with which she supported its unparalleled and complicated evils. There were moments, however, when her soul was nearly overwhelmed with the perception of her wretchedness, and when she even admitted a doubt whether death, inflicted by her own hand, was not preferable to a being like hers.

Mournful sensations happened to be particularly prevalent on this occasion, and she lay sleepless and listening to the signal which should announce her father's approach. This signal was at length heard, but it was obliged to be frequently repeated before the slumbers of the girl, who remained below, were broken. Louisa shuddered on reflecting on the probable consequences of this negligence. Her fears, in this respect, were not groundless, and Calvert no sooner obtained admittance than he proceeded to inflict on the culprit the most barbarous chastisement.

The sufferer, whose name was Althea, had been the play fellow, and was the affectionate attendant of her young mistress. Her form and features were delicate and regular, and her complexion so remote from jet, that the conjecture was generally admitted that her father was Calvert himself. These circumstances, in addition to the loneliness of her state, and the want of suitable associates, fostered in Louisa a sisterly affection for her waiting maid. She partook in all the studies and amusements of her mistress.

From the nature of her functions, in the performance of which she seldom had need to enter into the presence of the tyrant, from the unwearied diligence of Louisa to screen her from animadversions, and, perhaps, from some movements of paternal tenderness, she had hitherto, for the most part, escaped that treatment to which her companions in servitude had been condemned.

Every blow which she now received struck upon the heart of Louisa, and she bitterly lamented that she had not, by remaining below, encountered his resentment. Her thoughts were quickly recalled to the consideration of her own safety, for, in a few minutes, Calvert relinquished his present victim and burst into her chamber. He began with heaping on her those reproaches which were usually the prelude to personal violence. This she summoned up her magnanimity to bear without repining. Having exhausted his abuse, he proceeded to inform her of his solemn resolution, that she should not remain a moment longer under his roof, and commanded her to rise instantly and leave his house.

Menaces to this effect had frequently been uttered by him in the career of passion, but they were considered as momentary suggestions, and when his paroxysm had passed, were mutually forgotten. Now, however, he did not content himself with threats, but showed himself immoveably resolved.

Louisa enjoyed the compassion of all, but the friendship of none. She was little less than an absolute stranger to everyone beyond her father's threshold. Exiled from this roof, she knew of no place of refuge, or even of momentary entertainment. In vain she endeavoured, by intreaties, to avert this sentence, or at least to delay the execution of it. Her opposition only exasperated his rage, and transported him beyond all bounds of humanity. He seized her by the hair, and dragging her to the door, thrust her forth without mercy, and locked the entrance against her.

Her dress consisted merely of a thin and long robe which covered all her limbs, but her neck and feet were bare. Winter had already began its progress by disrobing the trees of their leaves, and whitening the ground with frost. It was midnight, and the atmosphere was cloudy and tempestuous. Such were the circumstances in which this inhuman father thought proper to turn his child out of doors.

For a time, she flattered herself that as his passion subsided, he would see the monstrousness of this act. She waited at the door in vain. The dullness of the atmosphere began at length to be felt. Despair at length took possession of her bosom, and she dragged her trembling limbs to a short distance from the house.

The plantation next to that of her father was bounded by the opposite side of the road. Annexed to it were two barns, one of which, smaller in size, and but little used, was sixty or eighty feet from Calvert's door. The first impulse was to go thither and screen herself from the piercing wind, by interposing this building between her and the northern blasts. She hoped likewise to find some hay scattered in its neighbourhood, by which her feet might be protected from the cold. Both of these purposes were in some degree answered, and she found herself at leisure to ruminate on the deplorableness of her condition.

The proprietor of the next plantation was a man of a very different character from Calvert. He had marked with disapprobation the excesses of his neighbour, and sometimes endeavoured, by remonstrances, to check his career. Some occasion had required him to leave his bed on this night, and his station happened to be such as to make him a witness of the scene that took place at Calvert's threshold. He followed the lady to her retreat, and quickly making himself known to her, easily prevailed upon her to take shelter under his roof.

Next morning he paid a visit to her father. I have said, that Calvert, in his intercourse with the world, was a strict observer of politeness. His treatment of this guest was by no means an exception to his maxims, but he absolutely refused to re-admit his daughter.

My mother was a distant relation of the sufferer, and the only person in America from whom relationship gave her any claim to protection. Louisa's present protector willingly assumed that province, and would not have consigned it to another with any other view than to the superior advantage of this young lady. He applied, therefore, to my mother for her advice on this occasion. My mother had recently lost her husband, and was just established in her new profession. She could not hesitate long how to act in this exigence, and Louisa thenceforth enjoyed under her roof, all the delights of social intercourse, and the benefits of maternal superintendance.

For a time, her father appeared wholly careless of her destiny. Being at length informed of her condition, his jealousy of paternal authority, and his malignant temper, made him desire her return. He deemed himself entitled to her implicit obedience, and therefore demanded the unconditional possession of her. Had Louisa been left to her own guidance, no doubt she would have readily complied, but my mother interfered, and prevailed upon her to continue in her new abode. No small firmness was required to resist the authority and menaces of Calvert, and fortify the wavering and timid temper of his daughter.

The cruelty of Calvert, by occasioning, as was strongly suspected, the death of her favourite Althea, took away her most powerful inducement to return. This event might be partly owing to regret for the loss of her young mistress, whom she tenderly loved, but there was likewise reason to ascribe it to inhuman treatment from her master. For many years after, her fate could never be thought upon by Louisa without impatience, or her name be mentioned without tears.

Calvert, finding my mother inflexible, informed her that he would not only refuse to discharge the expense of his daughter's subsistence, but would punish her disobedience by excluding her from all share in his estate after his decease. These threats were not likely to influence my mother's conduct. The inheritance of his estate would by no means compensate Louisa for the privation of all instruction and enjoyment during his life. Besides, she trusted to the favorable influence of time, and believed, that the approach of death would make a change in his views.

From this period till the dissolution of her little college, Louisa was my mother's companion. The same generous benefactor who bequeathed a portion of her property to my mother, gave to Louisa the property of three bonds, on the interest of which, by the practice of the rigidest economy, she was able to subsist. To effect this purpose, she was obliged to limit her expenses to little more than necessaries, and to perform many personal and household offices for herself. The abode which she selected, and which was recommended by its cheapness, its picturesque scenes, its salubrious air, and its vicinity to the residence of her dearest friends, was eight milesfrom the town of Lancaster. Here, she pursued occupations and amusements which, at first, were prescribed by necessity, but soon became the dictates of choice.

My mother's plan of education was wholly singular and unexampled. Hence, her pupils, while they were bound to each other and to her, by similitude of tastes and opinions, were placed in irreconcilable opposition to the rest of mankind. That friendship, which residence under the same roof and perpetual intercourse for ten years, were calculated to produce, did not languish or expire during their separation. Half the year was usually spent, by Louisa, at the house of one or other of her friends.

All intercourse between the parent and child had ceased from the moment when her final resolution was known, to avoid her father's habitation. He acted, on all occasions, just as if she had ceased to exist. Surrounded with the slaves of his will and shut out, partly by necessity and partly through choice, from intercourse with the rest of the world, he spent several years in the unrestrained indulgence of his passions. At length, he was attacked by an acute disease, which shortly brought his life to a close.

It was now to appear whether he had carried to his grave the enmity which he had fostered against his daughter. If her claim to preference should be disallowed, it did not appear that there was any other person in the world entitled to this preference. Those by whom he was surrounded were his slaves, to whom he was actuated by no sentiment but that of hatred. The rest of mankind were unknown, and must, therefore, be supposed to be indifferent to him. What, therefore, must my astonishment have been, on receiving a letter, shortly after his decease, from a respectable inhabitant of Philadelphia, announcing himself as joint executor with me in the will of Calvert, and informing me that, by this will, I was constituted successor to all his property.

Calvert and I had no intercourse, and my mother must have been to him an object of resentment. No event, therefore, was more adverse to my expectations. It was a new proof of the capriciousness of this man's temper. My surprise quickly yielded place to considerations as to the mode in which I should conduct myself in my new situation.

I was now become proprietor of three hundred fertile acres, in a commodious and healthful situation, a spacious and well furnished mansion, and fifteen negroes. My wants were already copiously supplied, and any deficiency was ready to be made up by my English cousin. With relation to myself, therefore, this event was no topic of congratulation. In a different view it was to be regarded with pleasure. The produce of this estate might be applied to far better uses than had been chosen by Calvert. His slaves would henceforth receive the treatment that was due to men, and their happiness be as sedulously promoted as it had been heretofore counteracted. I could not fail to perceive the superiority of Louisa's claim to this property, both as the daughter of Calvert, and as a being of uncommon worth, destitute of the means of agreeable and respectable subsistence. I needed not to be stimulated by my mother to an act of justice, and speedily resolved to transfer this property to her.

Meanwhile it was necessary to visit and take possession of this estate. I prepared for an immediate journey. My unacquaintance with the world, and my speculative education, made this expedition of uncommon importance. I had hitherto pursued an humble and familiar tract, and was oppressed with a consciousness of wanting a guide and instructor in the new path on which I was entering.

I shall not dwell upon the sensations which novelty produces, and whose existence is necessarily transient. The requisite forms were easily dispatched, and possession of my new inheritance acquired. The land was in the highest state of cultivation, and habits of diligence and regularity had been so long established among the slaves, that affairs proceeded in their usual course, notwithstanding the death of the late proprietor.

In the management of a plantation like this, it is requisite to select one to whom the whole authority may be occasionally delegated, and with whom the master may divide the task of actual superintendance. In the choice of a deputy, Calvert had exercised his usual judgment. Caesar, the eldest of the slaves, had a perfect knowledge of agriculture, was fertile in expedients, vigorous in foresight, and of unblameable fidelity. Caesar, therefore, was invested with the office of steward. Habits of command, and the influence of example, had a tendency to deprave him, but this tendency was checked by the precautions of Calvert, who not only withheld from him the power of inflicting punishment, but even prohibited him from the use of harsh and reproachful language.

These measures were not adopted by Calvert from a beneficent regard to the welfare of his servants, and from a knowledge of the cruelty which is sure to characterise a slave in office. They proceeded from an imperious temper, which could not endure that any of his slaves should lose sight of his dependant condition, and was unwilling to part, even for a moment, with his tyrannical prerogatives. Hence Caesar was obliged to secure obedience to his mandates by a mild and equitable deportment, and hence their attachment to his person was proportioned to their antipathy for Calvert.

Their new master was by no means disposed to revive the system of oppression under which they had suffered so long. The management was continued in the hands of Caesar, and, after a short stay at Calverton, I returned to the city. I purposed to return to Burlington, but my curiosity detained me in the city for some time, as well as my scheme with regard to Louisa Calvert. This lady had contracted an engagement with one of her friends and fellow pupils, who was lately married, and settled in this city, to spend two or three months with her. A fortnight was to elapse before her intended arrival, and it had been preconcerted, that, after her visit to Mrs. Wallace was performed, she should bestow the favour of her company, for an equal period, on my mother at Burlington.

It will not surprise you that I eagerly desired an interview with this lady. The boon which I had to bestow was not inconsiderable, and there seemed some propriety in obtaining a personal knowledge of the object of this benefit previous to conferring it. A letter from my mother, introduced me to Mrs. Wallace, and her husband, whose profession was that of a lawyer, had aided me in the execution of Calvert's testament. Hence, in this family, I was admitted on a familiar and confidential footing, and here my opportunities of intercourse with their expected visitant, would be frequent and favourable.

I have mentioned that my character contained no small portion of enthusiasm. I had mused on ideal forms, and glowed with visionary ardours. At this age there is an inexplicable fascination attendant upon our sex, and I was, in an eminent degree, the slave of this enchantment. My fancy was perpetually figuring to itself a train of cousequences to flow from any casual occurrences, and, where marriage was possible to be introduced, it was never omitted. I had never seen Louisa Calvert, but had listened, on numberless occasions, to eulogiums on her character, pronounced by my mother. Her image,therefore, was oftener presented to my mind than that of anyother female. It could not but happen that my reveries would sometimes suggest the possibility of marriage, but this idea was thwarted by the timorousness of youth, which made me depreciate my own claims to such felicity, by the consciousness of poverty, and, chiefly, by the unlikelihood that, in our respective situations, any meeting would take place between us.

A surprising revolution had removed many of

these obstacles. From the conduct which I intended to pursue, I should derive some merit, and, at the same time, remove the obstacle which poverty had erected. My acquaintance with the Wallaces, and her residence in this family, would bring us to the knowledge of each other under the most favourable auspices. Love is an ambiguous and capricious principle. That I was prepared or resolved to love this woman, is not, perhaps, an adequate description of my state. The delineations of her form and mind had been vivid and minute, and these had been truly lovely. I entertained no doubt that my destiny, in this respect, was now accomplished. My anticipations of an interview awakened all those golden dreams and delicious palpitations which are said to characterise this passion. Must it not, therefore, be inferred that I was in love?

Still it is apparent that my passion was merely the creature of fancy, and, as such, liable to be suddenly extinguished or transferred to a new object.

My mother's consent to my remaining in the city was easily obtained. I did not conceal from her my views with respect to Louisa, and they obtained her ardent approbation. The tenor of her discourse and her wishes, frequently hinted, that she might live to see me allied to a woman equally excellent, had no small influence on my meditations. These were likewise assisted by the eulogies of Mrs. Wallace, to whom the virtues of her friend constituted an inexhaustible theme.

My social intercourse was limited to a small circle. Besides this family, I was conversant with no one but a young man, my equal in age, though eminently my superior in wisdom, by name Sidney Carlton. He was the brother of Mrs. Wallace, and newly initiated into the legal profession. I met him at his sister's house, which he constantly frequented, and where I supped in his company every evening. It was this man whose existence was the source of the first uneasiness which I had ever known, and who was indirectly the author of all my subsequent calamities.

As the brother of Louisa's friend, and as one entitled, by that relationship, as well as by his native worth, to the good opinion of Louisa, he quickly appeared to me in an interesting and formidable light. He was regarded by his sister with an affection little short of idolatry. He was almost an inmate of the house. His intercourse, therefore, with the visitant, would be without restraint, and almost without intermission. His sister would exert herself to unite two persons so equally and passionately loved, and his merit was of so transcendant a kind that all ideas of rivalship were vain.

These thoughts might have tended to repress all hope, but I was rescued from despondency by reflecting on the capriciousness of passion, on the contrariety that frequently subsists between the dictates of desire and the injunctions of reason. Love is a motley and complex sentiment. It is the growth, not of reason, but of sense. The concurrence of reason may be requisite to make it a principle of action in persons of unusual elevation and refinement, but not in ordinary cases. The understanding may approve, and fortify, and prolong the existence of the passion, but this can never be the source of its existence.

Highly as I deemed of the discernment and intelligence of my cousin, I did not believe her exempt from sexual impulses. I believed her capable of being dazzled and seduced by a demeanour, characterised by all the impetuosity and tenderness of passion, by dexterity and fluency of elocution, by romantic generosity of sentiment, and elegant proportions and expressive features. In all these particulars my vanity taught me to believe myself superior to Sidney.

In these reflections I found an antidote to my fears. I was attentive to the sentiments and conduct of Sidney and of his sister, and met with nothing to persuade me that the esteem which the former was always eager to express for the absent lady, was connected with love. No fits of abstraction, no changes of hue took place when her name was mentioned, or the circumstances of her journey were discussed. These perturbations were felt only by myself.

My tranquility, however, was destined to be interrupted. One evening, my cousin being mentioned, Mrs. Wallace told me that her coming was expected on the next day. These tidings were, as was easily guessed, communicated in a letter. But my surprise and embarrasment were not a little excited, when I discovered that this letter had been addressed not to Mrs. Wallace, but to her brother, and that an epistolary correspondence had subsisted between him and Louisa for a long time.

This proof of confidence between them awakened all my fears. My confusion and dejection could not be concealed, but the apparent folly of this motive, hindered my friends from suspecting its influence. My deportment was frequently regarded by them as enigmatical. My fits of hope and of fear, of dejection and vivacity, were to them wholly inexplicable.

I was at first deterred, by a thousand scruples, from requesting the perusal of this letter. The first intimation which I dropped was instantly complied with. Not only this letter was put into my hand, but an offer made to me of perusing all the letters that had passed between them. The offer was accepted with a mixture of trepidation and joy. I shut myself up in my chamber to peruse them.

I read with eagerness and wonder. The scene exhibited by this correspondence was new. Sidney was four years older than his friend, and their intercourse by letter had lasted during a period equal to this. It began with avowals of love on the part of Sidney, which the lady had rejected. This rejection-was unaccompanied with anger and contempt. It was softened by every token of regret, by every proof of reverence, and by pathetic intreaties, that her incapacity to love him might not prove a forfeiture of his esteem, or a bar to their future intercourse.

This procedure appeared to have been regarded by the lover in its true light. Professions of love ceased to be made. The passion, lately so vehement, seemed to be extinguished in amoment, and to give place to the solicitude and fondness of a brother.

A fearlessness of false construction, absolute purity of purpose, and an unbounded disclosure of every sentiment, distinguished the correspondence that ensued between them. Every sentence was pregnant with novelty and instruction. A degree of unreserve was mutually practised, the possibility of which, between persons of a different sex, uncon-nected by kindred or by passion, I should, without this evidence, have deemed impossible.

The perusal of these letters added inconceivably to my veneration for my cousin. The value of her love was augmented a thousand fold. I vowed, with new ardour, to devote my thoughts and efforts to this purpose. That Sydney had already been reject-ed, was the inspirer of new hopes, but the proofs of her intellectual and moral attainments which these manuscripts contained, tended to discourage me.

The perusal of these letters, and the reflections to which they gave birth, occupied the whole night. The new attractions which the image of this lady had acquired, and the expectation of a meeting the next day, filled me with intense musing, and a tremulous impatience. These tremors increased as the hour of her arrival approached, and I entered Wallace's house in a state of trepidation and embarrassment too painful to belong endured.

Such were the emotions which were excited in my heart by one whom I had never seen, and whose person and features I knew only by description. In this way did the lawless and wild enthusiasm of my character first display itself. I regarded my feelings with wonder and mortification. They reminded me of what I had read in the old poets, of heroes who wept away their lives for love, though the object of their passion had never been seen, and sometimes did not exist. These pictures, which Cervantes had taught me to ridicule or to disbelieve, I now regarded with altered eyes, and perceived that they were somewhat more than creatures of a crazed or perverse fancy.

On entering Wallace's parlour, my friend presented me to one whom he called my cousin. My confusion scarcely allowed me to receive her offered check, or to look at her. One glance, however, was sufficient to dissolve my dream, and quiet my emotion. I was restored, in a moment, to myself, and to indifference, and could scarcely persuade myself that this was the being whom my fancy had so luxuriantly and vividly portrayed.

She was diminutive in size, and without well turned, or well adjusted members or features. Her face was moulded with some delicacy, but it was scarred by the small-pox, and the defects of her skin, in smoothness, were not compensated by any lustre of complexion. Minute in size, inelegantly proportioned, dun in complexion, this figure was a contrast to what the vague encomiums of my friends, and my own active imaginationhad taught me to expect.

This disappointment created dejection, and even some degree of peevishness. I was absurdly disposed to quarrel with my friends for exciting, by their exaggerations, fallacious hopes, and not to have fulfilled these hopes, I regarded as a crime in my cousin. On this account, I not only despised, but secretly upbraided her. Reflection speedily cured me of this folly, and intercourse with the newcomer, by gradually unfolding her excellencies, fully reconciled me to her personal defects, or made me wholly overlook them.

This intercourse was without constraint, and almost without intermission. I saw her at all hours, and almost during every hour of the day. At home and abroad, in the company of strangers and friends, at times of recreation and employment, her person and behaviour were exposed to my scrutiny: a temper capricious and uneven, timorous or irritable, impatient of delay or contradiction, and preferring her own gratification to that of others, never, at any moment, appeared. She smiled upon all, sought from every one the knowledge which he possessed, and betrayed solicitude to please and instruct her companion in her turn. Her mind was incessantly active in analizing the object or topic that occurred, in weighing proofs, tracing inferences, and correcting her mistakes. She read much, but she talked more than she read, and meditated more than she talked. She frequently changed her place, her company, and her employments, but these changes wrought no difference in the ineffable complacency which dwelt in her eyes, in the activity of her thoughts, and the benevolent fervour of her expressions.

Me she admitted, in a moment, to familiarity and confidence. She talked to me of her own concerns, of her maxims of economy, her household arrangements, her social connexions, her theories of virtue and duty, and related, with scrupulous fidelity, the history of her opinions and her friendships. This confidence did not flow from having ascertained my merits, or the assurance slowly and cautiously admitted, that her confessions would not be misunderstood, and would not be abused. She spake to me because I was within hearing, and only ceased to speak when interrupted by another, or to obtain replies to her questions. She was not more liberal of information respecting herself, than solicitous to obtain a knowledge of me. For this end she dealt not in circuities and hints, but employed direct questions, and inquired into my condition and views, with all the openness and warmth with which she disclosed her own.

The thoughts which had occupied me most, related to herself. My design of gaining her love had been thwarted, or, at least, discouraged by first appearances. The transfer of her father's property, had been recommended by a sense of justice, but I will not deny that I was also influenced by other motives. These motives had governed me without my being fully conscious of their force. I had desired, by bestowing this benefit, to advance myself in her esteem, and I could scarcely conceal from myself that marriage would restore to me what I should thus have given away.

My feelings were now changed, and I found reasons for abandoning my purpose, or, at least, for delaying the execution of it. What I did not mean to perform, there seemed some reasons for concealing that I had ever intended. Though she frequently alluded to the event which had made me possessor of her father's property, interrogated me as to the condition of the land and tendered me her counsel and assistance in the use of it, she never gave proofs of being dissatisfied or disappointed by her father's will, of having imagined her own tide superior to mine, or of imputing any meanness and guilt to my retention of it.

What her candour did not condemn, however, my own conscience disapproved. It was difficult to stifle my conviction of being actuated by selfish and ignoble views. I saw that I had formed this design upon improper motives, and had relinquished it from motives equally sordid. I had not only my own disapprobation to contend with, but was terrified by fear of that of others. I had incautiously mentioned this design to my mother and to Wallace, and it would not be easy to account for, or apologize to them for this change in my plans. Still, however, my reluctance to give away so large a property to one, who, by her marriage, would give it to another, was too powerful to be subdued.

While my mind was in this state of indecision, I took occasion to visit my cousin one evening, on which she was alone. I had scarcely entered the apartment when I noticed some marks of disquiet in her features, which she immediately explained, by repeating the substance of a conversation which had just passed between Sydney and her. From him she had heard of the design I had formerly entertained respecting Calverton.

"I have just been informed," she continued, "that you intended to transfer my father's estate to me. Your motives, no doubt, were generous, and founded on an high opinion of my worth. You have not executed this design, nor, since my arrival, have even mentioned it to my friend or to me. I cannot help feeling some anxiety on this account. If I had not received your earnest assurances that your prepossessions in my favour have been fulfilled, and even greatly surpassed, I should ascribe this change in your plans, to the discovery of some unworthiness in me. This belief I cannot admit, after having listened to so many encomiums from your lips, and yet I am at a loss to account for it in any other manner. A sort of half-formed suspicion has found its way into my heart, that—shall I tell you what I think, even when my thoughts are disadvantageous to you? I cannot help suspecting you of some caprice or some faultiness. I have hitherto found you, or imagined you, an excellent youth, I loved, I exulted in your virtues, such as I have known them, by means of your mother's report, and such as I have witnessed them myself. To have formed this design, argued more generosity than I had ascribed to you, but to have relinquished it when once formed, evinces either a blameable fickleness or a laudable sagacity. From which of these it flows, I know not. I want to esteem you more than I do, but I am afraid, when I come to be acquainted with the true motives on which you have acted, I shall find reason for esteeming you less. Pray, my friend, let me know the truth."

While saying this her eyes were fixed with great

earnestness on my face. They even glistened with tears. I was affectedin a singular manner. These proofs of a tender and sublime interest in my happiness and virtue, affected me with pleasure, while the consciousness of the truth of her suspicions covered me with shame.

I had a difficult part to act. To acknowledge the truth, would, indeed, lower me in her opinion, a circumstance not less distressful to her than to me. To pretend that I was influenced by disinterested considerations, and by a sort of refined, though perhaps erroneous regard to her happiness, which her present frugal competence would more essentially promote, than the possession of extensive and cumbrous property, to insinuate that I had only delayed, in consequence of some fictitious obstacles, the execution of my purpose, would have been grossly culpable. I was fortunately extricated from this embarrassment by the entrance of a neighbour, whose prolix loquacity consumed the whole evening, and allowed me to withdraw before any further explanation could take place.

This incident led my thoughts into a new direction. It seemed as if the option of doing or forbearing was taken away. My reputation was made to depend upon my conduct, and the rebukes and contempts of my mother, of Sydney, and of the lady herself, were to be shunned at a greater price than this. I was determined, with whatever reluctance, to execute my first purpose.

My reluctance did not flow from any single source. Power and property are intrinsically valuable, and I loved them for their own sake, as well as for the sake of the good which they would enable me to confer upon others. I was willing to obviate all the necessities of this woman, but desired to retain the means in my own hands. I did not love her, but I drew pain from thinking of her as belonging to another. I did not wish her to be mine, but I believed that no human being was so worthy to possess her as myself. To enrich her, would be merelyenriching some being, who, at present, was unknown, and whom, when known, I was sure that I should hate and despise.

The necessity to which I had reduced myself of giving, and the aversion which the conception of her marriage with another produced, led me, at length, to reflect upon the scheme of seeking her myself. To reconcile myself to this scheme, I ruminated on her unrivalled and inestimable qualities. I said, I must not expect to meet with any one equally excellent. She is destitute of beauty, but what is beauty? It is transient and perishable. Time or indisposition destroys it, and its power over the senses depends upon its novelty. Conjugal familiarity never fails, in a very short period, to dissolve the charm. The true foundation of love is placed in the moral character, and the assurance of being requited with affection.

To know that I am beloved by a being like this, will unavoidably excite that passion in me, but, if it did not, still my regard for the happiness of such a woman ought to determine my choice. I believe that she already loves me, and it is my duty to ascertain the truth, and, in some sort, to abide by her decision.

Meanwhile to offer her this estate, which truly belongs not to me, but to her, is my first province. In doing this, all allusions to wedlock or love should be carefully excluded. They may, in a due interval, properly succeed, but ought not to accompany the offer. To proffer money and love, in the same moment, is ridiculous. It would appear like bribing her affections, and is absurd, since it would be equivalent to taking back with one hand what we bestow with the other.

But how shall I account for my delay ? She knows that I once conceived this design, and have since apparently relinquished it. My motives have, I fear, been selfish or ambiguous, and I cannot prevail upon myself to disclose them. The truth must be palliated or disguised. Some adequate apology must be invented. It was in vain, however, that I sought for some apology which would answer my end, without a greater breach of truth than my honesty would allow me to commit.

At length it occurred to me, that since I had resolved to tender her my hand, there was no sufficient reason for deferring the tender. I neither expected nor desired stronger evidence of her intellectual excellence than I at present possessed. If she loved me, the sooner her anxieties were at an end, the more should I consult her happiness. If her affection were desirable, upon the whole, the sooner it was ascertained and secured, the better. Besides, since an apology for my delay must be found, none was more plausible than that it arose from my having entertained a passion, which, if crowned with success, would render my intended gift unnecessary and absurd.

Such was the train of my reflections, in my way homeward from the interview, which I have just described. When I left the house, no conception was more distant from my wishes than marriage with my cousin, but before I reached my lodging, a total reverse had taken place in my sentiments and views. This reverse was of too much moment not to engross my deepest thoughts. I entered my chamber and threw myself on the bed. As soon as I came to reflect upon this union, as on somewhat that was destined to happen, I was industrious in tracing its consequences and revolving its benefits. Insensibly my fancy became heated, I grew impatient of delay, I shuddered at the obstacles to my success that time might produce, and at those which might, at that moment, secretly exist. I endeavoured to bury my forebodings and anxieties in sleep, but sleep would not be summoned.

At length I started on my feet, and exclaimed, why should I endure this uncertainty a moment? Why should I impose it on another ? A mutual understanding may be accomplished next month or next week: but cannot it be, with more propriety, effected tomorrow? and if tomorrow, why not tonight? No event can be more disastrous and intolerable than suspense, and this hour, when the Wallaces are gone to their repose, and Louisa has withdrawn to her chamber, not to sleep, but to brood over the tormenting images of my depravity, may terminate suspense, and stifle suspicion, and overwhelm the heart of this angelic woman with joy.

She does not go to bed till twelve. In such a moonlight night as this, she is probably seated at her chamber window, which is lifted, and which overlooks the street. Hence, it will be easy to obtain audience, and the conference to which I summon her will be worthy of the sacred silence and solemnity attendant on it.

Fraught with this idea, I left my chamber and the house, and speeded towards the street where Wallace resided. The air was mild and the moonlight brilliant, and many persons were seated at their doors and in their porches, gaily conversing, and inhaling the breeze, whose grateful influence had been enhanced by the fervours of the past day.

My expectations of seeing Louisa at the window, were fulfilled. Her voice was coarse and monotonous, and wholly unadapted to music, but she was nevertheless, fond of the art, and, when alone, was accustomed to sing. This, at present, was her occupation, and though its influence was unpleasing, inasmuch as it reminded me of her deficiency in an art, upon skill in which my imagination had been used to set the highest value, it likewise delighted me, by denoting her presence at the window.

On recognising my voice she betrayed no small surprise. My request to be admitted to an interview was immediately granted. She came down stairs, and, opening the street door, went with me into a back parlour. This meeting, said she, is very singular and unexpected. Something of no very trivial import must have induced you to come hither at such an hour. Pry'thee tell me the cause.

To explain the cause was a task of some delicacy. Her own quickness of perception, however, supplied my want of perspicuity, and the ardour of her own feelings made her overlook the fluctuations and coldness which the neutral state of my affections could not but produce in my tone and deportment. That she loved me was a suspicion not admitted without plausible evidence, but the transports of her tenderness, the sobs which convulsed her bosom, and took away all utterance, surpassed those bounds which my imagination had assigned to it.

These appearances were not anticipated. It

cannot be said that they excited pain, but they were contemplated without rapture. I was conscious to a kind of disapprobation, of which the inertness and insensibility of my own heart were the objects. I believed that I ought to have partaken in her transports, that the merits of this being, and the value of her love, were such as to make my near approaches to indifference a crime. In circumstances that ought to have been pregnant with delight, my complex feelings were tinctured with dejection.

At this moment our attention was called away by a distant and faint sound. It was the murmur of confused and unequal voices, mingling, and, at each moment, growing louder and more distinct. Presently a tolling bell was heard. The sounds were, at first, slow, and at long intervals , but suddenly the strokes succeeded each other with more rapidity, and other larums were rung in different quarters. The sounds gradually approached the door. The pavement without was beaten by innumerable footsteps, and the fearful warning, ascending from a thousand mouths, was "Fire! Fire!"

I was confounded and dismayed by this uproar. I had never witnessed this disaster in a populous city, and my fancy had connected with it innumerable images of tumult and horror. I knew not the place or the limits of the danger, and gazed around me as if it were uncertain whether the room in which we stood was incircled by the blaze.

From this stupor I was roused by my companion, who knew nothing but compassion for the sufferers, and who implored me to fly to their relief.

Who? Where? Whither must I fly?

Go into the street: run whichever way the crowd runs.

I obeyed without parley or delay, and, rushing into the street, allowed myself to be carried along by the stream. Presently I turned a corner, and saw, far before me, red gleams, wavering on the roofs and walls, and luminous smoke, rolling inimmense volumes above.

I ran forward with speed. Presently I drew near the house that was in flames. The space before it was crowded with gazers, whose tongues were active in augmenting the clamour, while their hands seemed totally unoccupied. I pressed forward with eagerness, though actuated merely by an impetuous curiosity, till I reached a narrow interval between the walls of the building and the middle of the street. This space was ankle-deep in water, supplied by the pumps and engines, which had been drained without success. It was, besides, scarcely tenable from the heat. Beams, and fragments from the roof were incessantly falling around it. No danger, therefore, was more imminent, and the crowd kept aloof.

I had scarcely breathed, after reaching the verge of this space, when I noticed a ladder, raised against the wall, and leaning on a window at the third story.

No one ascended it, from fear, as I hastily collected from the exclamations of those near me, that the roof would sink before he who should be adventurous enough to enter the house should have time to leave it. I found, likewise, that some one was imagined to be asleep in that chamber.

I was not qualified to judge of the progress which the fire had made, or on what ground this apprehension was built. Had I deliberately consulted my reason, I should, doubtless, have continued to hover at a cowardly distance from the scene of peril, but the impulse that governed me was headlong and irresistible. It pushed me forward, and I began to mount the ladder. In vain a thousand voices called upon me to come down, and exclaimed that the roof was already falling. I was deaf to their clamours, and, having gained the top, dashedthrough the window, which, on the outside, could not have been lifted easily, or with sufficient expedition.

The apartment was nearly filled with smoke, which, by my being suddenly immersed in it, had nearly stifled me. Nothing was distinctly visible, but, stretching forth my hands, I threw myself forward at random. I reached a bed, and laid my hands upon a sleeper. It was wonderful that the uproar of men, and the crackling of flames, had not awakened her. I had almost dragged her from the bed before she opened her eyes, and became sensible of her situation.

I had no need of words to explain her danger, or of arguments to prevail on her to fly with me. She had only to regain possession of her senses, to look around her and to listen. The staircase and the roof were wrapt in flames. The fire had already taken hold of her chamber door. The lingering of a moment would have been fatal both to her and to me. Snatching her up in both arms, I hurried to the window, and, darting out of it, had nearly reached the bottom of the ladder when the roof fell in. A cloud of sparkles and cinders flew upward, and on every side. The concussion shook the ladder from its place. I fell, but was fortunate enough to reach the ground upon my feet.

By this time the strength of my companion was exhausted, and she fainted. I did not perceive her situation till, having dragged her through the crowd, who opened me a passage, I reached the steps of an opposite house. Here I paused to collect my thoughts and examine the state of my companion.

We were immediately surrounded by several persons, who offered their assistance. One of them, pointing to an house at some distance, and which was not likely to be injured by the fire, desired that the woman might be carried thither. At the same time he applied to a by stander who, as it appeared, lived in the house, at the door of which we were seated, for a blanket or cloak, in which we might wrap the naked limbs of the sufferer. A cloak was instantly furnished, and the woman, still insensible, was carried in the arms of several persons, to the house before pointed out.

During these transactions, I was nearly passive. An asylum being thus provided for this woman, and succour being thus amply and readily bestowed by others, there was need of no new exertion from me. I had done my part, and it now behooved me to attend to my own safety. Coals and cinders had lighted on my clothes, and penetrated, in several places, to my flesh. The pain, hence produced, was acute. I had likewise, in my incautious haste to regain the ladder, after having entered the room, struck my head against the side of the window, with such violence, as appeared to have left no slight contusion behind it. I felt myself, however, able to move, and believed it proper to return home with as much expedition as possible. I quickly extricated myself from the crowd, whose curiosity and solicitude were more engaged by the woman's condition than by mine, and stopped not till I reached my chamber.

On examining my wounds, I found them to be of small moment, and to be such as to stand in no need of nurse or physician. The pain could be allayed by simple applications within my reach, and I forbore to disturb any of the family. Being remote from the danger, it had not interrupted their repose, and they were wholly unconscious of my motions.

After some time, the tumult of my spirits subsided, and I had leisure to reflect upon the extraordinary occurrences that had just happened. They appeared more like the transitions of a feverish vision, than the sober changes of reality. The being whom I had saved from destruction was a woman. This I had been able to infer, not only from a rapid view of her face and person, but also from her shrieks, whose acute tones sufficiently denoted her sex. Closed eyes and the wanness of death, were not all that the pale reflection of the flames enabled me to discover during the few moments in which she lay in my arms. There were features, and neck, and bosom, which were stamped upon my memory and fancy, in eternal characters. Though seen for an instant, they refused to disappear, and the image was so vivid that I almost stretched forth my hand to discover whether it were not really before me.

What were the lines and hues of this image? Did they coincide with those delineations of ideal beauty by which my solitary hours had been occupied? They were different from all that I had imagined or witnessed. They burst upon my senses with all the enchantments attendant upon novelty as well as loveliness.

But though I had seen her so nearly, she was probably profoundly ignorant of me. Involved in darkness and smoke, she saw me not in her chamber, and, before she reached a station where my features could have been distinctly noticed, she was sunk into insensibility. Some of those around me might have had previous acquaintance with my person, but it was more probable that I was totally unknown to the nearest spectators. I had lately arrived in the city, and my intercourse was chiefly limited to Sydney and the Wallaces.

I scarcely know how to convey to you just ideas of so motley a character as mine was, in my juvenile days. I was the slave of phantasies and contradictions. My preceptors were books. These were of such a kind as to make me wise in speculation, but absurd in practice. I had blended the illusions of poetry with the essences of science. My mind was fertile in reasoning and invention, and my theory was not incorrect, but my practical notions of happiness and dignity, were full of imbecility and folly. The idol which my heart secretly worshipped, and to which I habitually annexed every excellent and splendid attribute, was love. I snatched glimpses of a better kind of devotion, that which is paid to science, to ambition, to the happiness of mankind, but these were transient in their influence.

According to my custom, I was now busy in tracing the consequences to which this incident might lead: in reflecting on the emotions which the lady, on recovering from her swoon, and obtaining a knowledge of the means of her rescue, might admit into her bosom, and on the effects which an interview between us was likely to produce.

The pleasure which I found in these reveries, was quickly damped by remembering that sacred engagement into which I had entered with my cousin, and on the importance to her happiness of my adherence to that engagement. I likewise thought upon those obstacles which fortune, or parents, or a previous marriage, might raise between me and this new acquaintance. These thoughts made my soul droop. I began to upbraid my precipitation with regard to my cousin, to consider my proffer of love before it was actually felt, as a criminal imposture, no less injurious to myself than unjust to her.

The mind is ingenious in inventing topics of consolation. Gradually my thoughts returned to the contemplation of my cousin's excellence, of the seldomness of any union between personal and mental beauty, and of the preference which the latter might always claim over the former. I was likewise wise enough to discern the danger that would flow from intercourse with this unknown person, the tendency of gratitude for so signal a benefit, to produce a more fervent passion, and the hazard of yielding to temptation, which my unfortified virtuemight incur. For these reasons I determined to decline all intercoursewith this female, and to foster, by every means, that affection for Louisa to which she was so well entitled.

Next day the topics of general conversation were, of course, connected with the late fire. Wallace had been roused by the alarm, but had arrived upon the spot sometime after I had retired from it. His inquiries had made him acquainted with most of the particulars which have just been mentioned, but no clue had been afforded by which to ascertain the person of him who had exposed his life to so imminent an hazard.

Sydney had likewise been upon the spot. His knowledge was equally imperfect. I withheld the knowledge which I possessed, being much amused with the speculations and comments that were made in my hearing. I could not but remark the numberless deviations from truth which the story exhibited in passing from one mouth to the other. A score of eye-witnesses communicated each a different tale, and a different description of my person. I was sometimes a youth, sometimes middle-aged. To no two observers was my garb precisely of the same colour and form, and one person solemnly maintained, on the evidence of a pair of eyes, whose acuteness had, in this instance, being assisted by spectacles, that I was a negro man, about forty, who was formerly a slave of his own, and whom he had sought out and handsomely rewarded for his courage. It must be added, indeed, that this witness had not acquired much reputation for veracity.

I was much more inquisitive as to the character and condition of the family who occupied this mansion. I was told that it consisted of two old ladies and a female servant. The latter was she whom I had rescued from destruction. Her mistresses had seasonably escaped, and their confusion and terror had made them overlook, for some time, the danger of their waiting-maid. This being, at length, recollected, some persons had gone so far as to raise the ladder to the window, but their fears would not suffer them to mount it. There were some who confidently reported that the rescuer of the girl, was no other than her lover, a journeyman carpenter and a well-disposed youth, who merited, on this occasion, a public recompense.

So! the nymph whom my imagination had deified, and whose presence I was to shun with as much care as Ulysses shut his ears against the song of the sirens, proved to be nothing more than a waiting-maid, who, though not an unsightly girl, was affirmed to be illiterate and coarse in manners and sentiments. I was sufficiently disposed to question the truth of this intelligence, but these facts were not equally liable to misrepresentation and mistake, as those which related to me, and were supported by no implausible evidence.

The flitting and ambiguous light in which she had been viewed, and her state of insensibility, had probably decorated her, to my eye, with so many fictitious charms. I drew a useful lesson from this discovery. I learned to contemn the vagaries of my fancy, and to place more reliance on experience.

My secret struggles and fantastic regrets, which my reason had been unable to subdue, were now at an end. The idol I had worshipped proved to be a worthless stock, and I returned, with satisfaction, to the path of love and of honour to which my cousin had invited me.

Some days after, on entering Sidney's apartment, he pointed out a paragraph, in the gazette of the day, in which were these words: "we learn that the person who so bravely exposed his life for the sake of a fellow creature, at the late fire in Highstreet, is Mr. Felix Calvert, a young gentleman lately from Europe." This paragraph put an end to my concealment, and my narrative of this transaction afforded to Louisa and my friends a topic of much curiosity and congratulation. The assertion of my late arrival from Europe was a new proof of the fallacy of rumour, and I took no pains either to confute this error, or to detect the means by which my concern in this affair had been discovered.

Some time afterwards I was accidentally enabled to trace the channel through which this information reached the printer. A young negro, who belonged to Calverton, had spent the night of this conflagration abroad. He had excused his absence to my steward, by feigning that he watched by the side of a sick slave, belonging to a neighbouring plantation. In truth, he spent it at a carousal in the city.

Three days after this event, he was standing in

the marketplace, chattering with great vivacity to a companion. Their discourse was overheard by an apprentice in the office of theWeekly Gazette, who stopped near them to purchase a melon. It appeared that Cuff was relating what had passed at the fire, of which he was a witness. When he reached the incident of mounting the ladder, he continued thus:

"Ou' pop a man! uppa de latha like a rat. Ob bobbs! what de debble! Prime, says I, is'n da massa Cavut? No! ees! ees! it ee massa Cavut. What de debble if ee see me? the Ceesa gim me floggin! Way! scampa! scud!

"No, no, says Prime, top he be kill. Run uppa de latha. Massa Cavut sure enough.

"So I top. Ebba body olla, downa, downa! Massa Cavut no ere em: run uppa lika querril up oaka tree. No debble runna like him. In ee pop. No liffa de winda, but in ee pop, trough glass and all. Quash! ebba body olla. Prime olla. Me ollamo dan ebba body. O massa Cavut! massa Cavut! massa Cavut era no body bum me. So ou' pop massa wid 'oman in 'is'and. Down de latha ee runna, mo fass dan ebba, 'oman in 'is'and 'till. Den I runna too, fear ee see me: teh Ceesa gimme floggin."

"Pray," said the apprentice, "Who are you talking of, Blackee? The man who got the girl out of the window the other night, at the fire? Do you know who he was?"

"Be sure I do. He my massa: ung massa Cavut.

He be lif oba Kukill. I be lif wid im. He be come estaday oba de watta."

Massa Cavut was translated by a market-man, who lived near Chester, into Mr. Felix Calvert, and this intelligence being transferred to the printer, it found its way, by his contrivance, to the public. Thus, though many different representations will be given of every incident, yet it may always be, that one among the number shall be true.

This event and its consequences were, in a short time, generally forgotten. It determined the colour of my destiny, but the period was not yet arrived when I was enabled to discern the extent of its influence. Meanwhile, my thoughts were occupied by schemes of love and happiness. Each day admitted me to a nearer view of the mental beauties of my cousin, afforded new proofs of the warmth of her affection, and gave new tenderness to my own feelings.

There is but one goal to which the wishes of lovers point. Having ascertained the mutual existence of love, and no impediment arising from considerations of fortune, all that remained was marriage. Having proceeded thus far, I was eager to accomplish the remainder, and a suitable opportunity occurring, I disclosed to her my wishes.

Either the vulgar portraits of women are groundless and absurd, or my cousin's deportment was an exception to those rules which ordinarily influence her sex. I am disposed to adopt the former opinion, having rarely found any of those distinctions that abound in books exemplified in real life. Woman has been painted as a mass of scruples and doubts, as studying concealments and disguises, as inviting and withdrawing from importunities, as perpetually distrusting the tendency of her feelings, and sifting the professions of her lover, as wishing, and deferring the attainment of her wishes when fully in her power, as practising a thousand stratagems and frauds, and cloaking her hypocrisy under the specious names of dignity, self-respect, modest reserve.

We are taught to expect that a woman will assiduously counterfeit indifference till the man has avowed his affection, that the secret of her heart, instead of spontaneously flowing to her lips, can only be extorted, that tremours, flutterings, and misgivings, a proneness to recede and delay, are to accompany every act of condescension, and every acquiescence in necessity, that these are feminine attributes, and are not only dictated by reason and duty, but are interwoven with the female constitution.

My teachers and guides had been the coiners of fiction, the preachers of duplicity, the moralists who talk of virtue as of one thing in man and another thing in woman, of mind as modified by sexual differences, like the hue of a skin and the texture of a muscle, and of duty and decorum as prescribing an opposite demeanour in similar circumstances.

Hitherto my theories had been only thwarted and contradicted by the conduct of my cousin. Love had made no inroad on her candour and her unreserve. Her preference of my society, even before she had reason to suppose me a lover, was never concealed. Her eyes sparkled with new pleasure on my entrance : her attention seldom strayed from my countenance and words: her anxiety at any token of disquiet in me was openly expressed, and once, on a sudden meeting, she so far overstepped the customary boundaries, as to wrap me in her arms and kiss my cheek. No self-reproof or blushful consciousness ensued this act of unguarded tenderness, though, indeed, it took place without a witness.

Knowing the benevolence of her temper, her perfect artlessness, and her assurance of her own rectitude, I was doubtful for a time whether to ascribe these appearances to more than friendship. I imagined that love was the parent of reserve and dissimulation, that it would produce a seeming unwillingness to answer my inquiries or comment upon my theories, that she should desire my exclusive company, but labour to conceal that desire, and so manage, that the attainment of her purpose should always appear to flow from accident, that her expressions, when addressed to others, should be fluent and unstudied, but, to me, should be selected with caution, and uttered withsome degree of hesitation, attention, when least apparent, should be most powerful, and when she listened with most eagerness, her eyes should seem most occupied by a different object.

On this occasion my vague prognostics were no less totally confuted. My intimations were understood before they were fully expressed. They obtained not a dubious acquiescence, but a vehement assent. It was unwise to defraud herself of the happiness of wedlock by the least delay. Next week was a period preferable to next month, tomorrow was still more to be desired. Nay, she would eagerly concur in the ratification of this contract on that very night. Domestic arrangements might follow with as much convenience and propriety as precede. The house of Wallace would be glad to receive me as a more permanent guest.

She hated the ostentations and formalities attendant on the rite of marriage. These made her regard, with some timidity, that which, on its own account, was productive of nothing but good. Why not lay these aside with the contempt which they deserved? Why tolerate a longer delay, or pass through more forms than were absolutely indispensable?

Her good friend, Mr. Aylford, knew of the engagement of her heart. She owed a visit to that reverend and excellent man. Let us begone this moment, she continued, and seek him in his closet, where he is busy in preparing the religious exercises of tomorrow. Let us claim his immediate assistance in uniting us beyond the power of fate to dissolve the union. We need not leave his house till tomorrow, when we will return hither, and afford you the opportunity of introducing to the Wallaces your wife.

I was almost startled by the abruptness and novelty of this proposal. Its adventurous singularity, however, was congenial with my character, and I eagerly assented to it. But where, said I, shall a witness be procured? Mr. Aylford will not be willing to dispense with the presence of another.

Neither would I be willing. A witness must doubtless be had, and that witness shall be Sidney. His approbation and his presence are wholly indispensable on an occasion like this.

At this moment Sidney entered the room, The lady, with her usual confidence in his affection, repeated the proposal which she had just made.

While thus employed I diligently observed the countenance of Sidney. I had never forgotten that he was once the lover of this woman. It was inconceivable that love so rational should have wholly disappeared. That Sidney, whose talents and integrity were revered by Louisa, should never have gained a place in her affections, had always appeared an inexplicable problem in my eyes, but it was still more difficult to comprehend how the love which Sidney had once admitted could have ceased to exist, when the intercourse between them, and the interchange of good offices, continued the same, and when no new passion had arisen to supplant the old.

I had seen, in him, however, no tokens of uneasiness or jealousy. He had marked the progress of our mutual passion with tranquil approbation. He had spoken of it with an air of serene contentment, and his frankness and affectionate demeanour, as well as his general cheerfulness, appeared not to have been lessened, but augmented by this event.

On the present occasion, he smiled, and said, I believe your wishes cannot be gratified to night, unless some other clergy man will answer your purposes as well as Mr. Aylford, for he left town this morning, and will not return till tomorrow evening.

Louisa declared it impossible for any other to supply his place, and professed her willingness to defer the ceremony till the morrow. On the whole, said she, it will be best. Mrs. Wallace would censure me with justice for taking so momentous a step, not only without her company, but without her knowledge. You, Sidney, and she, shall accompany us tomorrow to Mr. Aylford's, and be witnesses of the happiness of your friends.

Some incident now occurred to separate the company, and put an end to our discourse. I returned to my lodgings, and, till the next morning allowed me to visit my cousin, passed awakeful and feverish interval. The coming event I regarded with tumultuous impatience. So far from being able to sleep, it was impossible to enjoy a moment's rest. My limbs bore me mechanically to and fro. I marked the vibrations of the pendulum, and eyed the index of the clock as it stepped from one second to another. Time, surely, has no measurer but the progress of our own sensations. Fear and hope will prolong days into years, while the oblivion of insanity or sleep leaps overdays and years as if they were not.

Every moment seemed to annihilate some hazard that beset me, while, for one peril that it removed, several were created anew. As I approached the period that should accomplish my felicity, my terrors were augmented. While fettered by these panics, I seemed conscious of the folly of my bondage, that it existed only in my own imagination, that my eyes were deceived by mists which a single penetrating and vigorous glance would utterly dispel. Still the effort could not be made or could not be sustained. If the mist vanished for a moment, it returned in the next moment, harder to dispel, and more pregnant with monsters and chimeras than before.

The sun consoled me, at length, and encouraged me by his presence. Earlier than usual I hasted to Wallace's house. All the disasters that are incident to man had infested my nocturnal reveries. A thousand evils impended over my cousin, any one of which was sufficient to raise an insuperable barrier between us.

Fire might lurk in the walls or floors of her dwelling, it might burst forth in the midst of her security, as on the occasion formerly mentioned. Danger might assail her from within. At this moment she might be seized with the pangs of a mortal disease, and death might snatch her from my arms.

Short-sighted wretch! The evil which thou dreadest, was that which was to take this woman from thy possession. Whence but from some casualty or some disease, could this evil flow? That any moral impediment could arise, never occurred to thy conceptions. In thy widest and most lawless excursions, the possibility of treachery or change in this woman, of prevention or delay from moral considerations, never entered thy thought. All that knew us, were apprised of our mutual passion, all whose approbation was of value, were lavish of their approbation, all to whom Louisa was accustomed to apply for counsel, had been strenuous in their commendations of her choice. My mother had expressed her delight at the prospect of obtaining this woman for her son, had testified impatience at delay, and was eager to receive us under her roof. There were no bounds to the reverence and love which Louisa entertained for my mother. To contribute to her happiness, had almost been an irresistible motive for accepting the son, though her own heart had been neutral, but her heart added to untainted fidelity and probity, an affection that was unacquainted with restraint, and all her wishes were absorbed in that of being indissolubly and speedily united to her cousin. What then but some jarring of the elements, some shock of nature, some coincidence of physical disasters, could raise an impediment in the way of my hopes?

As I approached the house, my fears subsided, no vestiges of earthquake or fire were to be seen. The house exhibited the usual tokens of safety and tranquility. As I reached the door, Sidney came forth. We accosted each other with smiling civility. His cheerful brow dissipated any remnant of uneasiness that was not already removed.

I found Louisa alone in an upper room. She was sitting in a museful posture, leaning on her hand. For a moment my heart faultered with doubt, whether this was the attitude of thoughtfulness or dejection. On my entrance she looked up, and I perceived that she had been weeping. She assumed a tranquil appearance at my approach, but there were tokens of constraint sufficiently visible.

My heart sunk within me at this reception. I scarcely opened my lips to bid her good morrow, but placing myself by her side, waited, in fearful silence, for an explanation of this scene. At length, in the confusion of my thoughts, I muttered some inquiry respecting her health.

"No," said she, "I am not well. Sick. Heart-sick."

Good heaven! What is the cause ?

"The want of fortitude, the want of virtue. A sacrifice is claimed at my hands, which my pusillanimity does not hinder me from making, but I cannot make it cheerfully. My reluctance, the growth of folly and passion, refuses to yield."

Of what sacrifice do you speak? Louisa Calvert is equal to the performance of her duty.

"Yes, but she is unequal to the seasonable discovery and steadfast apprehension of her duty. I saw it clearly a few minutes ago, but now it is misty and ambiguous. I waver, and I see that my waverings proceed from cowardice and passion. This does not render me steadfast. It does not restore my resolution. It only heaps anguish and misery on my head." Saying this, her looks betrayed the deepest distress.

My alarms were importunate, and, at length, throwing herself, with a burst of tears, into my arms, she continued: "not for me only, my friend, but for thee also, do my tears flow. Self-denial is a lesson which I learned in my infancy, and in my father's house. The school of disappointment and adversity has taught me long ago what you are beginning to learn."

This was a terrible prelude. She proceeded, but I anticipated the stroke she was about to inflict.

"This evening was fixed for the period of our union, but that union must be deferred for many years, perhaps forever."

How say you? Forever ?

"All engagements between us are at an end. They must not be renewed in less than five years. Meanwhile, you must comply with your cousin's invitation, and go to Europe."

To Europe? Must comply? What language is this? Yesterday you knew it not. What frenzy has seized you? The contract that made you mine is sacred, and all that remains to perfect it must be performed this very day. I do not solicit your compliance, but exact it. You have bereaved yourself of the power of retracting, and are bound to my mother, to myself, to your friends, by an irrevocable promise.

"Alas! be it sacred or not, it can never be performed. It was made while ignorant of consequences, ignorant of my duty, I am now enlightened upon that head, and have uttered my unalterable resolution."

I was lost in astonishment at the causes that produced this change. For a time I persisted in denying that such a change had taken place. She was not anxious to convince me of the truth by loud exclamations. Her mournful silence, and her tears, were sufficient indications that the scheme of my felicity-was blasted by some untoward event or malignant counsellor. My entreaties to be told by whom these resolutions were suggested, and on what motives they were built, were answered in broken accents, and reluctantly.

"I am not able to repeat the reasons which were

urged. I only know that they were valid, that they enjoin upon us a temporary, and, perhaps, an eternal separation."

Who was the reasoner that has made such stupendous discoveries, who has taught you to act against your promise, against the dictates of your own reason, the expectations and opinions of the world, and what motives could his accursed ingenuity invent sufficient to sway you?

"Talk not thus vehemently. If this reasoner has erred, I have erred no less. While censuring him, you censure me. I was indulging my gay visions this morning, when Sidney came and besought an interview. The reasons which he laid before me, for postponing my marriage and dissolving the engagement between us were just." Sidney? Carlton? He dissuaded you from marriage? What motives could he urge?

"I am not qualified to explain them, in the present state of my feelings. I should not state them clearly and impartially. If you will go to him, he will tell you what has passed. He wishes to confer with you on this subject."

His wishes shall be instantly gratified. I will go to him immediately.

I entered Sidney's apartment in a state of perplexity and anger, which made me careless of all forms. Ideas floated in my brain which assumed no distinct shape, but they were connected with remembrances of Sidney's ancient pretensions to my cousin, and vague suspicions of malevolence or treachery.

He was sitting at a table, with books and papers before him. So, said I, abruptly and advancing towards him, here are mysteries which it must be your province to explain. Yesterday Louisa Calvert consented to become my wife, but today, it seems, she has changed her mind, and, she tells me, you have been the author of this change. You have urged reasons for not merely postponing our alliance, but even for wholly dissolving the contract. You will not be surprised that this disappointment should distress me, and that I should expect from you the reasons of so strange and unexpected, and, indeed, unwarrantable interference. What have you discovered to make my marriage with my cousin less eligible now than formerly? Till this moment, I have seen in your conduct, no marks but of approbation, and have relied upon you as my strongest advocate, but now, it seems, the tide has changed, and you have persuaded her to recal all her promises, and thwart every expectation of her friends.

During this address, Sidney's countenance became grave, but without embarrassment or dejection. After a pause, he replied in a sedate and mild tone,"it is true." There he stopped.

True! But why have you acted thus ? What objections have you found to this marriage? What vices or enormities have you detected in me which unfit me for being the husband of Louisa Calvert?

"No vices or enormities. Nothing but the want of age and experience. But my objections are not limited to you. They relate chiefly to your cousin. Her qualities, in my opinion, make this alliance improper. It is more likely that misery will flow from it than happiness. I have endeavoured to convince her of this, and have, beyond my expectations, succeeded."

Qualities in my cousin that make marriage improper? Pray, of what kind are they ? They have entirely escaped my sagacity, and I should be grateful for the assistance of a friend in drawing them to light.

"I doubt much," replied he, unaffected by the ironical severity of my looks and tones, and eyeing me mildly and steadfastly. "I much doubt the fervency of your gratitude for a service like that, and yet I have no mean opinion of your generosity. You are passionate and headstrong, but there is, in your character, a fund of excellence, which, if not checked by untoward events, will hereafter render you illustrious. You have won my esteem, and I love you so much that I am willing to promote your happiness even at the expense of your temporary gratification. I would save you from an alliance which would operate to your mutual destruction."

These intimations startled me. I re-urged, in a milder tone, my inquiries into those defects in my cousin which were adapted to produce such disastrous consequences.

"It is useless to discuss them," said he. "Instead of regarding them as defects, you will account them excellences, and excellences they truly are. Those qualities which have given birth to your passion, are the same which disqualify her for being your wife. In proportion to her candour and benevolence, to her tenderness and constancy, is she unfitted for an indissoluble alliance with a youth, raw, unexperienced, with principles untried and unsettled, impetuous, versatile, liable each day to new impressions, and enslaved by a thousand romantic and degrading prejudices. I do not beseech your patient attention to arguments and exhortations. I do not seek to convince you that Louisa Calvert, in proportion to the purity and elevation of her character, is unfit to be your wife. By my conduct on this occasion, I expect only to excite your rage, and to draw upon myself your upbraidings and suspicions. If any other emotions were excited, my objection to the marriage would not have existed. It was agreeable, however, to my conceptions of duty, to act and to speak thus. I think I foresee all the consequences of my actions, and as this foresight has not shaken mypurpose, these consequences, whatever they may be, will not molest my tranquility."

It is impossible to describe the emotions which were produced by these words. A secret conscience whispered me that Sidney was right, that I was, indeed, that versatile, romantic, and ambiguous being which he had described, that the passion I had fostered for my cousin was built on inadequate foundations, was unsupported by congeniality of character, was more allied to the impulses of sense and to the instigations of vanity, than to any better principle. This whispering conscience, however, was scarcely heard, and its intimations were neglected. I viewed the subject not through so cold a medium. My desires, though ambiguous in their origin, and, perhaps, transient and mutable, were vehement, and acquired new strength from this unexpected opposition. These desires dictated my opinions and my language. The interference of Sidney, in a transaction in which he had no direct concern, his attempt to control his friend in a choice where her happiness alone was to be consulted, appeared to me audacious and presumptuous. I was likewise sufficiently disposed to question the purity of his motives, to impute his conduct to mean jealousy and rivalship. I did not hide these thoughts, and was, by no means, sparing of surmises and reproaches.

He listened to me with unaltered features. At first I was inclined to suppose that my reproaches had possessed some influence, but when I gave him opportunity to speak, he declared that the light in which his interference had been viewed by me, and the resentment which it had excited, fully agreed with his expectations. My reproaches argued all that impetuosity of temper which he had already, in the secret of his own thoughts, ascribed to me. It added, if possible, new force to his objections against any union between me and his friend. "Your errors," continued he, "are of no rare or prodigious kind. They are incident to persons of your immature age, and contracted experience, and secluded education. They entitle you to sympathy and succour from those wiser and older than yourself. I am your senior by a few years, and if I possess any superiority over you, am indebted for it to wiser instructors and larger observation.

"I have made no secret of the love which I once felt for your cousin. That love was founded on proofs of her excellence, which time has multiplied instead of lessening. That love, therefore, has not been diminished, but enhanced by time, but the happiness to flow from her union with me, must mutually exist, or it cannot exist at all. If undesirable, if unproductive of felicity to her, it must cease to be desirable, cease to be productive of happiness to me.

"You imagine that my opposition has its root in selfish considerations, that I labour to prolong her single state, in hopes that time and assiduities will win her favour to myself. Even while you utter these surmises, you are doubtful of their truth, and you fully expect that I will earnestly assert the purity of my motives. These expectations will be disappointed. I am far from supposing myself raised above the frailties of my nature, that my conduct is exempt from all sinister and selfish bias. I know that they sway us in a thousand imperceptible ways, that they secretly pervert those resolutions, and vitiate those reasonings, which, to our hasty view, appear the most enlightened and benevolent. I claim no merit but that of honestly, and strenuously labouring to discover and exterminate the suggestions of self-interest. I know very well that I am far from constantly succeeding, and the detection of my own mistakes, is the irksome, but inevitable fruit of every new meditation.

"It is true that I love this woman, that no man on earth estimates so justly, and admires so fervently her virtuous qualities, that no one is so qualified to make her happy, provided love was not wanting on her side. I know that this love may, on some future occasion, start into being. Need I say that I desire this event? That I regard, with aversion, any obstacle to its occurrence ?

"It is true that she loves another, that her heart is devoted to you. I am grieved that her heart is thus devoted. I would willingly free her from this inauspicious passion, and restore her to that indifference which I desire that she should relinquishonly for my sake, I repine at her choice, because I am not the object of it, but I should be guilty of falsehood and injustice if I allowed you to suppose that this was the only cause of my repining, and that hence only arose my opposition to your marriage. No, it is founded on accurate examination of your character, and proof which, to me, is incontestible, that the misery of your cousin, and your own misery, would flow from your alliance.

"You will imagine that prejudice and selfishness create, to my view, those disadvantageous qualities which I impute to you. I will not deny it. It is possible that I mistake your character. Hence the diligence of my scrutiny into your deportment, and into my own motives, has been redoubled. Hence my decision has been protracted, and my interposition been delayed to the present hour. Hence I have not, as you seem to think, advised your cousin to dissolve all connection with you, but merely to postpone her marriage for a few years, during which that steadfastness of views and principles in which you are now wanting, may be acquired by intercourse with the world, and exposure to its temptations and vicissitudes.

"You have hitherto dreamed away your life in solitude. You have no practical acquaintance with yourself, or with the nature of the beings who surround you. You have nothing but distorted and crude conceptions, and passions lawless and undisciplined. You are governed by the present impulse, rebel against all restraints, shrink from all privations, and refer nothing to futurity. Your attachments spring from vanity and physical incitements, they are transient as the hour, and variable with every variation in the objects which surround you. To link Louisa Calvert, by ties that cannot be unloosed, to such an one, would be devoting one being, whom I love beyond all mankind, and another, for whom, in spite of his defects, I have considerable esteem, to bitter regrets and incurable calamity. I cannot think of it."

These representations, urged with the utmost pathos and simplicity, produced a temporary effect upon my feelings. Without being convinced, I was at a loss for an answer. After a pause of some minutes, I left the house, and, returning to my lodgings, employed myself in revolving the topics which Sidney had urged.

The impression which his last words had made upon me, speedily vanished. The more I brooded on the subject, the more equivocal his motives, and fallacious his reasonings appeared. I began to see nothing in his conduct but the stratagems of a selfish competitor, and called up all my courage to the contest with him. To compel him to recall his prohibitions, was not possible. To betake myself to solicitations and intreaties, was sordid and dastardly. My genuine province was to change my cousin's resolutions by intreaties or arguments. Inthis task, I imagined that little difficulty would occur, and relied, for success, on my own talents, and on the warmth of her affection.

Shortly I obtained another interview. Her

deportment wa sno longer the same. Instead of the cheerfulness, and even gaiety, by which she had been formerly distinguished, and manners flowing from the union of affection and candour, she was melancholy and full of solicitude, which she was at no pains to conceal. She eyed me with visible dejection and apprehension.

My discontents were sufficiently apparent, and augmented that anxiety which her conduct betrayed. A look, cast upon Mrs. Wallace, indicated her desire of conversing with me apart. Her friend seemed acquainted with the new embarrassments which had arisen between us, and left us to ourselves.

As soon as we were left alone, my cousin placed her chair close to mine, and pressing my hand between her's, said, in broken accents,"You have been with Sidney. He has talked to you, but not convinced you. He has repeated your discourse, and I see, too clearly, the inefficacy of his reasonings. O! my friend! would to heaven you could think with him and with me! and imitate that self-denial which duty imposes on me."

You mistake, said I, impatiently. Duty would prescribe a very different conduct. Should you listen to that, a lesson would be taught you very different from the suggestions of envy and jealousy.

At these words, her countenance changed into some expression of resentment. She withdrew her hand from mine. This resentment, however, passed away in a moment, and resuming looks of kindness, she replied, "I can bear injustice when committed against myself. I can also bear it even when committed against my friend. You misapprehend the character of Sidney, and I ascribe that misapprehension to causes that do not make you culpable. You have not enjoyed the means of knowing him, and your equity is blinded by passion. The time will come when that blindness will be removed, and your confidence in his integrity be equal to my own.

"On this subject I desire not to reason with you, forreasoning will make no conquest of your opinions, but will expose my own resolutions to be shaken, and lessen my tranquility. And yet I fondly cling to the hope that reflection will convince you of the rectitude of my scheme."

Your scheme! I know not your scheme. What scheme have you adopted?

"I have mentioned it once already. Spare me the anguish of repeating it."

You have uttered doubts and surmises, but I know not what it is that you finally intend. I have, indeed, talked with Sidney, but I will not suffer him to be your representative, and the announcer of my fate. What is it that you determine with regard to me? These words were uttered in a tone that excited the consternation of my cousin. She looked at me with streaming eyes, but without speaking.

What is it, continued I, you mean? To reject

me? To banish me? What have I done to merit the treatment of an enemy? Have I failed in any point of respect to you, or to my mother? Have I violated any law? Have I offended, in any instance, against virtue or decorum? Has a single day brought forth such damning proofs of my depravity? What is the crime? Let me know it, and let me be confronted with my accuser. Save me from the odious necessity of imputing fickleness and hypocrisy to the object of my devotion.

"You have talked with Sidney, and must, therefore, know my resolution, and the grounds on which it is built."

I know nothing from him but that I am a sensual, selfish, and hypocritical slave. That alliance with me will be, to Louisa Calvert, degrading and calamitous, that, instead of affection and esteem, I merit only to be detested and shunned. This, then, is the sentence you pronounce on me. He whom yesterday you loved beyond all mankind, in whose character you found no inexpiable blemish, and to whom you were willing to consecrate all your feelings and wishes, has, to day, become a being hateful or terrible. Make haste, I beseech you, to inform my mother of this change in your opinions. Show her the extent of her error in imagining her son worthy of your esteem. Persuade her to despise me, to relinquish the hopes which she had formed of seeing my happiness and virtue established by union with you.

"Felix! This is too much from you. You have deceived my expectations. I had more confidence in your moderation and your justice. It is impossible that Sidney should have spoken thus. Heaven knows that my love for you has no wise diminished, that I esteem you as much as ever, but I deem it necessary to postpone an event which cannot be recalled, and to stay till your character is matured by that age and experience in which you are now deficient. And what, if your love be virtuous and sincere, what objection can be reasonably made to the delay of a few years? Your absence will improve your understanding, your morals, and your fortune, and will not bereave us of the advantages of a pure and ardent friendship. Communication, as frequent and copious as we please, may subsist between us. Mutual sympathy and counsel may be imparted, and, by the practice of self-denial, we shall insure our claim to future happiness."

These reasonings were but little suited to appease my discontents. I endeavoured to demonstrate the visionary folly of her scheme, and dwelt upon the pangs of that disappointment which she would inflict, not only upon me, but upon my mother. You can scarcely expect, I said, the approbation of my mother, whose fondest hopes, with regard to her son, have been fixed upon this alliance, and who will charge you with caprice and levity.

"Indeed," she answered," I fear her censure, but

I confide in the candour of my deportment to prove
to her, at least, the purity of my motives, though my
arguments may fail to make any impression on her
understanding.   I will explain myself fully to her,
and if I should be so unfortunate as to have offended
her beyond forgiveness, it will, indeed, be a painful
aggravation of my calamity, though it ought not to
change a determination built upon such grounds as
mine."

My vanity, as well as my passion, led me to
imagine that my cousin's objections would easily
be overcome. Her scheme appeared so wild and
absurd, that I could scarcely argue with her patiently. It was modelling conduct by such artificial refinements and preposterous considerations, that it was
more the topic of ridicule than ratiocination. Her
purpose was so new, so remote from all her previous
views, and so adverse to that scheme of happiness
which she had formerly adopted with undoubting
confidence, that I was prone to regard it as a kind of
frenzy, which might maintain its hold for a time, but
which would speedily fall away of itself, if it were
not removed by argument.

At present, little more was said on either side. I
shortly after withdrew to ruminate on this strange
revolution. The more thought I bestowed upon
it, the more impatient and uneasy I became. My
indignation and aversion, with regard to Sidney,
increased. I began to suspect not only the disinter-

estedness of his conduct, but even that of my cousin herself. The change that had been effected, flowed, I imagined, from some unexplained cause, some cause which the parties were ashamed to avow.

This imagination was confused and wavering, but it gave birth to complaints and insinuations, which were heard with grief, and repelled or confuted with calmness and steadfastness. They were recounted in my presence to Sidney, on whom they appeared to excite no resentment, and whose deportment was unaltered by my reproaches. I was not studious of concealing from him my opinion of his interference. Finding his power over my cousin's sentiments was absolute, I laboured to convince him of his error, and, when arguments failed, resorted to the most pathetic entreaties. These, however, availed nothing, and our interviews always terminated in anger and upbraidings upon my side.

These obstacles added new fuel to the flame which consumed me. If my affections had been cold or neutral, previously to these transactions, their nature was now changed. The danger of losing this prize appeared to open my eyes to its true value. The thought of postponing our union for years, was equivalent to losing her forever. Nay, I derived more torment from these delays and suspences, arising, as I conceived, from perverseness or caprice, than from our total and everlasting separation. My vehement temper pushed me forward irresistably to the goal of my wishes. I would not believe but that the attainment of this good was within my power. I would not believe that, should all my efforts be frustrated, I could endure to live.

The ardour of Louisa's sensibility was the advocate on whosea ssistance I relied. Nothing but perseverance in her new scheme created a doubt of the sincerity of her love. I had innumerable proofs of her tenderness, and, therefore, was confident of vanquishing her scruples.

No wonder, that, with an heart full of softness, compassion, and rectitude as her's, she should sometimes hesitate. My impetuosity overbore all resistance. While she listened to my pleadings, she was ready to yield. Frequently I imagined my success complete, and exulted in my happiness, but the scruples which disappeared in my presence were sure to be reinspired by a single conversation with Sidney. On repeating my visit, when every obstacle was supposed to have been annihilated, I was always fated to discover them anew.

These incessant disappointments took away my hopes. I had exhausted every expedient and argument in vain. Every new day showed me that Sidney's power was not to be shaken. My confidence in my efforts languished and expired. I resigned myself to gloomy suspicions, sullenness, and utter dejection. My vivacity and smiling prospects were flown. I regarded myself as one unjustly treated and betrayed. I found a mournful satisfaction in secretly upbraiding the perfidy of Sidney, and the inhumanity and fickleness of my cousin. My visits to theWallaces became less frequent, they were shorter, and passedwithout any conversation from me. They produced nothing but pain, and were willingly postponed or exchanged for the solitude of my chamber or the fields. I seldom failed to meet Sidney at his sister's, and the tranquility of his deportment, and affectionate manner in which he continued to be treated by my cousin, I construed into insults upon myself. These mortifications I endeavoured to avoid by shunning the house.

My deportment, it was easy to see, was by no means regarded with indifference by Louisa. She eyed me, when present, with an air of ineffable solicitude. She could not escape the infection of my sadness. Her attention was alive, as formerly, to all my looks and words, but the vivacity which they formerly inspired, was now changed into grief. When we chanced to bealone together, she expressed her tenderness and her regretswithout reserve. On such occasions she renewed her declarationsof confidence in the propriety of her deportment, and endeavouredto win my concurrence.

These interviews and these contests, by always affording new proof that her determination was irrevocable, became irksome. I ceased to contend with her objections, but listened, in a silent and sullen mood, to all she could urge. If an answer was extorted by her intreaties, my words were dictated by resentment. They charged her with unfeeling obstinacy and infatuation, with treachery to me, and ingratitude to my mother. The last topic had always produced a more powerful effect upon her feelings than any other. She frequently confessed that her decision would be greatly, if not irresistably, influenced by my mother's choice. She was inexpressibly anxious with regard to the light in which her conduct would be viewed by my mother. She had written a copious letter to her friend, in which she had explained the reasons of her conduct with the utmost simplicity, and endeavoured to prepossess her in favour of her scheme, insinuating, at the same time, that my mother's authority would be of more weight with her than that of any other human being, and that the imputation of error or ingratitude from this quarter, would be avoided by any sacrifice, and at any price.

The sentence which was so much dreaded by Louisa, was not, in the same proportion, desirable to me. I had other passions besides love, and these lessened, though they did not annihilate the value of a gift, conferred, not from submission to reason or affection, but merely from deference to authority, and for the sake of avoiding unreasonable imputations. In truth, these imputations were not to be expected from my mother. After an intimation that her authority would prevail where her arguments failed, she would be anxious to maintain a neutrality. It was far from certain, that with a mind dispassionate, sobered by age, and prone to refer all events to their remotest consequences, she would not side with her niece, and fortify her present resolutions. Hence no hope was founded on my mother's interference.

This state, so fertile of calamity to me, could not long be endured. After musing on the same detestable impressions, and growing hourly more weary of their uniformity, my mind betook itself to the contemplation of that scheme which had formerly occurred to me with powerful recommendations, but which my engagements with Louisa had suspended. In the scene around me, there was nothing but provocations to melancholy. Every object reminded me of the blessing which an untoward destiny had ravished away, and contributed to deepen my gloom. I, therefore, determined to resume my ancient design of visiting Europe.

This design was strongly recommended by Sidney. It will appear to you by no means incompatible with the continuance of affection, and even of one kind of intercourse, between Louisa and I. To me, however, my departure was the extinction of all my hopes. Three thousand miles constituted an interval like death, and the absence of years was equivalent to eternity.

This design had been vaguely suggested by my friend, but she had, by no means, insisted upon it. She seemed contented that marriage should be postponed, but regarded my voyage to Europe with a reluctance she was unable to conceal. On this head, indeed, Sidney's arguments had not produced the same conviction as on others. She could not see but that my present situation abounded with sufficient motives to virtue, and trials of fortitude. That on the busy theatre of Europe, I should forget both her and my country, was not improbable, and this change was likely to banish all ancient impressions without reflecting any great degree of guilt upon me. This dread was confirmed by my own representation, which confounded the postponement with the dissolution of the contract, and my assertions that if I left my country, it would be with no design of ever returning. Her knowledge of my mother's views, who was, for various reasons, an enemy to this design, augmented the reluctance which she felt to concur in it.

Her aversion to my voyage, operated, in some degree, as an argument in its favour. I conceived that though she had resisted every other plea, it was possible that she would revoke her determination, if that alone would detain me. At all events, residence in my native country was grown intolerably irksome, and I resolved to stay on no condition but that of her immediate compliance with my wishes.

The arrangements necessary to my departure were easily made. Having fixed the day of my sailing, and made suitable preparation, I determined to pay my cousin a last visit, and exert all the powers of which I was possessed, to vanquish her scruples. I resolved to recapitulate and enforce every argument which had hitherto been urged, and to offer her the alternative of accepting me, or of seeing and hearing from me no more.

It happened, seasonably for my purpose, that, about this time, Louisa had gone a few miles from the city, on a visit to a venerable lady, who usually passed her time without company or any species of amusement. Louisa proposed to spend two or three days with this person, during which no other visitant was likely to intrude. Sidney, too, was called by some engagement, to a distance, and would not, therefore, be at hand to counteract myefforts. I designed to go to this house, in the evening, and taking my cousin apart, make a final and vigorous effort in the cause of my happiness.

For some days previous to this interview, my thoughts werefull of tumult and impatience. I was fully aware of the importance of my undertaking. On the success of this interview depended the condition of my future life. According to the event which should then take place, I should either be blessed with the possession of this woman, I should continue in my present abode, in the discharge of dutiful offices to my mother, in the enjoyment of conjugal felicity, and the improvement of my patrimony, or I should wander, homeless and unattended, through the world. I should separate myself forever from my family, my friends, and my country, and should seek, in a distant land, a new society, new enjoyments, and new motives. My sanguine temper led me to anticipate success rather than failure. When I reviewed the proofs of tenderness which I had received from my cousin, of the reluctance with which she admitted the possibility of my voyage, and the intrinsic force of the reasons which I should be able to allege in favour of wedlock, and the favourable circumstances, the lonely and solemn season when our interview should take place, and especially the absence of Sidney and Mrs. Wallace, who had hitherto been strenuous adversaries of my cause, and without whom none of these impediments would ever have subsisted, I trusted that I should extort from her some avowal or some promise, which she should be unable to recall.

The day, so momentous to my happiness, at length arrived. I was not sorry to find it dark and inclement. Storms would increase the probability of finding her alone, and add to the solemnity of our meeting. I designed to wait till night-fall, and then repair to her dwelling, whence, if my attempt should not succeed, I would hurry to New Castle, where lay the vessel in which I intended to embark.

On how slender threads does the destiny of human beings frequently depend! The caprice of a moment, an inexplicable and transitory impulse, in consequence of which our steps move one inch forward or on one side, will sometimes ascertain the tenor of our whole life, will influence the happiness and govern the activity of one man, and through him, control the destiny of nations and the world.

Throughout this day, my mind was but ill suited to any social occupation. I was too deeply absorbed in weighing the consequences of the impending interview, to spare much reflection to the claims and interests of others, but this theme became, by degrees, painful. My impatience was heightened into agony, and before noon had arrived, I resolved to hasten the meeting with my cousin, and set out immediately upon my visit.

While equipping myself and my horse for this purpose, some untoward chance called to my remembrance a person who lived near my ancient abode at Burlington, and with whom I had maintained a cordial intercourse from an early age. He had lately assigned me a commission which my abode in the city made it easy to perform, and which it was of some importance to him to have speedily and faithfully performed. It was merely to call on a kinsman who resided in the city, and inform him, in three words, that a certain person had returned to Burlington, who had formerly absconded, in consequence of debt. This person was in debt to my friend's kinsman, and as he had resumed his place in society, with a seeming confidence and fearlessness, it was to be hoped that he might be compelled, by legal means, to fulfill his former engagements.

This affair might be dispatched in ten minutes, and to have neglected it would have been wholly inexcusable. I set out, without delay, for this end. I had walked about three squares, when turning a corner, suddenly my attention was slightly attracted by a sound, issuing, as it seemed, from the upper windows of an house, near at hand. It was a faint shriek, uttered, apparently, by female organs. It was a feeble effort of the voice, and followed by deep silence. It was too indistinct to inform me whence it came. I could merely guess that it came from above, and from within some dwelling hard by, but from which of the houses in sight, and whether it denoted grief, or pain, or surprise, or affright, I was wholly unable to determine. I checked my steps an instant, and looked upward and around, but saw nothing to confirm or assist my conjectures, and therefore quietly resumed my way, and re-entered on the meditations which had been suspended by this incident. The circumstance could not be perceived to possess any relation to me. Its true nature was not likely to be discovered by any inquiries which were possible to one in my condition, and possessed no claim upon my curiosity.

Such is the indifference and heedlessness of one who spies the flash of a musket in the thicket, but is unapprised of the existence of an enemy. He imagines it a glow-worm or a meteor, and rests in supine security. Instead of headlong flight, he loiters till the lurking foe has refurnished the pan, and a second attempt urges the fatal bullet to his heart.

I found the person of whom I was in search, and imparted the tidings which I brought. He expressed much gratitude for this service, and inquired if I had any purpose of writing to his kinsman. I answered, that there was, at present, no urgent demand for a letter, that my engagements would lead me a different way in a few hours, and I had not designed to write to him during several weeks, or perhaps months.

He apologised for making this inquiry, by saying that an unlucky wound in his right hand, had, during some time, disabled him from writing, that no one was at hand to perform for him the office of an amanuensis, that the present affair was of a very urgent and momentous nature, that his future welfare and subsistence depended on the recovery of the sum which was owing by this fugitive, and that the slightest delay might preclude him from this recovery. If I had designed to write to my friend, it would have been an extraordinary favour to him to perform that office immediately, and to insert in my letter some directions with regard to the measures to be taken on this exigence.

To comply with this request, made diffidently, but with great earnestness, would, in a very slight degree, encroach upon my plans. It would fill an hour, and enable me, with more patience, to wait the coming of the period which I had originally fixed upon as most proper for a meeting with my cousin, I therefore consented to write immediately, and having received such information as he chose to give, returned home to compose my letter.

The letter being written, it was necessary to put it on board a vessel going to Burlington. I went in quest of the vessel, and, having deposited the script in suitable hands, returned home, designing to set out forthwith on my projected visit. It was a fortune equally untoward that made me re-enter my lodgings, instead of mounting my horse, which stood ready for my use at some distance. Knowing that my absence might last forever, I felt reluctance to depart, without leaving affectionate adieus with the good lady at whose house I lived.

Having entered the house, I was informed that a messenger had been in search of me, and had waited for my return some time, but being weary, at length, or in haste, had gone, leaving, however, a billet, which was put into my hand. This billet, containing compliments to Felix Calvert, and a request that he would call at the corner of Front and — streets, at three o'clock in the afternoon. On inquiry I was told that the bearer of this billet was a young female, of a foreign countenance and garb, and with an air and demeanour that seemed to prove her a waiting maid or upper servant. She had expressed much impatience and anxiety to see me, and had left the most earnest request that they would not fail to deliver me the billet. This impatience was visibly increased by the information that I was preparing to set out upon a journey, from which the period of my return was wholly uncertain. She repeated that the receipt of this billet, and compliance with the request contained in it, were of the highest importance, and that no consideration must induce them to neglect delivering it.

The surprise which this circumstance was adapted to produce, was heightened by observing that the corner of Front and — streets was the very spot at which the shriek just mentioned had excited my attention. A vague suspicion was suggested that some connection subsisted between the invitation just received and that mysterious voice. My acquaintance in the city lay in quarters distant from this, and there was no circumstance within my memory, or observation, enabling me to guess at the character or situation of the tenants of this house. It was spacious and magnificent, was probably inhabited by persons of the better class, and the messenger belonged to a female, since none but a female was likely to charge a waiting maid with a commission of this kind.

This new incident exercised a strange dominion over my thoughts. My attention, burning as it was with eagerness and impatience respecting my cousin's deportment, was diverted into a new channel. I did not hesitate in resolving to comply with this summons. An hour had been mentioned sufficiently early to permit the performance of my previous engagement. Between three o'clock and dusk, the interval was long enough for many an interview, and the dusk of evening was the period most suitable for my visit to Louisa.

My anxiety to gain some basis for conjecture as to the character and views of my inviter, led me to reflect upon the possibility of making some inquiries on that head previous to my visit. I now remembered that, some weeks before this, I had stopped at a shop nearly opposite to this mansion, to purchase some trifles, for which I had just received a commission from my mother. The seller, by name Mrs. Rivers, was a little, talkative, courteous woman, who was likely to have dealt as much in the history of her neighbours, as in the prices of laces and ribbons. The money I expended with her gave me a titleto respect, and much lively discourse had passed between us, not strictly connected with the quality and cost of her wares. She was quick, communicative, affable, and made any laborious advances to acquaintance superfluous. Her I resolved to visit, and, by duly managing the conversation, endeavour to extract from her all the knowledge of her neighbour she possessed.

I went forthwith to the shop. Salutations were exchanged. The price of this and that was required and given. Gloves and hose were spread upon the compter. One article was pretty and another cheap. She had sold this for two-pence more than she now asked, and that being the last pair remaining, she would let go for a shilling under her customary price. While her tongue was thus employed, I was meditating on the best means of leading the discourse to the desirable object.

Meanwhile, there entered the shop, a young woman, who asked for something, for which she paid, and immediately withdrew, yet not till Mrs. Rivers had uttered a score of interrogatories, such as "How d'ye do, Jenny? How is Miss Neville this morning? Does she never go out now-a-days? Why don't she call? When does she leave town? Don't she leave town this summer? How can she bear to stay? Has she got shet of her cold? Was the cruel of the right colour? Does she want anymore of it?" and so forth. These inquiries were made without intermission, and apparently with no view to be answered. The girl, however, stammered out yes or no, and showed a sort of consciousness and trepidation that attracted my notice.

While viewing her, I noticed her garb, aspect, and

general demeanour to be nearly such as had been described as belonging to the bearer of the billet. A suspicion arose that this was the same person. This suspicion was changed into certainty when I saw her trip across the street, and enter a gate belonging to the corner house.

Pray, said I, to my companion, pointing to the house in question, who lives there?

"Don't you know ? You look as if you knew. I'll warrant you, you know, but ask —"

Why? Why should I ask if I knew already?

"I can't tell, but if you really don't know, I'll tell you. 'Tis a young lady who came not long ago from England. Her aunt or mother (I am not sure which, I confess, for my part, I doubt, but they commonly think her aunt) came first. Mrs. Keith, a good lady, give her her due, and an excellent customer to me. Many a penny has she put into my pocket. Poor lady! I was quite inconsolable at her death. She began to droop just after the young lady's arrival, and died eight months ago."

Was Mrs. Keith a foreigner?

"Yes, no. She was partly one and partly 'tother. She was born in Jersey, and married early, in this town. Mr. Keith was of an ancient and rich family, and a lawyer. He made a great deal of money by the law, and went home* to enjoy it. Poor man! He died

---

* Before the revolution, Europe, and especially Britain, was universally called, by the American colonists, home.

just after he got ashore. This is several years ago, but Mrs. Keith returned, to lay her bones, as she said, in her native country, and, poor woman, she did, in a short time, the very thing which she came to do. She died, and left that house, and a very handsome property, to her niece, Clelia. Clelia Neville."

Is this lady married, or likely to be so?

"Not that I know of. She is quite young and handsome, but goes out but little, and sees scarcely any company. The death of her aunt was a severe stroke. She has been melancholy ever since. Jenny tells me, that from one month's end to another, she never goes out of her chamber and her garden, and sees not a living soul besides her own family. She dresses and lives very genteel. She is quite the lady. A mighty reader, Jenny says, writes much, paints landscapes, and plays very tastily upon the–something– it is an hard, outlandish name. This is all she does. She never does an hand's-turn at any kind of work. Not for want of knowing how to do it neither, but because she thinks it vulgar, or because she likes reading and playing better.

"She lives a very strange life. To tell you the truth, I am half a mind to think, that there's something like a sweet-heart at bottom, some disappointment of that sort, in England, that made her come out here. Her aunt did not know of her coming. It was very unexpected, and not at all liked by the old lady. The first time they met, Mrs. Keith was quite ill, and the young lady did not behave like one who had found a welcome reception. There was abundance of tears and of sad looks between them, then, and a good while after. Something, for certain, more than the death of her aunt, who was quite old and might look to die soon, is the matter with her now, but what it is, I can only guess.

"Jenny knows, I am sure she knows, but she is prim and close-mouthed about it. I could never get a hint of any thing from her. This is quite a topping dame. She reads and paints as well as her mistress, and won't stoop to be familiar with servants or any body. She often comes here to buy any thing, in my way, that the family wants, and talks about her mistress, but very cautiously. She is no tattler, that's the truth, and I know little but what I pick up myself (our houses, you see, are opposite) and from the neighbours, but still—"

Mrs. Rivers's loquacity was here diverted by the entrance of a new customer. Three o'clock had nearly arrived, and I imagined that my informant had nearly exhausted her stores of knowledge. I wanted an opportunity of reflecting on what I had already heard, and, therefore, putting my purchases in mypocket, I took my leave. I made a circuit of half a mile before I reached Miss Neville's door.

I was young, romantic, and without experience. There was somewhat in this adventure, wonderfully fitted to excite my curiosity and rouse my hopes. The slight portrait that had been drawn by Mrs. Rivers, exhibited a captivating person, elegant accomplishments, dignity of birth, and opulence, and, in a sufficient degree, an unblemished reputation. What motive could induce such an one to demand a visit from me, was a theme of perplexing, but no undelightful inquiry.

These inquiries were, at length, terminated by my arrival at her door. I had been summoned hither, but the summons was anonymous, and the cause was unexplained. I was somewhat at a loss, therefore, in what manner to demean myself, for whom to inquire, or what motive to allege for my visit. This perplexity hindered me not from knocking. The signal was speedily obeyed. The girl I had seen at Mrs. Rivers's appeared at the door and, before I had time to open my lips, desired me to walk in, and ushered me into a drawing room, on the second story.

Here I walked to and fro, for some minutes, alone. All the misgivings of youth, the timidities of inexperience, and the indefinable hopes and fears congenial with my visionary and enthusiastic temper, took possession of me. I looked at one door, and at the other, and listened. I mistook a casual sound for that of approaching footsteps. These fallacious omens, were, after some time, succeeded by unquestionable ones. The door from an inner chamber, opened, and there entered, in a sort of hurry, and with various tokens of embarrassment, a lovely female, arrayed in mourning.

I made my obeisance with an ill grace, and, on being requested, in a tremulous and soft voice, to sit down, with difficulty found a seat. She seated herself near me, and, after a short pause, said, "I am not so fortunate, sir, as to be known to you, and scarcely know how to apologise for the liberty which I have taken in requesting this visit. I am conscious that it may bear a strange and disadvantageous appearance, but my heart acquits me of any impropriety. My motive has been gratitude, for the greatest service which it is possible for one person to performfor another. You have saved my life, at the imminent hazard of your own, and I could not forbear seeking this opportunity of presenting you my thanks. The obligation can, indeed, be never discharged, but your benevolence and intrepidity entitle you, at least, to know that she whom you have rescued from the worst of deaths, is not ungrateful for the benefit."

At this address, I lifted my eyes and fixed them on the speaker. The blood thrilled at my heart in recognising, in this person, the form and features of her whom I had borne in my arms from a house in flames, and whom I had seen as for a moment, and whose image, impressed in such vivid hues upon my fancy, I had supposed to have been indebted for its charms to the illusion of my senses. Every line of that portrait was now visible. My surprise was equal to my delight, and these strong emotions overpowered, for a while, my timidity and awkwardness. I started, involuntarily, on my feet, and expressed my pleasure at this meeting, with an eloquence and fervour that were new to me.

She listened with emotions which I was unable, at that time, to interpret. Her eyes were downcast, her cheeks glowed, sorrow appeared to contend in her features, with joy, and confidence with doubt. Her tongue faultered in expressing her sentiments, and every gesture betokened a confusion of feelings, inexplicable, but bewitching.

This perplexity and reserve gradually lessened, and our conversation reverted to the events that brought about this interview. I mentioned the mistake in which I had been hitherto involved, as to the person I had saved, inquired into the situationof the ladies whose roof it was, and by what means she became exposed to the danger.

"I was merely a visitant of these ladies," she replied. "I spent the day with them, and they prevailed upon me to remain during the night. One of them was indisposed, and there was some reason to dread the increase of her indisposition. Hence I was more willing to stay.

"On fully recovering my senses, I found myself in the arms of an hospitable lady of the neighbourhood. I was not hurt, and the terror was quickly removed. I procured myself to be removed hither to my own house, as expeditiously as possible. I did not distinctly see my deliverer, and some time elapsed before the newspapers acquainted me with his name. My servant procured, by some means, information of the place of your abode, and my eagerness to render you the thanks that are so justly due, has made me overlook forms."

Let me thank you, said I, in my turn, for this negligence of forms. The mistake into which I was led, at the beginning, respecting your person, made me remiss in profiting by so favourable an opportunity of knowing you. I hope you will allowme to repair my error and authorise me to see you frequently.

She admitted my request with looks of the utmost benignity and satisfaction. The discourse passed to topics of a general and speculative kind. The transition was not effected by me. She led the way, almost imperceptibly, into new tracks, and glided from one theme to another, with dexterity and gracefulness inimitable.

Very far was my companion from forward and loquacious. She was merely earnest and full of thought. She spoke much, and with mellifluent volubility, but this arose from organs, flexible beyond any that I had ever known, and from a mind incessantly versatile and active, drawing with a facility, almost sportive, from inexhaustible stores of sentiment and language.

Our topics tended but little to throw light upon

the real incidents of her condition. There was the fullest display of her opinions. There were details of her intellectual education and the progress of her understanding. Transactions were related or alluded to, in which she had been a witness, and some in which she had been an actor, but these exhibited her modes of judging on abstract subjects, and threw very faint and reflected light upon her principles of conduct.

Books came, at length, to be mentioned. She appeared to be no unimpassioned votary of reading. She had, at almost an infantile age, imbibed an invincible attachment to books. She had read, for a long time, with indiscriminating appetite. Amusing and frivolous productions occupied her attention for a while, but her taste gradually acquired refinement. She distinguished between faults and beauties, between substance and show. Her facility of approbation, and her eagerness for novelty, abated. While some performances lost all or much of her esteem, others acquired stronger claims to admiration. The habit of inquiring into the reasons of her choice, of pausing and sending forth her mind upon discovery, of calling up and expatiating among the ideas linked with the suggestions of the writer, became vigorous and permanent. From seeing and feeling, she had long since proceeded to investigate, select, and arrange.

To me this spectacle was wholly new. I had met

with persons of extensive knowledge, but their minds were not pliant and elastic. Their discourse was jejune, disjointed, and obscure. Their mind gave out its stores, if I may so express myself, with difficulty and reluctance. Their expressions were meagre and coarse, inadequate and vague. Their tone was an insipid sing-song, or a monotonous uniformity. Their utterance was stammering through precipitation, or drawling through sluggishness. Their stock of words was too small to allow them to select suitable expressions with the requisite speed. They erred through perverse habit, or a vitiated taste.

The picture now before me was a dazzling reverse of these imperfections. Nature, accident, or education, had given her so large a store, and such absolute command of language, that she had nothing to do but to adjust her pause, her accent, and her emphasis. The stream was spontaneously and ever flowing. All her care consisted in leading it through proper channels, and giving melody and meaning to its cadencies.

My conceptions of the dignity and beauty of eloquence, of that power of utterance which bestows the utmost grace and force upon our own conceptions, or on those of others, were, probably, carried beyond the due bound. My education, in this respect, had made me a mere Roman. From much converse with ancient orators and rhetoricians, I had been taught to regard speech as the faculty of greatest value and power. Excellence in this, was most worthy of generous ambition, and to this the power of retaining and arranging ideas was subordinate and secondary.

Our modes are very different from those of the Latins. We have not lived long enough in a warm sun to acquire the vivacities of utterance and gesture which distinguish the Italians. Our northern extraction makes us sober and dispassionate, andour government raises a wholesome mound against populartides and billows. The perfections of speech have scope onlyon private occasions. There is no scene of deliberation wherethousands are convened, where every auditor is qualified, by education, to comprehend and relish the refinements of speech. Eloquence, in the Roman sense of that term, is driven fromamong men. It expired when the forum, from a theatre of government,sunk into a marketplace, and advocates and statesmenwere supplanted by butchers and herb-women.

But there is another sense in which its value and its efficacy are as great as ever. Persuasion and instruction are employments of as frequent recurrence, and as great moment now, as at any former period. The instrument is no less powerful to charm the eyes and ears, to sway the reason and affections of one or a few. Hence, the rhetoric of conversation awakened, in the highest degree, my juvenile enthusiasm. I prized myself more highly on account of my attainments in this art, than for any other accomplishment, and no excellence in others, gained more fervent veneration, than their skill in conversation, their power to adapt their theme to all persons and occasions, without sinking into levity or indecorum, of guiding and bending attention at pleasure, of joining sagacity to promptitude, and correctness to fluency. Hence, in listening to my new acquaintance, I derived pleasure beyond what I had ever experienced from the exhibition of intellectual excellence.

In the midst of our discourse, the evening overtook us. Four hours had passed away with imperceptible speed. I looked up and recalled my previous engagement to remembrance, but it appeareel with the dubiousness and faintness of a dream. It threw me into a temporary perplexity, and being aware that my visit had been longer than decorum usually prescribed, I took my leave.

I should in vain attempt to describe the state of my mind after this interview. A deep and thorough revolution had been wrought in it, of the full extent of which, however, I was not yet aware. The image of Miss Neville, clothed with nymph-like and fascinating graces, hovered in my view, a tumult of delicious feelings was awakened, which I cherished with diligence, and, during some time, avoided every act or meditation tending to divert my thoughts into a different and customary channel.

Gradually this tumult subsided, and allowed me

calmly to survey my real situation, and to figure to myself the consequences which this incident must produce. Irresolution and despondency took place of my rapture. I thought of all that had passed between Louisa Calvert and myself, of the earnestness with which I had sought her hand, of the obstacles which had occurred to my hopes, of the toil which I had undergone to overcome these obstacles, and of the measures which my recent despair kad dictated.

The first sentiment which now rose in my heart, was that of self-upbraiding. I had acted with the blind impetuosity of a lunatic. The dupe of deceitful rumour. I had stifled that emotion which the image of the rescued lady had excited. I had laboriously shunned the smooth and forthright path, and bent all my infatuated zeal to accomplish my destruction and that of my cousin, but my error was now not to be retrieved. I had gone too far to return, to stop, or even to linger.

What! Had I then ceased to love Louisa Calvert? Was a short interview with this stranger, in which nothing but the specious surfaces were visible, sufficient to change into indifference or aversion, that headlong zeal, which, an hour before, had burned in my heart, had urged me to the brink of despair, had made me determine to abandon my mother, my friends, and my country! How fully had I justified the censures and precautions of Sidney! What a monument of mutability and caprice should I make myself, should I now relinquish my pursuit, and devote to another those wishes and affections which had so   lately belonged to my cousin! This would be ignominious and disgraceful beyond any guilt which my nature could incur.

And yet, had not Louisa rejected me? Had she not determined to postpone our union to a remote and indefinite period? Was not our betrothment utterly dissolved? Were not my happiness, my safety, my life, voluntarily offered as a sacrifice to the prejudices of another ? I had persisted in contesting with her determination, long after the prospect of success had vanished. I meditated flight and exile, the sorrow of my mother, the neglect of my patrimony, the desertion of my friends, why? Because this woman had chosen to reject my vows, to preserve, unimpaired, her haughty independence, had refused to place trust in my rectitude and constancy, had loaded me with scorn.

Of this folly it was surely time to repent. It was time to discontinue my base and servile supplications, to leave her to consult the wisdom of Sidney, and to cultivate her own means of dignity and happiness. Let me claim to myself the same privilege. Let me seek happiness from one more able and more willing to confer it, who is governed by sentiments and principles harmonious and congenial with mine, who is not the slave of the ambiguous and cold-blooded scruples of another. Why should I decline my intended visit? Why not seek my cousin and afford her the satisfaction of my acquiescence in her schemes?

She was right. Sidney's knowledge of my character was more accurate than my own. I have been too precipitate. There are points of difference between Louisa and myself, incompatible with conjugal felicity, and which no time would probably annihilate. Parting will be best. Let me hasten to her presence, let me assure her of my full conviction of the propriety of her schemes. It will afford her the purest and most rapturous joy. Her sympathetic heart has long been agonised at the sight of my sufferings, and her ear been wounded by the murmurings of my injustice. It is time to dissipate her griefs, and restore her to complacency and cheerfulness.

Such were my reflections , in consequence of which I pursued my way to my cousin's habitation. These sentiments were not inequitable. They diffused a serenity and calmness through my bosom, to which I had long been a stranger. It did not occur to me to note the abruptness of this change, and to mark how little I had been indebted for it to the force of reason. Before my interview with Clelia Neville, these considerations were overlooked. The voice of equity was then too low to be heard, but now I had suddenly started up into a dispassionate and rational being. I could perceive and acknowledge the justice of her conduct, and acquitted her of all malignity and folly. Such is the imposture which men practice on themselves. Such are the folds under which self-ishness and passion hide themselves, and so easily are their boastful and arrogant pretensions to disinter-estedness and magnanimity admitted by their fond slave.

These reflections were succeeded by others relative to my new friend. I pursued, with intenseness, the comparison between the virtues and accomplishments of these women. I dwelt with delight upon the personal attractions, the polished understanding, the affluent and musical eloquence, the studious and seclusive habits of Miss Neville. I dwelt upon the propitious omens that attended the beginnings of our intercourse, the fervency of that gratitude which so eminent a service as that of saving her life, at the almost inevitable hazard of my own, was suited to produce, and which, the extraordinary mode adopted by her, to convey her thanks, sufficiently testified. I was her only visitant. She had given, even in so brief an interview, indubitable proofs of being highly pleased with my demeanour. She had accepted, with eagerness, my offers of continuing and advancing our acquaintance. She was a stranger in a foreign land, unfettered by obligations, springing from kindred or marriage, or poverty, unamused by varieties of company, and the shifting scenes of dissipation, fond of loneliness and books, and musing. Was it possible for invention to assemble more charms in one form, and more auspicious incidents together? Was she not the unknown type, after which my fancy, in the solitude of Burlington, had delighted to fashion the images of friend, mistress, wife ?

But what was my cousin? No music in her utterance, no vigour or grace in her elocution, no symmetry, no lustre, no bewitching hues, no radiance in her glances. She is an object of esteem. Her virtues are divine, but they alone cannot give birth to that ineffable passion which blends two beings into one. And yet, is virtue nothing in the balance of him who meditates wedlock? Is it nothing that Louisa loves with tenderness and constancy, that her character is fully known, and is void of blemish? Are integrity and moral sensibility, and rare genius, so easily outweighed by mere external qualities, whose intoxications are sure to disappear in nuptial familiarity, and to sink to the level of their opposites? What know I of this stranger that is inconsistent with innumerable foibles and frailties? She is plausible and smooth, but may she not conceal, under this delusive mask, a thousand weaknesses or prejudices?

It is true that she may be no less excellent in mind than in person. There is nothing destructive of each other in the perfections of form and of mind. This alliance, however, is yet to be proved. It remains to be discovered whether there do not secretly exist insuperable impediments to the wishes that I have formed. What are the means of this discovery? How does it become me to demean myself? Not, surely, in such a manner as will terminate every hope with regard to my cousin. Does she merit to be made unhappy by a full disclosure of my feelings? What if further and more intimate acquaintance with Miss Neville should prove my first impressions to be false?

Should I then declare to my cousin not only my change of opinions with regard to her, but my newborn preference of another? What will that be but to give her torment, which the failure of my expectations, and my wishes, with regard to Clelia Neville, may prove to be wantonly and needlessly inflicted? What will that be but to rob myself of the power of reverting to my ancient path, and loosing totally my hold of my cousin's affections? Far am I yet from loving this stranger. Farther still may our future intercourse place me from loving her. This new occurrence has only shown me the possibility of happiness without my cousin.

What then is incumbent on me? Let me hasten the intended interview. Let me yield to her remonstrances and projects, consent to consider our betrothment as dissolved, maintain with her, henceforth, the intercourse of friendship, and meanwhile cultivate the society of the stranger. Study her character, endeavour to comprehend her situation. If in those there be no impediments to a more intimate and sacred union, endeavour to effect that union. If there be such obstacles, then may I adopt some new scheme of happiness, and either revive my claim to Louisa Calvert, or bid an eternal adieu to these shores.

These principles appeared to me just. They argued, perhaps, a kind of sensibility, less ardent or less permanent than is commonly found in upright and ingenuous youth, but the speculative maxims that countenanced and sanctioned my deportment were not immoral. It is easily seen, however, what perils and temptations I was going to multiply around me. How hard I should find it to avoid, in adhering to this plan, falsehood and duplicity. The sequel will show how little qualified I was to resist these temptations.

Late in the evening I visited my cousin. I found her alone. Her friend had retired to her chamber earlier than usual, and left her to pursue her reveries without interruption. She was sitting, with a paper open in her lap, her arms folded, and her eyes moist with tears.

She endeavoured to assume a cheerful air at my approach, but her sadness was imperfectly concealed. My curiosity was naturally excited by these appearances. On questioning her as to the cause of her apparent discomposure, she gave me the letter.

"From your mother," said she. "I have just received it. You may read it."

I accordingly perused it, hastily. It was a copious epistle, written in answer to one received from my cousin, in which the reasons of her treatment of me had been explained. It was dictated by maternal candour and affection. My cousin wasapplauded for her fortitude, the sacrifice of inclination to reason. She was exhorted to continue under the guidance of the same principle, and was gently chidden for laying stress in questions so immediately pertaining to her own happiness and duty, on the assertion or authority of others. This rebuke related not to my cousin's deference to the councils of Sidney, but merely to her appeal to my mother's wishes, and her declaration that my mother's reason or will should be the rule of her conduct. This submission was earnestly rejected. She was exhorted to act with single views to her own felicity, that being the object of supreme regard to my mother, and that being incompatible with wedlock contracted without the utmost independence of choice, and the entire acquiescence of the understanding.

She then proceeded to state her reasons for dissenting from Louisa. She dwelt upon the flexibility and ductility of the youthful character, how much it depends upon the incidents befalling it, and how delicate those contingencies are by which the ultimate rank and condition of men are governed.

She acknowledged that her son's principles were yet unformed, but she believed his biases and propensities to be good, and that no circumstance could be imagined more favourable to the growth and stability of my virtue, than marriage with one of my cousin's excellence.

She had not failed to study my character. She trembled on perceiving my susceptibility of new impressions. Her zeal for my welfare had made her anxious to screen me from the contagion of bad example, to avert all temptations incident to my age, to the possession of opulence, and to freedom from restraint. She had particularly deprecated my voyage to Europe, where my appetites would be provoked, and my prejudices fostered in that sphere of nobility and luxury in which my birth would inevitably place me. The surest and only anchor of my felicity and her's, was marriage with a virtuous woman, together with abode in my native country, and conformity to its simplicity and rectitude of manners. One of these advantages she knew was inseparably connected with another. Nothing but success with my cousin, would prevent my departure. This event was more irreconcilable with her maternal feelings than any other, but she trusted that her fortitude was not unequal to the trial.

These considerations were urged with pathetical simplicity, and with a candour which insured their success. Having finished the perusal, and laid down the paper, I said, and what effect has this letter produced.

"You may easily guess at its effect. It has plunged me into perplexity and grief. I cannot endure to offend your mother and mine. That, indeed, I need not dread. She knows the goodness of my motives, and will pardon me, but I cannot endure to make her unhappy, or even to put her happiness to hazard. Your voyage is dreaded no less by me than by her. As her reason and her love are equally averse to it, so are mine. Should you persist in this resolution, I shall not condemn you. The impetuosity of your feelings makes you unhappy in the sight of that good, which, in your apprehension, is unreasonably withholden from you. You want to fly from sorrow and to put an end to fruitless hopes, by flying from your country and from me. You descry no danger in your path, and are therefore fearless and rash. I imagine that I see those dangers, that your youth will not escape them, but am unable to communicate my feelings to you, and to reconcile you to the practice of a salutary self-denial. Should you go, according to your late intimations, should any evil befall you in your way, or should our fears for your integrity be realized, what will be your mother's anguish? What will be mine? I see, too clearly, that life would be insupportable." These words were accompanied withflowing tears, and every muscle of her face swelled with grief.

My nature could not make me insensible to these tokens of a generous and disinterested affection. Their tendency had hitherto been thwarted by those excruciating regrets, which these very tokens, by adding new strength to my passion, were adapted to produce. Those fears for my safety, those proofs of her virtue and her love, gave new edge to my desire, and made her conduct, respecting me, appear still more to argue infatuation and folly. The difficulty of embracing her conditions, of acquiescing in merely amicable intercourse, and my resolution to end the fruitless contest by eternal separation, were augmented in proportion to her aversion to my voyage. I likewise was careful to remember that this ground might insure my victory, and hoped that marriage would be chosen by her in preference to absence.

The last opinion was enforced by the circumstances of our present interview. It was plain, that by assailing her constancy in this failing moment, I should triumph over her scruples, but the late occurrences had secretly modified and given new direction to my thoughts. My abode in America was no longer a source of unsatisfied craving and despondency. My visions of happiness were no longer collected round this point. I could now endure to think of my cousin as a sister or a friend, and to exchange courtesies with her without the poison of resentment and of jealousy. Agreeably to this change of sentiments, I now said to her:

I designed, on this visit, to leave with you my last farewell. I am hopeless of subduing your scruples, which my heart and my reason condemn as injurious to yourself and to me. I have, therefore, made every suitable preparation for my voyage. My clothes are packed, my trunks prepared, and my passage bespoken. The ship lies at New Castle, ready to profit by the next favourable wind, and I designed to have reached the ship this evening.

My companion turned pale, her limbs trembled, and she seemed ready to swoon. This weakness was counteracted by a powerful effort, and she continued, with apparent composure to listen.

This resolution, continued I, will not create surprise, will not be wondered at, will not be condemned by you. It is true, that I have no fears for my integrity. I see not more numerous or more powerful temptations in that scene than in this. On the contrary, my abode in Europe would make me happier and wiser. My own interest, separately considered, would be in every respect promoted by it, but I cannot, and ought not, to have an interest separate from my mother's and from your's. My resolution, ardent and strenuous as it was, is now changed. I will not go.

This unexpected and abrupt conclusion, excited in my friend as much surprise as joy. She looked at me with an air of doubt. "What!" said she, hesitating. "How is this change?"

Are there not sufficient motives for it? Is not the sacrifice of my inclination, in this point, fully due to my mother and to yourself?

"Alas! There is nothing due to me. My scruples appear to you groundless and absurd. My conduct argues, in your opinion, an heart callous, and cold, and indifferent to your welfare. With such sentiments, and such is my unfortunate condition, that my conduct cannot fail to give birth to such sentiments, you cannot conceive any sacrifice due to me."

You have a very contemptuous opinion of my understanding and my heart. Hitherto I have deserved that opinion, but not now. I still deplore the error into which a phantastic prudence and an unwise counsellor have led you, and would willingly root it out. To do this, I have tried in vain, and I now give up my scheme in despair: but I am no longer blind to the purity of your motives, I acknowledge and revere them, though I owe to them my misery.

At these words, a serene pleasure lighted up those eyes which had, for a long time past, betokened nothing but melancholy.

"And is it so, my beloved friend? Now, indeed, shall I find my resolution in danger of yielding. I have grieved at perceiving your injustice towards me, for, not to have seen the goodness of my intentions from the beginning, was to be guilty of injustice. My affection has, in some degree, been lessened with my esteem, but this precious acknowledgment has restored you to your former dignity, to your first place in my affections, and has made me happier than words can express.

"But you know my wishes with regard to you. They are not limited to merely your staying among us. There are other conditions, which, perhaps (I am inclined to hope every thing from your magnanimity) you will consent to, and consent to cheerfully."

Let me know them.

"Do not you know them? You must give me very much of your society. I must see you and hear from you continually, there must be no limits to your confidence, but, for some years to come— Recollect your youth, your unformed sentiments, your mutable affections, the influence of time, and observation, and experience to new-mould the character. For some years to come, you must be only my friend."

I do not mean, said I, after a pause, to make an incomplete and partial sacrifice. What you wish, I will be.

This promise was accepted with eagerness and gratitude. She gave a thousand artless proofs of her joy, her tenderness, and her confidence in ray integrity. The feelings which this deportment excited in me were far from joyous or tranquil. I couid not but reflect on the causes of this change in my resolutions. I saw that I deserved not the eulogies and thanks of my cousin, that she ascribed magnanimity to me to which I was a stranger, that the present state of my thoughts demonstrated the wisdom of her conduct, since they proved me to be as capricious, fickle, and prejudiced, as her friend had represented it as possible for me to become.

But while her praises inspired me with nothing but humiliation and compunction, my false shame hindered me from confessing the true state of my feelings, and unveiling the genuine motives of my actions. I betook myself to searching for apologies and arguments in favour of my dissimulation. I endeavoured to persuade myself that concealment was but justice to my cousin, whom the disclosure of my thoughts would render needlessly unhappy and whose estimate of human conduct was superfluously rigid. I flattered myself that time would speedily determine my destiny with regard to Miss Neville, that if my love for her was frustrated or immatured, it was equitable, on the whole, to conceal from my cousin that it ever existed, but that, if it were conducted to a prosperous issue, it might be disclosed without injury or difficulty. I should be without guilt in the eyes of my cousin, since she had voluntarily loosened the bonds of our betrothment, and had denied me the name, privileges, and expectations of a lover.

These sophistries quieted, for a time, my self-upbraidings, but they were sure to be awakened anew, and every proof of her affection and confidence in me was a sting, goading into new sensibility my slumbering conscience. The anxiety and fluctuation that hence arose, were to be stifled and stilled by new arguments and subtleties, whose influence was, in like manner, merely temporary. This disquiet did not escape the piercing eye of my friend. Bring void of suspicion, she was inclined to impute these appearances to my hopes, respecting herself, assuming occasional dominion. When her demeanour was most affectionate, tender, and confiding, my compunctions were always most acute, and the discomposure of my thoughts most apparent. It was at such times, that had my conduct been truly disinterested, those regrets which her candour ascribed to me, would naturally have arisen and acquired new strength, and thus was she unavoidably confirmed in her error.

The emotions which, on these occasions, her looks testified, were of a very complex and mixed kind. Those tokens of unhappiness in me, conjoined with the cause whence she imagined it to flow, and with that magnanimity which enabled me to withhold all crimination and complaint, and, in a short time, to regain my usual composure, excited her admiration, her pity, and her love. Her ingenuous manners always betrayed the sentiments of her heart, but sometimes she expressed these sentiments in words, and employed terms which, while they were designed to fortify my resolution and restore my tranquility, only gave new edge to my remorse, and rendered my self-condemnations more bitter.

Every day made the disclosure of the truth more

difficult, for every day added to the number of my artifices and subterfuges, and, by increasing my guilt, augmented the humiliation of confession. I saw the nature of her error, but could not rectify it without unlimited disclosure. I was frequently compelled to answer her interrogatories, or comment on her remarks. I was frequently denied the middle and equivocal path of silence, and was obliged to countenance her error, not only by ambiguous looks, but by false assertions. She did not allow me to passover my interviews with Clelia Neville in silence, but having rendered to me, at each meeting, a full account of her own transactions, she always proceeded to demand from me a similar account of the disposal of my time. I foresaw the consequences of even mentioning the name of Clelia Neville. Curiosity would immediately exert itself to know her character, her situation, the circumstances leading to our acquaintance, and accompanying every interview. Surprise and suspicion would be awakened by the concealment which I had hitherto practised. Painful, elaborate, and, perhaps, inefficacious artifices and fictions must be, thenceforth, employed to divert or elude her conjectures. She would immediately procure an introduction to the stranger, and that union of sagacity and frankness which she so eminently possessed, would speedily unravel the maze. Wholly to suppress her name, therefore, and to pretend a different employment of those hours that were devoted to her, were unavoidable. This task was rendered less difficult by the removal of Mrs. Wallace's family to a villa, at a small distance from the city. At this season, it being midsummer, they maintained as little intercourse with the town and its inhabitants, as possible, and were seldom visited by those who could molest their benign repose by tales of slander. Sidney's engagements continued to detain him abroad.

Meanwhile, my first visit to Miss Neville was followed by many succeeding ones. The second visit was paid agreeably to her invitation. This passed away without producing any new impression. General topics of morality or literature were discussed with complacency and eloquence, and the admiration at first excited by her talents, was no wise diminished.

The interval between this and a succeeding interview was occupied by one set of ideas. My mind pondered incessantly upon her features, accents, and words. Having been reviewed and dismissed, they returned anon, and were once more mused upon and scrutinised. All other occupations were tedious and impertinent. I lay upon my bed, or strolled in the fields, beset and haunted by this image from morning to night. I looked forward to the hour when decorum would permit me to go to her house with impatience, and with a thousand perplexities and misgivings as to the seasonableness of my visits. These perplexities were always dispelled by the manner in which I was received. It was always with the blushes of agreeable surprise, and the smiles of a fervent welcome.

The hour, thus devoted, was generally in the evening. I insensibly preferred its friendly obscurity to the garish eye of day. At this time, I hoped to find her more disengaged from social and domestic occupations than at others. In this respect, I quickly found that all hours were nearly alike. She had no intimate companions of her own age, no unceremonious and familiar visitants. She enjoyed the protection of a few respectable families, relatives or friends of Mrs. Keith, and as much of their society as she chose to exact, but there being much dissimilitude in age, taste, and especially in religious opinions, between them, the intercourse was rare and brief. At this time, likewise, two of these families with whom she had been most intimately connected, had withdrawn from the city's sultry precincts to the country.

She was almost constantly alone. She chid me for adhering to the formality of knocking at the door, which I, thenceforth, omitted, and, entering always without ceremony, found her seated in a garb of elegant negligence, either in her drawing room, or, if the air permitted, in the summer-house, placed at the farther end of an extensive garden. This latticed building was embowered by a vine, originally brought from the Canaries, whose purple clusters were plucked by her waiting maid, and presented to us on a china plate, accompanied with nectarines or peaches, produced in the same garden, and with lemonade or sherbet. Except at these times, our interviews were wholly unmolested by the presence or the fear of intruders.

You must permit me to dwell somewhat longer on the incidents of that period. I now look back upon them as on the tissue of some golden dream. Their bewitching influence on my juvenile feelings, was enforced by their novelty, by the suddenness and abruptness with which they succeeded to the homely enjoyments and clownish occupations of my previous years, and by their agreement with those fictions of fancy with which a romantic education had made me enamoured, and which I hadpursued with an utter hopelessness of their ever being realised. Were it not for that endless series of disasters and calamities that originated here, I should be disposed to confound the circumstances of these interviews with those of the dreams which haunted my seclusion at Burlington.

There was, indeed, nothing wanting to complete the enchantments of that scene. All the refinements of a polished education, the luxuriances of youth, and the attractions of beauty, were possessed by my friend, but she joined music to her elocution, and taste to her knowledge. Her favourite instrument was a viol d'amour, from which she extracted the most soothing and voluptuous tones, and to which she was wont to add a voice of boundless compass and inimitable flexibility. These filled up the intervals of conversation, and spread such a hue of fanciful delight and romantic dignity over the accompanying circumstances of moonlight, solitude, a garden, and a bower, that they can never be remembered without tremulous emotions of wonder and pleasure.

In the course of our interviews, I was naturally inquisitive as to the genuine condition of Miss Neville. I was anxious, likewise, for the establishment of confidence between us. I wanted to know every thing concerning herself, and was not unwilling to impart, in my turn, most of the particulars of my own history. My notions of politeness hindered me from accomplishing either of these ends by simple and direct means, by bluntly inquiring into her history, and unceremoniously unfolding my own. I conceived that some curiosity was necessary to be betrayed on her part, before I could justly be explicit. Some opening or invitation, either tacit or expressed, which might gracefully lead to questioning on one hand, or confession on the other.

These invitations or openings never occurred. I frequently introduced such topics as were favourable to my purposes. I talked of Europe and Britain, of emigration to America, of the motives which usually lead to emigration. I imagined and related the adventures of emigrants, and painted innumerable motives which were possible to incite to emigration. I made these imaginary circumstances approach more or less to a resemblance with her own, or what I guessed to be her own. Her own sex, age, single state, her relationship to Mrs. Keith, and such incidents as the talkative shop-keeper had communicated, were adroitly interwoven with my narrative, and the effect of these resemblances on her countenance and demeanour diligently noticed.

All these ingenious stratagems were useless. They served no purpose but to diffuse over my companion an air of thoughtfulness and melancholy. I believed that I saw in her features the workings of her mind. I saw her busy at one time in reviewing her past condition. I marked that she shrunk from the remembrance with aversion and grief, or with sundry tokens of embarrassment and trepidation, that she solicitously started other topics, and that ease and cheerfulness returned merely in proportion as we lost ourselves in general and literary speculation.

These appearances, while they baffled my contrivances and slackened my efforts, gave new edge to my curiosity. Every resolution which I formed in solitude, to trample upon forms, was defeated by my awkwardness and diffidence, and by the unseasonable return of those scruples which forbade me to extort from another what that other was apparently unwilling to communicate.

The same motives made me no less unwilling to

expatiate upon my own private history. I imagined that there was want of dignity in discussing the particulars of our household and our revenue, or in anticipating curiosity by dwelling on one's birth and parentage. I was aware that the mention of my mother and my cousin might lead to expectations or requests of being introduced to them, or to surmises and conclusions respecting the condition of my heart, unfavourable to the end which I proposed in cultivating her society. I was studious to describe myself as one standing, in a considerable degree, alone, as having few or no connections in my present situation, as having lately arrived, and as being merely a sojourner and guest in the city where I dwelt. I endeavoured, particularly, to inspire the belief that my hand and my heart were unappropriated by any foreign or previous engagement, and my manners tended to evince a state of mind, if not actually enamoured of herself, yet unfortified against, and liable to such impressions.

One motive of curiosity, in relation to herself, was weakened by her manners. It was obvious to suspect or imagine obstacles to the success of my views, arising from her former oractual situation. This suspicion was quickly removed by a kindness in her manners, that approached, at certain seasons, to tenderness, by glowing hues and downcast eyes, when certain topics were discussed, and certain situations experienced, by a yielding sensibility, which made tones and glances more eloquent and more expressive than any words.

On these occasions, intelligence between hearts is communicated long before the proffer and formal acceptance of vows, verbal confessions are, indeed, necessary to our happiness, but merely to dissipate that uncertainty created by the magnitude of the good which is sought. By augmenting our desire, it enhances our anxiety, impatience, and doubt.

To this crisis, however, which my impetuosity continually brought near, my diffidences made it long before my actual arrival. An half score times have I gone to her with a full resolution to explain my feelings, but the nearer I approached the eventful moment, the more significant and more nearly bordering on sincerity was the topic of our conversation, the more commodious, protracted, and conscious were the pauses of our general discourse, the more turbulent were my sensations, and the more invincible my incapacity to speak. There was, at those times, a physical obstruction to speech. My utterance was palsied, and, to articulate a syllable was no less impossible than to lift a mill-stone. To lay my hand on her's, though almost courted to do so, was no less impracticable. The will was strong, but its command over my muscles, whencesoever it arose, was annihilated.

It was impossible for things to remain long in this state. Feverish circulation, ardent musing, incessant watchfulness, and repeated disappointments, were rapidly injurious to my health. My vivacity in Clelia's presence, the earnestness of my discourse, was sensibly diminished. Her company was sought with more fondness than ever, but I grew despondent, museful, prone to silence, and inquietude was deeply written on my cheek.

These tokens did not escape her notice. They were not fully understood by her, but they added new pathos to her features, and tenderness to her accents, and they finally produced these measures on her side, without which my silence would never have been broken.

The constitution of man is compounded and modified with endless variety. The wisest and soberest of human beings is, in some respects, a madman, that is, he acts against his better reason, and his feet stand still, or go south, when every motive is busy in impelling him north. He cannot infer from his conduct, on one occasion, how he shall act when the same or asimilar occasion hereafter occurs. It is vulgarly imagined, and perhaps truly, that the sexes are eternally distinguished by their conduct when under the influence of love, that nature has unalterably assigned to woman the passive or retreating, and to man the active province, that lovers, confident of their success, are bold, forward, and more abundant, and impassioned, and impetuous in their rhetoric, than at any other time. This maxim was realised in my deportment to my cousin. There I was, precipitate and bold. I hearkened to no scruples, and brooked no delays, but now my feelings and demeanour were totally reversed. I was not doubtful of success. I believed that as much felicity would be imparted as received by my confessions, and yet was I dumb.

One evening, when seated in Miss Neville's drawing room, the conversation had been carried on with less vivacity than usual. As the moment of parting approached, my inexplicable despondency increased. At length, just as I was preparing to leave my seat, and the last "good night" was ready to fall from my lips, my friend placed herself beside me, without formality, apology, or invitation. Hitherto she had given me no proof of equal familiarity. My blood flowed with new swiftness, and the flame that burnt at my heart, spread over my countenance a new crimson. She spoke, not without some faultering, but in a tone of exquisite tenderness.

"Stay a little longer. You must not go yet. You have first a small account to settle with me."

Indeed! said I, much alarmed and half suffocated with emotion.

"Be not frightened," resumed she with a smile, "it is true, you have offended, but I shall not be extremely rigid in exacting the penalty."

Offence? Have I, indeed, offended you? Nothing was farther from my purpose. The hand that injured you, I would cut off, the heart that fostered a single thought to your prejudice, I would tear from my bosom.

"Your hand has not offended me. It is your heart that has been criminal, and I take you at your word. Yet, you need not do violence to your heart, but only to the feelings which have so long been harboured in it. Put me in possession of these feelings. Lay them open before me, and drop, at length, that veil of odious and unfriendly secrecy which has shrouded all your sentiments and feelings. Think you I have not noticed your inquietudes? That I have not shared in them? That I have not longed for an opportunity to lessen or remove them? Indeed you mistake. I have caught from you all your sadness, have mourned over your unknown misfortunes, but have more bitterly wept at seeing that you deem me unworthy of partaking your sorrow. I have endured your silence and injustice long enough, and am now determined to wrest from you that confidence which is my due."

Is it not strange, that even this address had no tendency but to make motion and utterance more difficult? After a pause, she resumed:

"How have I deserved to be treated as your enemy? Has any thing been wanting to convince you how dearly I prize your happiness? What farther proof is needed? There is none which I will refuse."

Half dubious and reluctant, she now put her

hand in mine, and continued. "You are an invincible man. You are cruel and unjust. You refuse to confide in me, and will not enable me to give that proof of my claim to your confidence which you think necessary. Whatever proof you demand, I will give. I will withhold nothing."

Nothing?

"Nothing. What do you ask?"

Your love.

"It is yours."

Of all moments in the life of an human being, surely this is most pregnant with felicity. One like me, ardent with youth, inattentive to futurity, unchastised by reason, unsobered by experience, it was calculated to bewilder and intoxicate. Those lips, whose sweetness and whose music had hitherto charmed me at a distance, were now near enough for the softest whisper to be heard. They were now opened only to enchant me with the oft repeated assurance, "it is yours: long, very long, has it been yours." They were shut only to confirm the vow by testimonies still more tender. The spell once dissolved, the scruples that had so greatly tormented me, vanished in a moment,and left me in a state in which moderation and forbearance became lessons as necessary to be taught, and as difficult to practise, as confidence and self-reliance had been before.

That night was spent in a tumult and elation of thought approaching to delirium. The image of my cousin rarely intruded. It was only when some sleep had been obtained, and a new day arose, that the transactions of the preceding evening began to assume a more tranquil aspect, and I had leisure to inquire, what is now to be done? Speedy and auspicious beyond the painting of my most daring hope, has been the terminating scene of this drama. Only five weeks are past since, lying in this very chamber, I was mournfully ruminating on the incidents of a voyage on which I was the next day to enter, and which was to bear me forever from my native soil. Howshould I have held that folly in derision which should then have teazed the ears of my despair with a tale of such events as have since occurred, and have endeavoured to illumine my benighted soul by persuading me that such was the destiny reserved for me!

But what must be my future conduct? Has not the period arrived when dissimulation and concealment must be laid aside with regard to my cousin? I love another, and my passion is accepted and returned. That which she wantonly, or arrogantly, or rashly cast away, has been found, and is cherished as an inestimable good by another. I must go to her this very day and tell her that my hand and heart must never be hers.

Unhappy girl! How little will such tidings accord with thy fond hopes! Thy eyes, whenever I meet thee, beam with benignity and pleasure. If thy vivacity be sometimes tinged with a shade of sadness, it is from observation of that melancholy which my deportment has hitherto betokened, and which thou fondly ascribest to the struggle between my devotion to thee, and my reverence for virtue. Thou imaginest that, however hard the conflict, the victory has ultimately fallen to the side of magnanimity and duty, and congratulatest thyself on these proofs of constancy and worth in him whom thou lovest with a passion the purest and most ardent that ever glowed in the female bosom.

How wilt thou be astonished on discovering the truth, at finding that this tissue of appearances was merely the garb of hypocrisy! How bitterly wilt thou deplore, not merely the sudden ruin of that structure of happiness to which thy heart was devoted, but this defection from sincerity, this revolt from gratitude, this trampling upon duty, of which I shall appear to be guilty!

But why should I thus haste to make her miserable? Do I build my confidence on sufficient grounds? Have I not had bitter experience of the instability of human resolutions? The frailty of schemes composed of the elements of hope and fear? Clelia loves me, of that she has afforded me sufficient proof. But, in spite of the illusions of passion, I cannot hide from myself my ignorance of her real situation and her character. What untoward events may not arise to postpone, or forever to preclude that blissful consummation which wedlock bestows? Ought I not, at least, to ascertain her acquiescence in the desirableness of marriage? Ought I not, at least, to gain her consent to ratify irrevocable vows at some definite, however distant period? Having accomplished this, the disclosure of my situation to Louisa will then be seasonable and proper. Before, it will be but hazarding my reputation and my safety on a fluctuating and deceitful sea. This night shall she be persuaded to fix the nuptial day.

Full of these turbulent feelings, I hastened, at the usual hour in the evening, to Miss Neville. She was alone, and afforded me a welcome more fervent than usual, and fraught with that tenderness which became our present situation. After some cursory topics, she glided into a description of those surmises and conjectures which led her to adopt the conduct of last evening, the considerations of decorum, which had long deterred her from pursuing any means for extorting from me my feelings, and inquired into the reasons of so singular a backwardness on my part to claim that friendship from her, which I could not but have discovered in her a perfect readiness to bestow.

This inquiry was made with symptoms of anxiety in my companion which I could not fail to notice, and which I thought disproportioned to the occasion. It seemed as if her fancy pictured to itself some cause of a formidable nature. Whethert his cause related to myself or to her, whether her apprehensions sprang from the belief of my knowing some particular in her own condition, or from surmises respecting my mother and my cousin, it was impossible to conjecture.

These reflections were suspended while I laid before her the truth.

Sheer bashfulness! said I. I loved you, but my tongue refused the office of interpreting my sentiments. I believed that my passion was not unanswered, but this emboldened me not. It is strange. I am unable to explain it. My timidity had no basis in reasoning. It existed only in your presence, and in spite of resolutions formed in solitude.

She looked at me with a scrutinising and anxious glance. "Is that possible?" she emphatically exclaimed.

Why not? What other cause could exist? I am confident of your integrity, I am conscious of my own. Situated as you and I are, what bar could arise to obstruct the declaration of our feelings? They are innocent and laudable, and, to obey them, forfeits no fame, and violates no duty.

She cast down her eyes at these words, yet her perplexity, though not removed, was lessened. A secret witness, in my own heart, whispered a censure which made me fully share in her uneasiness. The possibility that my betrothment to my cousin, and the mistakes under which she laboured, had, by some untoward chance, been made known to my new friend. The unfavourable judgment she might pass upon my conduct, and the embarrassments or obstacles to my felicity which might thence be created, overpowered me with terror. I repeated more earnestly, is not our affection innocent and laudable? Know you aught of me that would make it otherwise? Tell me, I beseech you.

"No," she replied, "I know nothing of you but what redounds to your glory, and places you among the first of men. I know you better than you at this time imagine. Long have I known you, and can bear witness to that unparalleled magnanimity which makes you worthy of the devotion of a pure heart."

These encomiums were strange and unexpected. She knew more of me than I imagined! And for a longer time! My conduct has been disinterested and wise! Had she exerted indirect means to obtain this knowledge? Had she been deceived and misinformed, or was her judgment such as to bestow approbation upon that which my own conscience had condemned? These words, however, had confuted my first conjecture. I had no longer to fear the effects of a morality too scrupulous, or a sagacity too eagle-eyed.

Yet, whence then could flow a perturbation so visible? Was it from reflections on her own misconduct?

This image was of too awful and portentuous a

kind not to make me shake off my puerile embarrassments. After a considerable pause, I addressed her thus:

Clelia Neville! We are now arrived at a critical moment in our destiny. It becomes us to walk erect, with a thorough knowledge of our path, and with no possibility of being entangled by suspicion or overtaken by repentance. There are marks in your countenance of apprehension and distrust. You have ascribed my former diffidence to some cause unknown to me. Doubt and fear have found harbour in your thoughts. Whence do they proceed? What is the meaning of those solicitudes which I now witness? You have acquitted me of any guilt. As you value our mutual happiness, be explicit and sincere, and tell me whether there be any thing in your own conduct that should lessen you in my opinion, and bereave you of that love which I have proffered to you.

"No," she replied with some degree of sadness. "There is nothing. I have had the faults of inexperience and youth, but my intentions have been free from malignity. My heart ispure, and is as worthy of you as the heait of woman can be."

I believe thee, said I, folding her in my arms, and let me on these lips seal my vows of everlasting honour. Thus do I devote my life to the cause of thy felicity. Now my soul knows no wish but one, a wish in which thine, if thy assertions be sincere, will as eagerly participate. There are ties without which our union, and of consequence our happiness, is incomplete. I can know no rest till these ties are formed. When shall that event take place? When shall a solemn rite make Clelia Neville my wife?

Instead of that blushful and tremulous rapture which I expected this intimation to produce, a sudden shock pervaded the frame of my companion, she uttered a shriek of terror and surprise, and shrinking from my embrace, threw herself on a sofa in an agony unspeakable.

The effects of this scene upon my sensations, may be easily imagined. The first momentary dread that some fatal stroke of disease had fallen on her, was supplanted by different forebodings. Their object was terrible, indeed, but vague, misty, and obscure. They menaced nothing less than extinction to my new-born and darling hopes.

I seated myself by her side. I took her hand and pressed it to my lips. I dared not lift my eyes or utter a word. She did not withdraw from my kindness, but leaning her face on my bosom, poured forth incessant tears. I struggled, after the first burst of passion was exhausted, to obtain words.

You do not answer me. Have I vaunted of my happiness in vain ? Have I, in seeking your love, done no more than pull ruin upon my head? Speak, I conjure you. Will you not be mine?

She answered only by new grief.

Torture me not with suspense. Whatever be my doom, let me, at least, have the consolation to know it. Tomorrow, tonight, this very hour, will not Clelia Neville consent to be mywife?

Still I could obtain no answer but tears and the deepest sighs. I had too much reason to infer a denial from these appearances, but my happiness was too deeply involved in this discovery to make me satisfied with vague surmises. I urged my question with augmented vehemence.

At length, she with difficulty articulated: "Alas! Not now. It must be postponed."

Postponed! Blast not my ears with that accursed word. Recall that sentence if you wish me to live.

She shook her head.

I continued: Postponed! God grant me patience! For how long? For months? For weeks? Let me have the foresight, at least, of respite to my misery, of end to my pangs. How long must marriage be postponed?

"I cannot tell. An overruling fate must decide. Perhaps for years, perhaps forever."

At these words, my equanimity wholly forsook me. My mind was plunged into the gloomiest despair. I fixed my eyes upon the floor, and, forbearing to notice my companion, pursued the disastrous tenor of my own thoughts. This reverse was as fatal in its influence on my happiness as the events preceding it had been auspicious. I could not trust to my senses that informed me of this reverse. They had deceived me. Comforted with this reflection, I started from my dream and turned my eyes on my companion. In her features I read the confirmation of the tidings. Flowing tears, and sighs rising from the bottom of her heart, were tokens of their truth.

But what was the obstacle to my felicity? Was it such a groundless scruple as had actuated my perverse cousin? Might I not hope to remove or rise above it? Was the character of this woman made up of the same refractory materials? Would not her aversion be subdued by intreaties or by arguments? Somewhat revived by these hopes, I again addressed my weeping companion.

"You tell me that our union must be deferred. The period is uncertain. Whence arises this uncertainty? Whence comes this obstacle? It must, it shall be disregarded or surmounted.

"It cannot be."

Cannot be! Let me judge of its insurmountable nature. Tell me what it is.

She was silent. She had no power to answer.

Will you banish me forever from your presence? Will you discard me from your love? And shall I not know in what I have offended? Shall I not join with you, and trample down impediments with which your single strength cannot cope?

"Alas! No earthly power can remove them. Slight obstacles, superable by human force, I should set at naught, but this—"

Shall be set at naught. Thou art mine. It will be vain to refuse or hesitate. Whatever rite, divine or human, is necessary to cement, to ratify our vows, shall be made. I hearken not to scruples. Denials I will not hear. No power of others or yourself, shall stop my way to the possession of your hand. In this resolution I will no longer repine. I will argue or supplicate no more, for thou shalt be mine.

"Alas! Good youth! Thy confidence is vain, thy efforts will be fruitless. I cannot be thy wife, for I am–*a wife already!*"

A wife! Clelia Neville a wife! She belongs to another! The obstacle, indeed, is not to be surmounted. My happiness is gone. My trust in the sincerity of others, in the blandishments of fortune, in the fictions of probability, in the suggestions of my own discernment, in the consolatory accents of hope, is gone.

A wife! That little word was sufficient wholly to reverse my sensations, to throw me from my pinacle of joyous confidence, and leave me whelmed in the utter darkness of despair. I can scarcely tell what were my first gestures, or what were the words I uttered after my senses had been struck by this fatal intelligence. My heart swelled with horror, indignation, and grief, with indignation at that hypocrisy which I imagined to have been exercised to entice me to the verge of this precipice, horror at the guilt to the commission of which I seemed to have been rushing, grief at the closing of my prospects, at the fruitlessness of all my efforts after happiness, of all those humiliations and artifices which I had employed to prolong the ignorance and elude the suspicions of my cousin. Thus had the wiles of the deceiver thrown back upon himself the well-earned penalty of disgrace, disappointment, and despair.

I broke from her presence in a mood half made up of sullenness and rage. I shut myself up in solitude. I avenged myself by curses on my evil fortune, by muttering to the unconscious walls my abhorrence of her dissimulation and concealment, by half-formed vows of abjuring the society of mankind, of flying from my hated country, of withdrawing from life.

From upbraiding Clelia, my infatuation passed to wreaking my impotent resentment on my cousin, whose perverseness, by driving me to search elsewhere for happiness, exposed me to this misery and ignominy. Sidney was likewise devested as the primitive cause of my misfortunes, as the great dispenser of ill, whose malignant agency would never fail to blast my most auspicious and best concerted projects, and from whose wanton persecution I could only hope to escape by placing oceans and continents between us.

This fit of passion gradually remitted its violence. After some hours, spent in a kind of frenzy which only wanted duration to be as ferocious and destructive as any that receives the name, my thoughts began to flow in a more equable course. Time hushes every storm, and when the hurricane has ended its career, every flowing of the billows is less impetuous than the last, till, at length, the tranquilising power "summa placidum caput extulit unda." Thus it is in the tempests of the mind. Hope breaks through the cloud which hung over us and shut out the day, and brings back serenity and radiance.

Insensibly my mind reverted to the contemplation of those events which preceded my first meeting with Miss Neville. I called back my ancient feelings with regard to my cousin. From regreting the artifices and concealments of which I had been guilty, I began to regard them as having been prudent and wise. I blessed myself for having thus long delayed the disclosure of my intercourse with this foreigner, and determined, henceforth, to act as if she had never been known to me, to resume my visits to my cousin, and find, in her ingenuous confidence, her artless affection, and the effusions of her pure and upright mind, a recompense for my recent disappointments.

You will ask if my passion for Clelia was thus easily annihilated, if the lapse of a single day or week was sufficient to free me from shackles which are usually the strongest which nature has imposed upon youthful hearts, if the extinction of desire thus rapidly followed the extinction of hope. This inference would be very wide of the truth, yet it was the inference which was drawn, at that time, by myself. My state was like that of a person who had rashly entangled himself in a fen, and, after panic fears and vehement struggles, has safely reached the firm ground. Exhausted by my efforts, I stood still to retrieve mycomposure and strength, and found a nameless delight in comparing my present safety with my past danger.

Such is the nature of passion, and, especially, of this passion. Our views of things are perpetually varying, and our feelings, conforming themselves to the change, are tranquil or stormy, torn by regrets or soaring into tranquility. The first belief that succeeded to the rage of disappointnient, was that of being free from the enchantments which, had hitherto seduced me. I imagined that my love for Clelia was at an end. Though my new emotions, with respect to my cousin, were merely those of brotherly esteem, and such as to enable me, with sincerity and cheerfulness, to conform to those conditions which she imposed on our intercourse.

In this state of fleeting and delusive calm, I resolved to visit my cousin. Almost a fortnight had passed since I had seen her last. By indirect expressions, I had given her reason to suppose that this interval would be passed at Calverton. She had remonstrated against so long an absence, but my state of mind made my interviews with her irksome and embarrassing, and I readily seized any means of avoiding them. I pleaded some necessity for staying at this farm, and, in truth, the intervals between my visits to Miss Neville had been chiefly spent in that retreat. Sidney was still abroad, and Louisa was still with her friends on the bank of Schuylkill, and to her, on the approach of evening, I repaired.

I found her pensively walking in an embowered alley of the garden. At my approach, pleasure took place of all other emotions, and she stretched out her hand. "Have you come at last, my dear cousin! Let me first bid you welcome, and then demand from you the cause of this unfriendly absence."

I stammered out some poor apology, and promised more attention for the future.

"Nay," she replied, "let your inclination guide you. Much as I love your company, its value must depend upon being cheerfully and willingly bestowed. And yet," continued she, checking herself, and after a moment's pause, "what a foolish saying was that! What a criminal effusion of selfishness and pride! I want your company much, and will solicit it, and claim it, even should you be averse or reluctant. It becomes me to vanquish that aversion and contend with that reluctance. I have wished for you, and looked for you every evening this week. I have thought of you very much, and longed to communicate my thoughts. Go, sit down upon that bench, and I will tell you all that I have been thinking."

Being seated, she took up a book that lay upon the bench. "See here, what I have been reading this afternoon. How hard beset will you think me, to find it necessary to resort to Mademoiselle Scuderi for entertainment. I found the volume in a garret. It was new to me. I never heard of it, or saw it before, and my curiosity, I promise you, was highly gratified by the first score or two of pages. Look at it."

I took the book, and the first words I met with were Statira, Lysimachus, Perdiccas. I closed the volume with a deep sigh.

She darted piercing eyes at me, and said "Why that sorrowful air? Do you know the book?"

Full well, I answered. If I ever grow old and reflect upon the events that formed my character, I shall mark out this book as the most powerful of all the agents who made me what I am. If I am fickle and fantastic, not a moral or rational, or political being, but a thing of mere sex, this it was that fashioned me. I almost predict that I shall owe an ignominious life, and a shameful end, to this book.

I again opened the volume, carelessly. A letter appeared between the leaves. It was superscribed "Louisa Calvert," and the hand writing was Sidney's. Something like jealousy and envy just then twitched me at the heart.

"Ah!" said she. "That is what I want you to read. It talks a great deal about you, and has told me something that has furnished its chief employment to my mind for these several days. It is that which has made me so impatient for your coming."

At these words my heart misgave me. Is it possible, thought I, that this audacious intermedler has betrayed me? But it cannot be. He is too far off to be acquainted with my movements.

I unfolded and read with some hurry and trepidation. All the while, the eyes of my companion were fixed upon me. They were usually languid and inexpressive, but now they had a strange and fascinating power. Full of conscious purity and benevolent meaning, she seemed prepared to read my inmost soul, and yet, not as a censor or accuser, but as forgiving and compassionate.

Angel of a woman! Methinks I see thee at this moment! Thy virtue was sufficient to irradiate even thy homely features! But I must not call thee thins vividly to my remembrance. I must forget that cruel fate that made me the engine to destroy thee. All is now past, and my story will benefit others, though it plunges me again into anguish and repining. That persuasion shall support me in relating it, in exhibiting my guilt and folly in their genuine colours, and in doing justice to thy memory.

The first part of this letter related to himself, his own situation and employments, but presently he proceeded to a new topic, and continued in these words:

You tell me that your time is chiefly spent without visitants, that Felix himself has deserted you, that he finds full occupation for his time at Calverton, and yet, you add, that you wonder what entertainment he can find in that unsightly and unwholesome spot, surrounded by black faces, parched fields, and long grass.

Your wonder is very natural, but in this case it proceeds from your ignorance. Calverton, in truth, has no charms for your cousin. Few of his hours are spent there. They are much more agreeably devoted to a new acquaintance in the city. This is some lovely female from abroad, on whom our young friend has already bestowed his heart. What is the exact nature of their intercourse I am not informed, but it is intimate and frequent. I greatly fear that the impetuosity of Calvert, has carried him forward with too much speed, or with too little circumspection. I shall very shortly return and counsel him as a friend. Meanwhile, I would have you procure a meeting with him, extort from him some hints respecting his genuine situation, and be that guardian of his virtue and happiness for which your good sense, and your affection for him, so eminently qualify you.

During the perusal of this, my confusion was inexpressible. Shame, at this detection of my imposture, and rage against the author of it, filled my heart almost to bursting. I threw the paper on the ground, and felt myself prompted to rush out of the garden. I turned my eyes from my cousin, and wished that some power would suddenly strike me deaf, that I might be screened from her reproaches. I expected nothing but the keenest rebukes, or the most contemptuous raillery. A pause of some minutes ensued. At length my cousin spoke.

"Why, my friend, are you thus disturbed? Have you been unfortunate? Is any disaster connected with your intercourse with the person here alluded to? Let me comfort you. Let me counsel you. Tell me who she is, and what has passed between you. Perhaps I may assist you. If your happiness requires it, I will be your intercessor, and your advocate."

Good Heaven! Do you not then upbraid me? Do you not scorn me, drive me from your presence as a villain and betrayer?

She shuddered at these words. She looked at me with eyes of terror and pity, and clasping her hands, "Have you, indeed, betrayed her? Have you debased yourself? Have you acted vilely by a woman and a stranger?"

I saw the nature of her error, and made haste to remove it. No, no. She has received no injury from me. Her character, her innocence, are pure as they ever were. I have not hetrayedor deceived her.

"Do you speak true? I beseech you, I conjure you,

tell me the truth. Have you not injured her?"

I averred my innocence once more.

"Why then charge yourself with villainy, with deceit? Whom have you deceived?"

These words involved me in new perplexity. Was she not aware of my imposture with regard to herself? Had I not encouraged her fallacious inferences as to the state of my mind, and allowed her to ascribe appearances, which flowed from my affection for another, from fear and remorse, to emotions connected with my former pretensions to herself?

Observing my silence, she continued. "Have you been guilty of deceit? Whom have you deceived, and on what account could you persuade yourself to act so base a part?"

Have I not concealed from you even the existence of Clelia Neville?

"Alas! You did not deem me worthy of your confidence. The interest that I take in your welfare, you rated too lightly. I have not succeeded in convincing you that I am worthy of your trust. You impute to me indifference, or selfishness, of envy, and hence have arisen your concealments. You imagined, perhaps, that I should be weak enough to derive unhappiness from your attachment to another, though I had, of my own accord, and against your inclination, unloosed all the ties that bound you to me, though I had voluntarily given up my claim to your heart, or wicked enough to hinder your success. You were reluctant, therefore, to make me unhappy, or to raise obstacles in the way of your wishes. Ought I then to blame you for concealment? Ought I not rather to regret the failure of my own efforts, to evince the consistency and rectitude of my sentiments, and to be more diligent for the future?

"Let me, then, persuade you to lay aside disguise, and to confide in me. Depend upon my council and aid in any good cause. Who is the woman that Sidney speaks of? Do you love her? Is she worthy? What wishes or views do you form respecting her? How arose your acquaintance, and whither does it tend? Pr'ythee tell me the whole. Without scruple or evasion tell it me, my more than brother, my friend!"

Was it possible to resist this bewitching frankness? To listen to such accents and not be brought a penitent confessor, to her feet? The motives of my former conduct had indeed been various and mixed. Those which she just ascribed to me, had some part in swaying me to secrecy, but these were not the whole, nor the chief. I feared the imputation of caprice. My doubts of the ultimate decision of Clelia made me hold fast my former claim upon my cousin, a claim which my frank avowals, I imagined, would weaken or wholly take away. But these were impulses of which her generous mind was not aware. She was prone to find in others, and especially me, a purity and self-oblivion like her own.

Should I now disclose to her the full extent of

my versatile and sordid temper? Should I give her the pain of knowing the depth and number of transgressions, of which I sincerely repented, and of which, with the usual temerity of inexperience, I ardently vowed never more to be guilty? Equally humiliating to me, and useless to her, would be such confessions. If hitherto I had not merited her good opinion, hereafter I would do nothing to invalidate my claim.

In this state of mind, I adventured to recount to her my introduction to Miss Neville, and the incidents that had since occurred. My narrative was somewhat different from that which I have just related to you. Incidents were truly related, but falsehood almost spontaneously and insensibly insinuated itself into the statement of my motives. The picture was incomplete, inasmuch as certain lineaments and shades were left out, but no spurious addition was admitted, no positive, though untrue assertion was made. How subtly modified are self-delineations, by vanity, or shame, or misjudging interest! How invisibly faint are the boundaries of truth and falsehood!

She listened with great earnestness. When I brought my story to a close, with the confession of Clelia, that she was already a wife, my cousin started and shuddered. A pause of deep abstraction and silence ensued. At length, she said:

"A wife! So long concealed her marriage from you! To mark the tendency of such intercourse, the progress of your feelings to love! To hear the confessions of that love without reluctance or sorrow! To sanction them, to meet them with corresponding confessions! To grant you those proofs of tenderness, which, in a wife, are surely unwarranted and culpable! Strange deportment!

"To the accents of love, she listened with complacency. By offers of marriage, she was terrified. Surprise was the master passion for a time. Why should she be surprised? Did she imagine you acquainted with her true state? And could she cheerfully receive offices of tenderness from one whom she knew to be apprised of her marriage? What rashness! What blindness to consequences!

"You say that she followed her aunt to America, that her coming was unexpected and unwelcome. It must, then, have been criminal, or, at least, indiscreet and rash. Could she have fled from her husband? Perilous, indeed, my brother, has been your situation. Let this event contribute to inspire you with caution. Be grateful to that succouring Providence which has saved you from ruin, and be, for the future, less prone to confide in the illusions of beauty, and the flattery of first impressions. What have you resolved to do? I hope this has been the last interview."

I assured her that it was so, and that I had unalterably determined never to see the foreigner again. She expressed the utmost satisfaction at this promise, and urged various considerations to strengthen my adherence to it. That evening was spent in her company, and I did not return to the city till next day.

When I retired to rest, my meditations were active and vivid. The events of this evening had given a new soul to my frame. I caught the sweet whispers of self-approbation, and had a glimpse of that felicity which is a stranger to foreboding and remorse. I admired the means by which this transition was effected, and contemplated my cousin's conduct with astonishment and reverence. Judging of others by myself, I had not preconceived the possibility of such sentiments and such deportment. It seemed to be a diiferent person to whom I had been introduced, and my earliest impressions, with regard to her, those which existed before our first meeting, and which arose, were generated by fancy upon rumour, seemed to be revived. My cousin's homely features and diminutive form gave place to symmetry and dignity, and I wondered at myself for having so long overlooked her loveliness.

Next day, after promising to repeat my visit very speedily, I parted from her, and returned to my lodgings in the city. For a time, I was sensible of no decay of my newly acquired zeal. I reviewed late incidents with satisfaction and tranquility. My fancy was engrossed by the looks and words of my cousin. Gradually, however, my attention reverted to the topics of our late conversation, and these recalled to my view, Clelia and her train of charms.

I mused upon the progress of our acquaintance, the delight which she seemed to receive from my discourse, and the fatal disclosure of her marriage now occurred to me, attended with all the indications of grief which were visible on that occasion. From an object of indignation, she insensibly appeared before me as entitled to compassion. That she had eloped from her husband, was sufficiently apparent, but it did not appear that she had fled with a seducer. On the contrary, she had sought protection in the arms of an affectionate and virtuous aunt, whose grief might have been excited, not by the crimes, but by the misfortunes of her niece , and who had, surely, affordedsome proof of her parental confidence and love, by bequeathing to her so large a property. Besides, what, reprehensible or suspicious, had been discovered in the conduct of Clelia since her arrival on these shores? The friends of Mrs. Keith were her friends. Her mode of life was a chaste seclusion, unapproached by any whose intercourse might contaminate her purity. She was free, not from actual degradation merely, but from slander and suspicion. Were not these circumstances of someweight in the scale?

True it is, that she is married, yet she has confessed her love for me, and is that so heinous an offence? If it may claim to be forgiven, surely that claim may be made with most reason on him who is the object of her love. Persecution and resentment, from any quarter, may be undeserved, but from him to whom her heart is devoted, and for whose sake her guilt, if any guilt has been contracted, would be, in an uncommon degree, barbarous and perverse. The motives of her flight may possibly have been such as to be excused, if not justified by a candid arbiter, and why should I decide upon these motives, and on the equity of her conduct, before I am acquainted with them?

I had withdrawn from our last interview in rage. Was this the treatment she had merited? What was her crime in suppressing the mention of that which possibly she imagined to be known to me already? My conduct was precipitate and cruel, but it cannot now be repaired. I have vowed never to see her more. My promise to Louisa is sacred, and must be preserved.

With these reasonings passing through my mind, I reached home. I had scarcely entered the house, when a letter was presented to me by my landlord. I started when I saw that the superscription was in the same hand with that in which the billet formerly received, was written. So! said I. A letter from Clelia herself! This is an evil omen. I hastily opened, and read as follows:

To Felix Calvert. You left me in anger and

contempt. What has happened to lessen me in your esteem? I deserve nothing but your pity. I demand your pity.

Your proposal astonished and grieved me. It astonished me because I had good reason to believe you acquainted with my situation, and because it was inconsistent with those opinions you had previously avowed. You taught me to believe that you could love me with the same passion with which you could love a friend of your own sex.

I am grieved to find you a stranger to my real condition. Had I supposed that ignorance, I should long ago have hastened to remove it. I beseech you, afford me the opportunity of justifying my conduct. You know me merely as a fugitive from my husband and my country, and you impute to me all that is criminal and odious, but the true reasons of my actions will show you that I am not without excuse. I request one last interview, that I may lay before you these reasons.

I invite you not to a renewal of intercourse. Neither my happiness nor yours will permit that. I would see you once more, that I may convince my benefactor that I am not altogether as unworthy as he thinks me, but, thenceforth, we must part forever.

I will expect you at the customary hour this evening.

C. N.

Was this summons to be obeyed? Compliance was but just. An invitation to a single interview, for a purpose like this, was innocent and laudable. What but good could flow from compliance? I had promised my cousin not to visit Miss Neville (for so I will continue to call her) but she, herself, would readily absolve me from this promise, were she apprised of the purpose of the desired interview. I will go.

My conjecture had been right. She supposed me acquaintedwith her marriage, yet, how could that knowledge have been obtained? Perhaps from her aunt's friends, with whom I might be naturally imagined to have some intercourse.

I paid my visit at the appointed hour. I found her as usual when the evening was serene, in the garden. She received me with some marks of confusion and distress. As I approached the house, my placidness and courage began to yield place to dejection and restlessness. These increased on entering the alcove, where so many pleasurable moments had passed, and the sight of her pale hues and downcast eyes, completed the subversion of my fortitude. My sensations on leaving her, at the former interview, returned upon me with scarcely less force.

I did not speak. I did not seat myself beside her, but opposite. I folded my hands upon my breast, and waited, mournfully, for what communications she should please to make. After some pause, she said, in a tremulous tone:

"I have invited you hither, without knowing whether you had any desire for the interview. I have offered to communicate the knowledge of events, which, perhaps, are to you indifferent. What I tell you, may only, in a slight degree, lessen your disapprobation, but I would fain restore myself to the esteem of one who has saved my life. I would elude the charge of having seduced your affections, by appearances of being willing to accept them, without the violation of my duty.

"It is true, alas, that I am married, but the man who claims my person, has no claim upon my esteem and my love. I have fled from his house, because it was a scene of depravity and tyranny. I have exercised no other liberty than that of forbearing intercourse with a wretch, polluted by the blackest guilt. To withdraw from his power, to regard him with aversion instead of love, was no crime. To feel gratitude for real services, to give esteem, confidence, and love to another who deserves it, is consistent with every duty to my husband, and I have fostered these emotions towards you without remorse.

"My father was a banker of Dublin. My mother died a few hours after my birth, and left me, the only consolation of my father. My early years were spent without any remarkable occurrence. At the age of fourteen I was permitted to take up my abode with my father's sister, Mrs. Keith, who, at that period,

came from America, and was left lonely and discon-
solate, by the death of her husband. She adopted,
and treated me as her own, and I was not wanting in
filial affection and gratitude.

"I had passed my eighteenth year, not without
many suitors. None of them were such as obtained,
at once, my own approbation, and that of my two
parents, and their concurrence, as well as that of
my own heart, was an indispensable condition of
success. I was an only child, and the heiress of both
my father and his sister, and both were deemed rich.
Hence there was no want of amorous protestors,
and disinterested wooers, but I erected a standard,
by which to judge of their sincerity, that none of
them could endure.

"At length one was introduced to me, by name
Belgrave. His family was ancient, and much superior in dignity to mine. He was possessed of great
fortunes, which he spent with magnificence, but
without visible profusion. He was in the bloom
of youth, graceful, elegant, insinuating. He had
received the usual education, and spent the usual
time in foreign countries, from which he had
returned, with all that speciousness and gloss about
him, which converse, on equal terms, with the great
and the gay, are adapted to produce.

"He quickly selected me for the object of his
devotion, and employed every means of gaining
my esteem. He conformed to all my pursuits and

opinions, applauded and condemned according to the example which I set him, and made himself, as nearly as possible, a copy of that model which my fancy had most delighted to contemplate.

"His efforts were in some degree successful. His manners, and his general conduct, were such as I readily and ardently approved. His external circumstances were liable to no exception, but still there was a nameless something in his countenance and carriage, which I could not prevail upon my heart to love. When called upon to state the grounds of my aversion, I could mention no strain of discourse, no mode of conduct which I disapproved. His tongue was fluent, and always prodigal of generous feelings, and heroic ardours, and his features were flexible and animated, and yet the look of true benevolence, an eye, ingenious and benignant, were never to be found by me. Doubts, misgivings, proneness to shrink, to cover up my feelings, as from one incapable of sharing in them, always swayed me in his presence, and when my attention was fixed upon his face. They were instinctive, and inexplicable. I could not clearly define them to another, and produce in another the same emotions with regard to him.

"After a due period of assiduity he besought my hand. It was refused. His humiliation and grief were unaffected, but wrought no change in my resolutions. My aunt and my father were engaged as his advocates. I could convince neither of them of the propriety of my objections. In their eyes, my scruples appeared absurd and capricious. They were hearkened to with disgust, and censured with asperity. Solicitations and commands, menaces of separation and displeasure, were liberally employed to vanquish what was called my infatuation and my folly.

"Hitherto I had known little but happiness. My aunt's and my father's approbation and love, had amply compensated me for the few ills and privations which had fallen to my lot, but these consolations were now withdrawn. I reverenced their judgments, but their arguments, while they taught me to mistrust my own impressions, did not weaken these impressions, or prevent me from sinking into grief, at the prospect of becoming the wife of Belgrave.

"This state of fluctuation continued for several months. Belgrave was indefatigable in his importunities, in his appeals to my compassion, and my reason, in his vows of eternal gratitude and boundless devotion, and my parents were no less urgent in contending with scruples, which they deemed fantastic, ridiculous and criminal.

"I will not dwell upon the feelings with which I endured this conflict. They cannot be described. They cannot be conceived but by one who loved with gratitude and fervor like mine, devoted to a revered parent, and idolising the penetration and generosity of my friend. Their rebukes became daily more severe, and my fainting courage became every day more unequal to resistance, My father, at length, disclosed obligations under which Belgrave had laid him, and which, as they had saved him from bankruptcy, had preserved me from indigence. These demanded every grateful service, and my refusal to become Belgrave's wife, would offend my father and my aunt beyond forgiveness. Subdued, at length, I resigned myself to my fate.

"Too soon were the forebodings of my fears realised. Those appearances were laid aside, which he had deemed necessary for the attainment of his purposes. Cohabiting with him, I became acquainted with transactions and scenes, which, at a distance, could not possibly have been suspected. Under a veil of darkness, propensities were indulged by my husband, that have not a name which I can utter. They cannot be thought of without horror. They cannot be related.

"In the bosom of my aunt, I was unacquainted with the existence of half the vices and evils which infest mankind. For some enormities, which my subsequent experience brought within my observation, so far from knowing them by name, they had never occurred to me as possible. In brooding over my suspicions with respect to Belgrave, I fashioned, as I imagined, the most horrid images of voluptuousness and insensibility, but far different, far more flagrant was the guilt, far more savage the pollutions to which he was habituated.

"My detection of the truth was gradual. Quickly did indifference and inattention succeed to insinuation and warmth, but these slowly gave way to peevishness, impatience, and, at length, to undisguised disgust. Momentary returns to kindness became fewer. Bursts of contempt and resentment became more frequent. Hasty intimations that my pride and my obstinacy, in so long resisting his entreaties, merited punishment, and that his perseverance was dictated by a desire of revenge, sometimes escaped him.

"This vengeance he proceeded to inflict, by treating me with rudeness and contempt, by thwarting all my most trifling wishes, by forbidding his servants to bear my messages or execute my orders, by affronting my friends and visitants, by interrupting me in my favourite employments of music and reading, or depriving me of the means of pursuing them. My father was shortly taken away by a sudden death, and his property, of course, devolved upon Belgrave. This property enlarged his gratifications, but contributed, in no degree, to my comfort or my deliverance from mistreatment. Nor did he strive to conceal from me that my wealth had been the great inducement in applying for my favour, and that the pecuniary assistance which he had given to my father, was merely designed to benefit himself, and to preserve, unimpaired, that fortune which he expected would one day come into his own hands.

"These evils were endured with some degree of fortitude. There were, indeed, moments of agony, of hopeless distress, and of complaint, but my complaints were poured into no ears but those of my aunt. She mingled her tears with mine. She expressed her regrets at her former importunity, but endeavoured to console me by pointing out the path of duty, and showing me the consequences of adhering to it in the approbation of my conscience and the smiles of a protecting God.

"At length, various circumstances set the depravity of my husband in a new light. For a long time I was blind to the obvious inferences which a person, much acquainted with the world, could not fail to have drawn from appearances. My husband's negligence of me I naturally ascribed to his attachment to some other woman. I could not readily believe what yet appeared to be true, that his associates were wholly of his own sex, and I gave him credit for a rectitude of conduct, in one respect, which was little in unison with other parts of his deportment.

"This illusion came, at length, to an end. Belgrave's contempt and hatred of me exceeded even his regard for his own reputation, and to his own safety, from the animadversions of the law. So open, so shameless was his conduct, that, at length, my own eyes were allowed to witness...

"I cannot utter it. I was frozen with horror. I

doubted whether hideous phantoms, produced by my own imagination had not deceived me. Till my memory, putting past incidents together, convinced me that they were real.

"My husband's presence, his house, became loathsome and intolerable. I flew to my only comforter, my aunt. I related what I had seen, and declared my desperate resolution never more to return to his house, to brave the contumelies of the world, which would never believe the wrongs which I had endured,a nd which, indeed, would never know the most odious of these wrongs.

"She contended with my despair. She joined with me in my abhorrence of Belgrave, but she endeavoured to reconcile me to my fate, to wean me from reliance on the world's opinion and the world's goods, to seek, in religion, a balm to my wounded spirit, and a basis for hope which the depravity of those around me could never shake.

"My aunt's exhortations were always earnest and pathetic to a degree that never failed to conquer my despair, at least, for a time. Her lessons instilled into me patience, at least, to sustain the miseries of my condition. I consented to return to an habitation polluted by abominable crimes, to hush my murmurs, and to meet the wretch who called himself my husband, without invectives.

"My aunt, shortly after, thought it necessary to return to America. She was the only friend which, in spite of the tyranny and malice of Belgrave, I had preserved. It was she only whose accents had any power to inspire me with fortitude. Her counsels and admonitions were perpetually necessary, and in her bosom I poured my sorrows, and found comfort. She was now going to desert me. She would pass into a distant world, from which she designed never to return. All useful intercourse between us would be cut off.

"I endeavoured to persuade her to relinquish her scheme and urged the necessity of her presence to prevent me from committing some fatal act of despair or resentment. She resisted my intreaties, and showed me the weakness of dependence on a fellow creature, whom so many accidents might snatch away from this state of existence. She urged anew the duty of seeking strength from an higher source, and, after many efforts on my side, and many arguments on hers, I consented, with a bleeding heart, to her departure, and to the loss of the only comfort that remained to me.

"I will not dwell upon the incidents that ensued her departure. My husband's conduct became more atrocious than ever. My life became more burthensome. My customary source of fortitude was withdrawn. I was overwhelmed with a consciousness of solitude and wretchedness. I endeavoured, in vain, to practise the lessons of resignation and devotion which my aunt had taught me. I looked after my beloved friend with unspeakable longings. My fancy accompanied her across the inhospitable ocean, and took up its abode with her on the shores of this new world. This employment possessed a strange power of delighting and tormenting me. I pursued it incessantly by night and by day. I loved to sleep, for my dreams were sure to unite me with my absent friend, and to annihilate that dreary interval by which we were severed from each other. I awoke to sorrow. To sorrow, that the scene was visionary and fleeting.

"By perpetually musing on the forlornness of my condition, the inquiry was gradually suggested, is it without remedy? Has my friend gone whither it is impossible to follow her? The ocean is passable by me as well as by her. What should hinder me from pursuing the same track? From seeking deliverance from the tyranny under which I now suffer, by flying to a distant land.

"This thought had not now occurred for the first time. When my aunt's voyage had first been mentioned, my heart involuntarily exclaimed, O! that I could be her companion, that I could fly from my country forever, from the power of my bitterest enemy, and the most profligate of men, and hide my head in a remote land of tranquility and innocence! This desire I never dared to utter, and made haste to stifle so flattering a gratification.

"To a scheme like that, I knew that my aunt would never consent. To know that it was harboured for a moment in my bosom, would give her exquisite pain, by showing her the futility of all her efforts to convince me of my sacred duty and irrevocable obligations. Now this scheme was anew suggested to my thoughts with more attractions than ever. The more I revolved it, the more practicable and eligible it appeared.

"What," said I, "are the impediments that hinder me? Cannot I withdraw from this habitation and this city, without exciting my husband's opposition? He little suspects that my despair could prompt me to an action like this. He will, therefore, employ no precautions against it. If I conceal my name, assume a different and plainer garb, and retire to some obscure sea port in the north, I may embark for America without molestation, and my place of refuge will never be suspected by those whom I leave behind.

"My flight will be regarded with pleasure by Belgrave, more than with anger. He will not know whither I have fled. He will suppose me lost in obscurity and indigence, and his savage heart will derive satisfaction from reflecting on the humiliations and embarrassments to which he may imagine me subjected. Instead of diligently pursuing my footsteps, and reclaiming possession of my person, he will be contented with my property, and rejoice at being freed from that restraint which my presence could not fail, in some degree, to produce.

"He may propagate some tale injurious to my honour, and my reputation may be blasted, but, free as I am from reproach, and notorious as my husband's vices have at length become, what have I to fear from his aspersions? On what ground has my conduct afforded him the possibility of building slanderous insinuations? And will he not be deterred by the uncertainty of my condition, and the likelihood, therefore, that I live to confute his falsehoods, and to avenge my injuries, by unfolding to the world those enormities which would not only cover him with infamy, but expose to danger his liberty, and even his life.

"My friend will be grieved at my conduct, but, surely, if it cannot be justified, it is yet not without excuse. Her wisdom will reconcile her to an event which cannot be recalled, and she will not refuse me her protection and her love.

"This scheme, after many difficulties and delays, was carried into execution. I escaped from Dublin without warning any human creature of my design, and without leaving behind me any traces of my flight. After a tempestuous voyage, I arrived in this city. Having found my aunt's habitation, I burst into her presence, and, throwing myself into her arms, poured forth tears of joy and shame.

"My maternal friend easily forgave the errors of her child, when it was no longer in her power to prevent them, but her wisdom could not reconcile her to an act which she deemed a violation of the most sacred duty. Long have I wept over her grave, and my grief has been embittered by the thought that my misconduct contributed to cloud the evening of her life, and, perhaps, to hasten that event which has robbed me of a guide, a protector, and a parent.

"I have no correspondence with my native country. I know not the condition of Belgrave, or the effects which my disappearance has produced upon him or upon others. I have had no desire but to live unmolested and in privacy, in the indulgence of mournful recollections, and in the moderate use of that liberty and those enjoyments which are within my reach, and which are innocent."

Here the narrator paused. I had listened with the deepest interest. I continued to listen. I readily acquitted her of all blame for leaving her country, but how were these events likely to be known to me, when it had probably been her earnest wish to hide them from all mankind, and when, indeed, her own silence, on the subject of her own adventures, had never been broken?

I did not conceal from her these thoughts. Her countenance betrayed embarrassment and perplexity. She hesitated to answer me, and, at length, said:

"It is true. I imagined you to be acquainted with my condition. I found in you one whom I wish to call my friend, because my unhappy situation will not allow any nearer claim. I am content to be the object of your fraternal love, but this is not sufficient for your happiness. I must, therefore, consent to lose the pleasures and advantages of your society, but I thought it due to myself to explain the reasons of a conduct which to you might appear culpable.

"I have suppressed the mention of my own misfortunes, at first, because the subject is painful in remembrance, because suitable occasions for the mention of them never occurred, because your curiosity never appeared to be awakened with regard to them, and you never, even indirectly, and at our most confidential moments, questioned me as to my former or actual condition."

But that deportment, replied I, eyeing her steadfastly, might arise from diffidence or false delicacy, from a thousand causes different from my knowledge of your true condition. Besides, how was I to obtain that knowledge? Who was there, beyond these walls, able to communicate it, and from whom I was likely, in my present situation, to obtain it? I have told you that I am nearly a stranger in this city, that there is none of its inhabitants but you with whom I have frequent or friendly intercourse.

Her embarrassment was increased by the steadfastness of my scrutiny. She answered, "I thought you knew it. It was vague conjecture, and fallacious, as the event has now proved. Perhaps I may have found such place in your esteem that you will credit my assertion without knowing the grounds of my opinion. I will not hide from you the existence of such grounds, which, at the same time, I cannot now disclose to you. The time will, perhaps, come, when the disclosure may be possible. Now it is not."

I renewed my questions, but she repelled them in the same manner. To tell her reasons for supposing me more knowing, in relation to her, than I was, was not fit for this time. The consequences of this error were not more to be lamented for my sake than for hers. It had deprived her of a friend.

Why do you speak thus? Why must this discovery raise an insuperable bar between us? Why should we not interchange our feelings and ideas as formerly?

She cast at me looks of surprise, mingled with affection. "Have I not betrayed you? Have I not misled you by false pretences, by appearances which did not correspond with truth? Is not this the light by which I am regarded by you?"

Not if I confide in your assertions that you meant not to deceive me, that you imagined me aware of that obstacle which forbade any intercourse but that of friendship between us?

Her eyes sparkled with delight at these words. "And do you trust me? Do you confide in me? Will you still be my friend? Will you add another and a greater benefit to that which you bestowed on me in saving my life, by allowing me the affections, the caresses, and the counsels of a brother?"

Such looks and tones accompanied these words,

that I yielded my assent, not coldly or reluctantly, but with undisguised and immeasurable fervency.

"I am a forlorn girl," she resumed. "I am an exile and a recluse. I have been the victim of imposture and cruelty. I desire not to mix with the world, or to disclose my condition. I have resumed my father's name, and disown the condition of a wife. What expedient the malice of Belgrave may employ to hurt my reputation, or regain his power over my person, I know not. But I know that my safety depends upon his ignorance of my retreat. My heart is formed for all the tender sympathies of nature. My soul melts when the images of wife and mother occur strongly to my fancy, and I sink into repining at the hardness of my destiny which has cut me off from all these duties and enjoyments.

"Since I have known you, my regrets are less painful. I love to paint myself as owing life and all its enjoyments to your hand. I love that boundless gratitude which swells my heart at the sight of you, and which your estimable qualities have converted into affection and esteem. My love for you is tender, but that love demands nothing but your affection, your society, and your happiness. On my own account, I scarcely regret those bars which hinder you from standing in any nearer relation to me. How happy shall I be, if there be no reason to regret it upon your account, if you can cheerfully consent to be my friend. Can you consent? Cheerfully?"

At that moment, and while listening to such accents, it was impossible not to repeat my concurrence. For some hours, my cousin was forgotten. My indignation was dismissed. My horror at the name of wife, my aversion to restraint, was no longer felt. I regarded my companion as a martyr to an ill fated marriage. Her misfortunes, her desolate condition, her dependence upon me for happiness, and the obstacles to our union not arising, as in my cousin's case, from her own perverseness, but from causes whose existence was as deeply deplored by herself as by me, added to the enchantments of her features and the graces of her demeanour, made me willingly renew my homage at this shrine.

When the interview was at an end, I began to review these incidents with more sobriety. I was struck with wonder at the difference between the consequences of this meeting and those which I had previously imagined would flow from it, at the rapid transitions which my feelings had undergone from indignation and horror, to complacency, and even rapture. Is there a human heart, said I, fashioned like mine, susceptible of such extremes, shifting guises and forms with such celerity, and delivering itself up to such opposite emotions within the same short period? And what is now to be done?

I promised my cousin never to repeat my visit to Miss Neville. Ten hours have scarcely passed since the promise was made, yet I have paid this interdicted visit, and have promised to be more assiduous in my attentions than ever! Will this disobedience be excused by my cousin? Shall I not disclose all that has passed? And will not Clelia be regarded by her as worthy of affection and pity?

I acquiesced in this resolution, yet I was not in haste to execute it. My hours of leisure I felt most disposed to devote to Miss Neville. The distance from my lodgings was less, and the attractions of her company far more powerful. I will see my cousin, I said, shortly, but not tonight. Tomorrow will be time enough. When the morrow arrived, my visit was again postponed. I readily admitted a stormy atmosphere to plead my excuse, and even the likelihood of rain was sufficient to reconcile me to delay. Thus day after day occurred. New impediments arose in my way to the Wallace's, and apology for absence became, at once, more necessary and more difficult.

My intercourse with Clelia was such as to intoxicate my juvenile feelings, and to shut out all foreign images. No pair of tongues were ever more voluble when they were set at liberty, and yet, on my part, I never made my own history the theme of my discourse. I loved to paint my visions of fancy, the images collected from books, but, chiefly, I was fond of questioning my friend in relation to her past life, and to the formation and the progress of her sentiments. On this subject she delighted to dwell. Her memory appeared to retain all the impressions of the past. The terms of every interesting dialogue, the looks, gestures, and minutest incidents accompanying it. Every hue of the quickest and most mutable feeling were exhibited with all the graces of a lucid elocution.

These topics were not of an exhaustible kind. They were more acceptable to me than any other. Others were excluded, not so much from any antipathy conceived against them, as because the time was more delightfully engrossed by these.

One evening, entering with my usual carelessness, I discovered Miss Neville in her drawing room, earnestly contemplating some object which she held in her hand. Her attention was so much absorbed by this object, that she did not notice me till I touched her elbow. She started, thrust something into her bosom, and averted from my eyes a face suffused with the deepest crimson.

What, said I, have I caught you? Why is that something so hastily thrust out of sight?

She stammered out the usual evasions of "Nothing. Nothing at all. A matter of no consequence," and made strong efforts to regain her composure.

I grew importunate. A. sort of vague suspicion darted through my mind, and whispered me that this was a picture, a picture which was not to be shown to me, though proper to begazed at when alone. I ceased to importune. I allowed her to change the conversation, but disquietude rankled in my heart, and I suffered the discourse to languish.

She quickly perceived the cloud upon my brow, and asked, tenderly, the cause.

What is that, I answered, which you put into your bosom? Her confusion returned, and my anxieties increased. She refused to produce it. She was too honest to mislead me by direct assertions, but she besought me to excuse her.

Readily, said I, gravely, I excuse you from performing what will give you pain.

She again attempted to engage me in sprightly talk, but my heart was pained. The gloom upon my countenance became more deep. I even made a motion as if I would go away.

"My friend, what is the matter with you? Why this sedateness, this reserve?"

It is your reserve that occasions mine. You will not tell me what you put into your bosom.

"Must you know?"

If it be not disclosed, I shall go away less happy than when I came.

After visible embarrassment and struggle, she drew it forth. It was, indeed, a picture. My heart sunk still lower. I had scarcely courage to examine it. What was my surprise and pleasure when, on glancing at it, I beheld my own image.

And what need was there of concealing this? said I. How could I fail to derive pleasure from this proof of your attachment?

By this time she had recovered her tranquility. "It was mere folly, I own. I am a wayward creature, but your kindness will forgive me. In time, I shall become more reasonable and consistent. I have just been altering it."

Altering it?

"Yes. When first taken, I committed some egregious mistakes. How I could fall into them, is incomprehensible. I thought I had obtained a perfect image, but, on closer scrutiny, I found I had strayed wide from the true proportions. Your hair is a shade darker than at first sight, and your eyes, instead of being of an heavenly blue, are of an hazel cast."

Strange mistakes, indeed, said I. But why did you not order me to sit while you copied my real face?

"There is reason for that," she replied, casting down her eyes and blushing with bewitching significance.

Certainly, but what was the reason?

Half sportively, "I will not tell you. That is still to be a secret. The time will be, I hope, when that and many other kindred mysteries will show themselves without disguise. Let it content you that the face is yours, and that I wear it here, within all these folds, and have worn it. Do you know how I have been employed today?"

No.

"I have been writing. An history. A secret history.

Though I have prated so much about myself, I have not told you all. I cannot utter everything, and what I cannot, I have consigned to the pen. You know nothing yet of my secret history. That will be a feast for you which I mean shortly to set before you."

Pr'ythee make haste, then, I shall have no rest while a secret remains. But who are the actors in these mysteries?

"Myself, to be sure, and another."

What other?

She cast most expressive looks at me, yet I could not satisfactorily interpret them. "Cannot you guess?"

I should hope that in a drama where two characters only are exhibited, and you were one, that I should be the other.

"You have guessed aright. And yet you know me not. I was masqued. But what am I doing? You will rifle my box of secrets before I am aware. I am telling you what I meant you should read. O! let me ask you how came that scar upon your left cheek?"

In leaping from an hay-mow, I fell and struck my head against the edge of a mattock that lay concealed beneath a wisp of straw.

"When did that happen?"

In my childhood.

She expressed much surprise. "In your childhood? And has it always been thus?"

Always since my tenth year.

She suddenly became thoughtful, but presently resumed her sprightliness. "This, likewise, was omitted in your first portrait, which is very strange. Methinks the mark is sufficiently conspicuous."

At our very first interview this scar was noticed by you, so that I conclude my portrait was taken before we met in this house.

This hint was followed by deep confusion. "Talk no more ofthe portrait. I was an unskilful artist, it is true."

She now called away her own thoughts and mine to some other topic, and I did not muse on these occurrences till we had parted. It was then that her secret history, her masquerade, the portrait formed previous to my knowledge of her, and concealed from me with such solicitude, occurred to my thoughts. My reflections were unattended by pain. They set me to conjecturing what had passed between her escape from the house in flames, till our actual meeting. I had spent that interval chiefly in the city, and many occasions might be conceived on which a glimpse of me might have been afforded her. These surmises were flattering to my vanity, and showed the deep impression which gratitude had made upon her.

On my return home, I found a billet from my cousin, couched in these words:

Why do you forget your promise? I want to see

you. Come to me tomorrow morning, and make amends for this forgetfulness or negligence. I shall fully expect to see you, so that you must not disappoint me.

This billet threw me into some perplexity. I was conscious how culpable I had been, and was at a loss what apology to make. I could not, however, hesitate to comply, and went next morning to Wallace's. My cousin received me with her usual frankness and affection, and, after a few minutes' conversation, in which her friend bore a part, she invited me to walk with her. The air with which this invitation was made, convinced me that something extraordinary engrossed her thoughts. This belief increased my embarrassments.

After a few turns in the garden, and when we appeared at a sufficient distance from interruption, she spoke with great earnestness, and, looking at me steadfastly, "Sidney returned home last week, and spent yesterday here. He tells me that you visit Clelia Neville frequently. You told me, when I saw you last, that you designed to have no more intercourse with that person. What has happened to change this resolution?"

I was silent. She noticed my embarrassment, and resumed, in a tone of irresistible tenderness. "Let not my brother deem me selfish and impertinent. My inquiries are dictated by regard for your welfare.

That welfare I believe to be, in some danger. Forgive me, then, for taking you thus to task. You have overlooked your promise to me, but that promise was exacted not merely or chiefly to gratify myself, but to screen you from the most formidable danger which can assail your youth. Far am I from intending to upbraid you for any negligence of me. I have, of my own accord, given up my claims upon your-faith, and cannot wonder that beauty, gracefulness, intelligence, and sensibility, far superior to what I possess, have enchanted you in another. For this you are not to blame. You are not to blame for anything, least of all for withholding your confidence from me, and declining to seek my advice. As soon as I can thoroughly convince you that my regard for you is void of selfishness and jealousy, this reserve will disappear, and I will convince you of it.

"You are the son of my mother. She who saved me from indigence and suffering, who took me to her home and her bosom, and gave me all the happiness that I possess, lives in your form, in your features, in your voice. When you are present, she is always before me. You are the pride and the hope of her life. Shall I not love you, then, for her sake?

"But that love is small in proportion to that which I bear you for your own sake. My woman's heart is yours. My very soul reposes in your bosom. I know no happiness but as you are happy. Are the transports of a wife and a mother not to be found in your arms? Are your affections to be given to another? It is well. I unmurmuringly acquiesce. I adopt that other for my substitute. I am anxious, only, that she merits your devotion. To see you betrayed, connected with a specious impostor, with a faithless wanton, would break my heart. Indeed it would.

"You are mine," she continued, putting her arm round my neck, and in a tone of new sweetness, "You are mine, and I will not part with you but to one that well deserves the precious gift. Beloved Felix! Clelia Neville deserves you not."

What were my feelings during this address? My heart was fickle and inconstant, but not yet callous. Tears rushed to my eyes. I was subdued. I was torn with remorse for my past insensibility to such excellence. I said, I have wronged you. Henceforth I put my fate in your hands. Direct me as you please. I will worship and obey you as my better angel.

"That is a good youth, but be not prodigal of promises. Show your sincerity by disclosing your feelings and motives. Give me a just account of what has happened during your absence. Why, on the evening of the very day we parted, did you go to Miss Neville? Why have so many evenings since been spent with her? From twilight to ten, twelve, and even two o'clock? And why, on leaving this enchantress, instead of seeking your repose, have you rambled to Schuylkill, and descried the dawn from the verge of Quarry-hill?"

I started. How came you acquainted with these incidents?

"They came to me from Sidney, who gained them from a friend who lives not far from Miss Neville's."

Sidney and his friend, thought I, are officious, and had better be employed about their own concerns. I suppressed these thoughts, and produced the letter which I had received from Clelia. There, said I, was my inducement to renew my visits.

She perused the letter. I then recounted the substance of Clelia's narrative. I mentioned the compassion which this story had excited, and my readiness to maintain a friendly intercourse with her. Nothing had since passed unsuitable to those duties which were incumbent on her as a wife. I regarded her as such, and was not ashamed to confess that I delighted in her company. I saw nothing in this intercourse that ought to offend the most scrupulous.

My cousin's eye was full of suspicion and uneasiness. After a pause she said, "She once confessed that she loved you?"

She did.

"Has she retracted that confession?"

Heaven forbid!

"She repeats still that she loves you?"

She does not deny it.

"She is not particularly circumspect? Reserved?"

Certainly she is, as much as she ought to be.

"More so than before the discovery of her marriage? Than when she demeaned herself as lovers are used to do?"

Not more so. In that respect, I see no difference.

"When you offer, she does not decline? She does not shrink from your caresses? She does not manifest displeasure?"

No. She is as affectionate in her deportment as you are.

"But I am your sister. I am more than your sister. I am not a wife. Has she never wept at those ties which obligeher to treat you merely as a friend? Has she never painted the felicity attendant on indissoluble union with you, and maligned the power which forbids it?"

I could not deny that she had.

"Have you never concurred with her wishes and her tears? Have you never sought relief from impatience and dejection in reflecting that every man must die? That Belgrave's vices will probably expedite his death, and that then you may seek the hand of this woman without a crime?"

It is true.

"Do not these fits of impatience increase in frequency and obstinacy?"

I cannot tell. They are more easily removed at one time than at another.

"At moments when your feelings are most active, does not a momentary doubt insinuate itself as to the validity of that bond which inthralls your Clelia to another? It was not strong enough to bind her affections and person to a ruffian. It hinders her not from imbibing and avowing an attachment to one more worthy, and whose heart gives her all its treasures in return. Why, then, (do you not sometimes ask) should it hinder her from giving the natural proofs of that attachment? Conjugal duty, it seems, has not prevented her withdrawing from Belgrave her love, her confidence, and her society. It has not hindered her from bestowing all these upon another. Having given thus much, the seal surely is broken, and duty will permit her to give all. Have not such reveries as these sometimes, however rarely, fluctuated in your thoughts, and rendered you insensible to midnight damps?"

I was silent.

"Have not soliloquies escaped you, at moments when memory was most full of the blandishments and graces of this friend, in which an hearer would distinguish such sounds as 'Unnatural restraints! Arbitrary institutions! Capricious scruples!' Tell me, honestly, Felix."

I could not speak.

"But these were merely creatures of a fancy, which, in being ever busy in creation, and always hovering round the image of this girl, must be expected to produce every shape, and to sport with every possible phantom. These images are fleeting.

They are chastised and banished by wiser thoughts, which show you that the effusions of the heart, the interchange of sentiments, and the acceptance and return of chaste caresses, are all that is of lasting value, even in wedlock. With these you resolve to be content, and to wait till circumstances arise that will sanction a closer intimacy."

There, said I, with eagerness, you do me justice.

"And yet, how often does that officious phrase 'and yet' interfere to break this equable tenor, to call up a regretful sigh? And yet, it is a pity. Life is wasted in delays. Belgrave may survive an half-century.' How often, at the conclusion of an interview, has a contempt of remote consequences, a faith in concealment, indignation at imaginary restraints, and the unjust obloquy of mankind, insensibly gained the upperplace in your mind! How often have you noted the repose of nature, the security of solitude, and whispered in her ear, 'Why must we part? Why should we be separated an hour, and why should this hour sever us?' And do you not still hear that sweet voice, which sighingly and whisperingly answers, alas! It must be so!"

I was overpowered with confusion. I shuddered as if a witness had really been present at our interviews. I was astonished and abashed at so faithful a picture.

"I forgive your silence," resumed my monitress. "You need not answer me. I see that my conjectures are true. Such must ever be the reveries of one young as you, with principles versatile, ungrounded in religion, or on that morality which is the growth of experience. And the tendency of these things, if not to undermine your virtue, to make you dissolute and callous to reproach, yet, to unnerve your courage, to enfeeble all your energies, to divert your attention from useful knowledge, the service of your friends and your country, you do not see!

"Clelia has hitherto been, in your opinion, blameless. She has been the victim of treachery and cruelty. She fled from the mistreatment of a monster. She stands in need, and she is deserving of a friend. Are not these your opinions?"

They are.

"And on what evidence are they built?"

I was disconcerted, and at a loss for an answer. At length I said, I have no evidence but her own assertion. I have told you the story which I heard from her.

"And is that evidence sufficient? How numberless and irresistible are the inducements to conceal what, if known, would redound to our shame? How easy to disguise the real motives of our conduct! Belgrave may have been the inhuman and depraved wretch which he is said to be. Aversion to his features, and impatience of his tyranny, may have existed, but were these the only motives to object to marriage and to abandon her country? Might not her abhorrence of

Belgrave partly have arisen from an unauthorised attachment to another? Mightnot his cruelty partly proceed from reasonable jealousy? And might not that attachment have been one of the inducements to elopement?"

These insinuations startled me. I had no time to weigh their truth. These being admitted by one of my cousin's candour and discernment, intitled them to some regard from me. I besought her to be more explicit. Were these her suspicions? On what grounds were they built?

"You know that she has friends and associates in this country. You know that there are many who have constant intercourse with Dublin. Have you made inquiries among these respecting your friend? Possibly some one might be able to corroborate or confute her story."

I confessed that I had made use of no such expedients.

"But ought they not to have been used? Would they not have naturally occurred to a cautious temper?"

I answered, that my recent arrival in the city, hindered me from forming acquaintanceships with many persons, that, however strong my doubts might have been, and my desire of foreign information, I was wholly at a loss to whom to apply for this end.

"Say rather, my friend, that your devotion to this

girl absorbed every thought, and all that time that might have been employed in enlarging the number of your friends, and in supplying you with materials of observation and reflection. You were a stranger to suspicion, and, therefore, reflected not that Mrs. Keith had been much known and respected in this city, that persons existed who had been serviceable to her in the management and disposal of her property, that her will, by which she made this girl her successor, must have had executors, and witnesses, who, probably, knew the character and condition of Miss Neville, and to whom one like you, might easily have found access. Ought not your caution to have suggested these expedients?"

I could not but acknowledge it.

"And these expedients which you ought to have pursued, would naturally be pursued by those who love you. Would they not?"

And have they been pursued?

"Sidney has obtained, from authentic sources, some information respecting this woman, which has just been communicated to me."

I was anxious to receive this information. I entreated her not to withhold from me what she had heard.

"Alas! my friend, this woman, thus amiable, thus studious, thus unfortunate, is a profligate. Her husband had some reason for his persecution. His character is wholly opposite to that which she has described. His reputation has fewer blemishes than are incident to most men of the same riches and rank. Before marriage, she bestowed her heart and her person upon a young man, insinuating and elegant, but, unprincipled and dishonest. He was her father's clerk. Her attachment to this youth was shameless, and overstepped all bounds of decorum. It has, indeed, been proved, that the first overtures to an illicit intercourse came from her. This intercourse continued after marriage, and she, finally, to secure his company, eloped with him.

"These truths are notorious in her native city, and have been circumstantially related to Mr. L___, whose probity you well know, in a letter from an Irish friend, whose integrity and means of knowing the truth, are unquestionable. Mr. L___'s modes of thinking are singular. He had much respect for Mrs. Keith and his widow, and is named trustee in the will of the latter. During her abode here, the young lady's conduct has been free from reproach. She has shunned almost all intercourse with the world, since the decease of her aunt, probably from a consciousness of her guilt, and of the danger of detection. Mr. L___ has disclosed his knowledge to no one, but has kept a vigilant eye over her. He is unwilling to destroy her reputation, as long as she acts with circumspection.

"You know Mr. L___'s friendship for Sidney. A meeting took place between them a few days ago.

Clelia was mentioned by the former, and the assiduity of your visits, some connection being known to subsist between Sidney and you was likewise mentioned. Sidney was desired to exert his influence to induce you to break off so dangerous an intercourse. For some time the true character of Miss Neville was concealed, notwithstanding Sidney's endeavours to extort from him his knowledge, but, at length, these facts were stated, and the letter containing them were shown, on condition that the discreetest and most sparing use should be made of them. They were communicated to me, that I might guard you against consequences so much to be dreaded from the uncommon fascinations of this woman.

"How very slender must be those talents which will not enable their possessor to frame a plausible tale, and how easily may looks of innocence and candour be assumed by a guilty heart?

"This woman is eminently lovely. Her attractions and accomplishments are dazzling, but she is sensual and fickle. No doubt she is susceptible of gratitude. No doubt your mind and person have enchanted her. She loves you as one like her is capable of loving, with impetuosity. Marriage is no bar and no requisite to the gratification of her passion, and her deportment to you has hitherto been such as no heart of true delicacy and chastity would ever have adopted. It has been skilfully adapted to your constitution and temper, and, if you do not instantly change your course, will lead you to ruin. I shudder to think how near you have already been to the verge of guilt. That you have not fallen, was owing not to her virtue, but to yours.

"She has artfully spread her wiles for you. She has chosen scenes and hours for your intercourse, most favourable to the oblivion of conscience and foresight. The songs which she adapts, according to your own account, to her magic instrument, tend to move the soul to love, and inculcate contempt of the future, and forgetfulness of virtuous restraints. Thank Heaven! In spite of her enchantments, your integrity is safe. Are you not, at length, convinced of your past danger, and determined to exercise more caution for the future?"

What could I say? These tidings sunk me into grief. The evidence thus produced, appeared to me incontestible. Clelia then was an adulteress, and a profligate? With such an one, it was impossible to hold converse. That love, to which I confided my hopes of happiness, could never lodge in the bosom of a sensualist and hypocrite. Her passion for me might lead to extravagance and phrenzy, but without the ornament of chastity, or a basis in integrity, it was to be shunned and abhorred.

My courage wholly deserted me. I melted into tears. I became, to my cousin, an object of commiseration. I became flexible and pliant to all her wishes, and readily consented to avoid this unfortunate girl in future.

My grief at this discovery, after the first burst of conviction was past, and when solitude afforded me leisure to think, led me to investigate Sidney's evidence more closely. I said, is it right thus hastily to condemn a being, whose situation necessarily exposes her to calumny and misapprehension? Am I sure that the whole is not a wicked artifice of Sidney's, to thwart my projects of happiness? That L___ has not invented this tale to blast the character of Clelia? That L___'s correspondent has not been a deceiver, or been himself misled?

She has given me proofs of tenderness, but, admitting them to be incautious, they are not, in themselves, criminal, and may surely be excused by her youth, her ardent feelings, and her confidence in me. Where is this lover with whom she is said to have eloped? Her conduct, since her coming hither, has been allowed to be proper, and what human creature may not repent of his misdeeds, and grow wiser by experience? What should hinder but that her past errors are now regarded withdetestation and remorse? That she has admitted a pure love into her heart, and will henceforth conform to its dictates? It was not I that, in spite of her concealment, detected her marriage. She spontaneously disclosed it. To this hour it might have been a secret, for she is not aware that her true situation is known to any one on this side of the ocean.

She had dwelt with the most picturesque, and, apparently, the most ingenuous minuteness on the incidents of her life, and especially those subsequent to marriage with Belgrave. She had related all the steps taken to effect her escape, all the events of the voyage, the name, character, and situation of the captain. Had she been accompanied by a lover, this narrative was vitiated not merely by omissions, but by falsehoods. All the difficulties and distresses which she painted, necessarily implied the want of a friend or protector. Was it possible that nothing in her tones or looks, nothing in a story so abundant in particulars, would have betrayed her falsehood? By affording me the means of inquiring of the captain, and her fellow passengers, one of whom was a resident in this city, did she not afford sufficient proof of her sincerity?

And what if she be calumniated? If Belgrave, by inhuman falsehoods, has blasted her good name, and thus perpetuated the mischiefs, which his vengeance had already inflicted, and from which, flight into another world has not been able to screen her, his enmity to her, and even his regard for himself, would naturally lead him to employ this engine to ruin her. Hypocrisy and artifice are easy, and she who might counter work or unmask the betrayer, was unconscious of his machinations. She lived, in the vain security that her name and her existence were forgotten, and that her reputation, at least, among the beings who surrounded her, was free from stain.

No, I will not desert her. I will not hastily believe her wicked, and will spare no pains to ascertain the truth. I will go to Sidney. I will make him introduce me to his friend. I will see this letter with my own eyes. I will scrupulously weigh its claims to belief. I will make inquiries of others, and even of herself. I will charge her with imposture in terms so direct, and with a watchfulness so close, that the truth shall not escape me.

With these sentiments I returned to the city, and hasted to Sidney's lodgings. He received me with that placid brow, and cordial familiarity which always distinguished him. Cursory topics were quickly dismissed, and I called his attention to my cousin and Miss Neville. I related what had just been told me, and required him to deny or confirm it.

"Your cousin has faithfully repeatedly my intelligence. All that is true."

All that, I quickly replied, is false. There is some deception, some stratagem to ruin this unhappy woman, and to ruin me.

He lifted his eyes, but looked forward with undiminished benignity, and spoke mildly. "Would you say that I have invented that tale?"

Forgive me. That insinuation was rash.

"Nay," said he. "It was suitable and proper. You ought to listen to such tales with reluctance, and not admit them on slight evidence. I ask you not to credit me on my assertion. Nothing should content you but the sight of the letter, which I will procure for you, and, so far from wishing you to believe before you see it, I exhort you to suspend your belief. Meanwhile, here is a copy, which you may peruse, and may compare with the original."

I took the paper and read it. It contained all that my cousin had reported. Sidney's character, the absence of all motives to deceit, on this occasion, since his interest as the lover of Louisa, and as my competitor, would necessarily induce him to favour, rather than to counteract, my pursuit of another, showed me the folly of casting suspicions upon him. There could not be a doubt that this letter, at least, was genuine. I laid down the paper and was silent.

"Perhaps," said Sidney, "your knowledge of this woman has supplied you with proof of the falsehood of this story. Perhaps you have indubitable evidence that she is not a wife? That she did not quit Ireland clandestinely?"

Both these, said I mournfully, are true.

"Indeed! How did that appear?"

By her own confession.

"What then are the facts which she denies, or which you disbelieve?"

She fled, but her fidelity to her husband has been inviolate. She fled, not to enjoy the company of a seducer, but to shun the cruelty of a tyrant.

Sidney shook his head, in token of incredulity, but, for a short interval, said nothing. At length he resumed:

"Nothing is more frequent than calumny. Nothing is more easy than to belie the actions and motives of a human being. Appearances against this woman are strong. Yet her innocence is not impossible. For her own sake, as well as for yours, I have resolved to ascertain the truth. She ought not to be kept in ignorance of what is believed respecting her. She ought, at least, to have an opportunity of avowing her integrity. After reading this letter, in the hands of Mr. L___, I determined to visit her, and lay before her the contents."

I started. And did you go? Did you tell her this?

My perturbations attracted his notice. They partly arose from surprise, at the abrupt mention of a project so singular and unexpected, and partly from inexplicable fears lest he might prejudice her mind against me.

"Be not alarmed," he replied, "I did not go. There was no need to go. My uncertainty was removed by differentmeans.

Are you then convinced of her innocence?

"No. The proofs which I allude to had an opposite tendency. They convince me of her guilt."

My heart drooped at these unwelcome sounds. I had scarcely courage enough to inquire into the nature of these proofs.

"They inform me that the paramour, with whom Clelia dishonoured herself before marriage, and whom the claims of an husband could not prevail on her to discard, is now in this city. That their illicit intercourse is still continued, her nights being spent in his company."

Horror at this news was quickly lessened by incredulity. I remembered that four evenings in the week were spent with me. That I went to her early, and left her late. The existence of a rival was impossible, for what motive could induce her to bestow tenderness and confidence on me. To suppose her affections thus equally divided, thus daily changeable, to suppose her, with regard to me, a dissembler, was, to the last degree, absurd! Why should she devote her time to any other besides him who possessed her affections? Why solicit and encourage visits, when those visits would merely interfere with, and tend to the detection of her intercourse with one whose society must be infinitely preferred. I saw her not at stated hours, or concerted intervals. Half the evenings of the week were devoted to her, but they were not pre-appointed. My approach was hailed with delight, and my departure witnessed with reluctance. No, this was a manifest calumny. I did not disclose all my reasons for denying my faith to this story, but I did not conceal my disbelief, and inquired what were the proofs?

"My evidence I cannot produce. The information was given on condition that the authors were concealed. I promised concealment more readily, because, if the intelligence were true, its truth might easily be ascertained. I, for my part, entertain no doubts. The evidence was such as not to be resisted. I am convinced of her depravity. Without this evidence, I neither desire nor expect you to believe it, but it must always be in your power to ascertain its truth by other means."

Be good enough to tell me how.

"The path is obvious. By charging her directly with this misconduct, she will hardly fail of tacitly confirm ing it. Besides, you know whether she has any acknowledged visitants besides yourself."

She has none. None, at least, but of her own sex.

"If she denies herself to him, in the presence of another, she must often deny herself to you. So much of her time must be shared with him, that your visits must be very unfrequent not to interfere with his."

My visits, said I, are not unfrequent, and they take place at seasons utterly inconsistent with the existence of such a connection.

"Indeed!" exclaimed Sidney, in a tone of surprise and disapprobation. "It grieves me to hear that. If this woman be criminal, it matters little whether it be with you or with another."

I was disconcerted and abashed at the inference thus drawn from my words. The inference was false, but such as a mind fastidious in its maxims of decorum, might easily draw from the frequency, the loneliness, and protraction of our interviews. I was unwilling to state the truth, in this respect, for fear of creating one suspicion, by the means employed for removing another. Meanwhile anxiety was strongly painted in my friend's looks. He resumed:

"Your visits must, indeed, be frequent and unseasonable if they interfered with his. Such intercourse loves to hide itself beneath the veil of darkness. It is awake and active when the rest of the world are asleep. Sufficient caution is, indeed, employed to prevent intrusion in the present instance. Should you call at the hours devoted to him, you would be turned away with 'she is indisposed ,' 'she is not at home,' 'she is engaged.' Doors and windows are closed and fastened, and the porter is commissioned to exclude every comer."

And pray, you, what are those seasons?

"They begin at eight or nine, and end before morning."

My heart now misgave me. Such were the periods of my own visits, but I saw her only thrice or four times in the week. The intervals, indeed, were regular, though that regularity had been accidental. Could those nights when I was absent be thus devoted? And what were my claims? I was no more than her friend. My pretensions interfere not with those of such a one as this. To me she gave her confidence and esteem, on another she bestowed her love.

How often, said I, does this intercourse take place?

"Not every night, but thrice a week at least."

This tended to confirm my fears. Indignation began to rise with my grief. I will burst upon her, said I, when she expects me not. I will detect her in the very arms of her seducer. This will be ample proof, and this proof is in my power.

Sidney marked the disquietude which these thoughts produced. He regarded me with looks of compassion. "Come," said he, cheerily, "things shall all be set right. You and I ,Felix, shall know each other better. Your cousin shall join us in a scheme from which we will contrive to extract pleasure as well as benefit. If you will spend this evening with me, I will disclose my plan."

I am in no mood, said I, to adopt new schemes. This unhappy mystery must be cleared up before I can take repose.

"Whence does this interest in a stranger arise?" said he. "Is it a disinterested zeal for the honour of a female, who, inconsequence of being a wife, is culpable for maintaining intimacy with any one but her husband? But this mystery is easily removed. It might have been removed last evening."

How?

"If, instead of pushing pieces of wood over a chequered table, you had applied at her door for admission."

What then?

"You would have been dismissed with a false, or evasive answer."

Last evening? Was this profligate in her company last evening? For how long?

"From ten o'clock till one, at least."

These few words instantly revived my fainting hopes. Evidence of the treachery employed against my friend could not be stronger than this. These hours were spent in my company. The grossness of the calumny was therefore apparent. My features brightened with confidence and exultation. Your informer has assured you of this? Or is it a conjecture? Is it built upon the same authority with the rest of the story you have told?

"I have no better evidence for any thing respecting this woman."

Then you are deceived, cried I, vehemently. Your informer is a lying and perfidious wretch. It is some wicked agent of her tyrant, who has endeavoured to abuse your ears, and to blast the reputation of an helpless and unfortunate woman.

He still preserved an air of doubt and anxiety." I fear that you pronounce too hastily," said he.

No. The falsehood of this assertion, at least, I have the means of discovering incontestibly.

"What means?"

Such as are more to be relied on than vague and

anonymous insinuations.. Nothing less than the testimony of my own senses.

He looked at me with new disquietude. "You talk in riddles. How could the testimony of your senses inform you in what manner, and with whom, this woman spent the last evening.

"Because I was neither blind nor deaf. Because, at the very time you mention, from ten o'clock till one, at night, I was her companion. There was not an interval of ten seconds in which I did not see or hear her.

"You mistake me," said he. "I speak of *last* evening, of Saturday evening."

Certainly, returned I, and I rejoice that you do, otherwise I might have wanted so unerring proofs of the falsehood of the tale.

He rose from his seat, and fixing more steadfast looks upon me, repeated,"Last evening, you tell me, was wholly spent by you with this woman."

It was.

He now turned away from me, and walked to and fro, with a troubled face. I imagined that I understood these tokens. He inferred an improper intercourse from an interview thus unseasonable. I was embarrassed in my turn. I was fearful of this inference, and therefore confessed thus much, with some faltering and reluctance, which inevitably tended to confirm his suspicions. Still the strongest emotion in my heart was delight, in discovering the falsehood of the charges made against Miss Neville.

"Felix," said Sidney, solemnly, and with a deep sigh, "I love you much. I think upon the danger which besets you, with pain, arising not only from the love that I bear you, but from my affection for your cousin, whose happiness is interwoven with yours. Till this moment I was not aware of all your danger, of the frailty, the fickleness, the pliancy of your mind." There he stopped.

Your fears, said I, on my account, are generous, butgroundless. This woman is nothing to me, but a friend, from whose society I collect greater pleasure and instruction than any other source will supply. She is a sufferer whom it is my duty to cherish. She has been maligned and persecuted, and while I am convinced of the iniquity with which she has been treated, ought I to act as if my convictions were opposite? Ought I to shun the society of one whom I know to be innocent and excellent, or refuse her conversation and her confidence, on terms consistent with every duty?

He seemed to pay little regard to these words, but, advancing towards me, with new solemnity, said: "Let me again ask you, let me conjure you to tell me the truth. How, and where did you spend last evening?"

Innocently, as I hope for mercy from a righteous and omniscient judge. I spent it innocently. Nothing passed between us. Nothing has ever passed between us, inconsistent with her obligations as the wife of another, nothing but what a sister might laudably bestow.

"But how, and where was it spent? In the presence of the same righteous judge, tell me how, and where was it spent?"

I have already told you. It was in my own lodgings till nine o'clock, from that hour till one in the morning, in the house, and by the side of Clelia.

Surprise, indignation and grief were mingled in the features of Sidney. He could with difficulty articulate,"is it possible? So young, trained up in habits of sincerity and purity, and yet capable, under a tremendous sanction, thus deliberately capable! Felix, I dismiss my hopes of you. This instance of depravity and falsehood exceeds what my worst fears had painted."

Falsehood! Depravity! What words are these? How have I deserved the charge?

"Enough. Nothing need be said, unless it be to retract a falsehood so hateful, so audacious!"

My blood began to boil. I have nothing to retract. I can only aver my truth and my innocence. If surmises and rumours, or fallacious inferences, are of more weight than my solemn declarations, I have, indeed, fallen low in your esteem. I disdain to expostulate with you. I shall make no efforts to retrieve your good opinion. If it can thus easily be lost, to gain it is impossible, and when gained, it is worthless.

What followed, tended only mutually to exasperate. We parted in anger.

My mind was full of vexation and uneasiness. I was oppressed with the proofs of Sidney's general integrity, persuaded of my own innocence, wounded by the charge of having basely lied, though conscious that the charge was unmerited, alternately consoled by the approbation of my own conscience, and afflicted by perceiving that I had lost the esteem of one whose discernment and integrity I had been accustomed to revere, and dubious of the grounds on which I stood, I was fearful that the evidence which swayed his belief was, in itself, sufficiently plausible and intricate to govern a dispassionate observer, fearful that the same evidence, and even the mere authority of Sidney, would undermine my reputation in the hearts of others, of the Wallaces, of my cousin, of my mother.

For the present, I felt no inclination to visit Clelia. I wanted some one in whose ear I might pour my whole soul, in whose bosom I might disburthen my heart of its Vexations. No one was more entitled to this confidence than my cousin, and to her I accordingly, on the next morning, repaired.

She received me without her usual smiles of affability. She had been weeping. She acceded to my wishes to walk in the garden, with half disguised reluctance. When alone together, she seemed disinclined to speak. I was chilled with a thousand different apprehensions. I already perceived that her mind was poisoned by what I deemed the artifices or malignities of Sidney. My courage forsook me at the thought of contending with an adversary so formidable.

At length I broke silence, and complained of her reserve.

"My reserve," she answered, "flows from my sorrow. What can I say to you? It is not my province to rebuke, or to censure you. Perhaps, if I once had acted differently, things would not have been thus. I acted, as I thought, for the best, but you will be of a different opinion. Your vices and your miseries you will not scruple to lay at the door of my pride and obstinacy. And how shall I repell the charge?"

Do you then believe me to be vicious?

"I cannot but believe it."

Good Heaven! What is the ground of your belief? You will not surely condemn me unheard?

"I have no doubts."

No doubt of my depravity?

"Alas! None."

Let me then take away from your sight, a wretch who is not even worthy to be heard in his own defence.

She wept, and sobbed. "Go, my once loved brother, the joy of my heart, leave me. Your presence is a source of pain too exquisite to be borne. Go, and may your eyes be opened to the ruin which lies in your path soon enough to shun it!"

And is it come to this? Shall I not, at least, know my crime?

"Your crime cannot but be known to you. Would you have me blast my own ears by repeating it? To connect with the name of Felix Calvert the odious appellations of villain, liar! 'Tis too much! I beseech you leave me! Never see me more!"

This, said I, is the fatal treachery of Sidney. It is he who has shut your ears against the claims of justice.

"Speak not of Sidney thus. You misapprehend, you know him not. Would to heaven there was more affinity between you, that a portion of his noble and enlightened spirit had fallen on my brother. But to hope is vain! Such felicity is not reserved for the lost Louisa!"

And is the word of Sidney to condemn me to infamy and exile? As an human creature, is it impossible for him to fail in knowledge, or in virtue? May not some unhappy error have misled him?

"No, there is no alternative. Either you or he is a perjured villain. Can I believe that Sidney hates my brother, that he deliberately utters abhorred falsehoods? That I must believe, or suppose you to be guilty of the like. I cannot hesitate which to choose, which to condemn." Her grief was now mingled with impatience. She continued, "I will not hear you. I will not see you more. If you continue here, my heart will burst. Go, ill-starred youth! Go. The sight of thee reminds me of thy mother, and I cannot bear to think."

My thoughts insensibly acquired firmness and consistency! Of those atrocious charges I was innocent. I knew not what these charges were. I cared not to know. If I were not worthy to be heard, to be informed of my offences, I would trample, in my turn, on such injustice. I would leave my vindication to time, to chance. It was enough that my own heart acquitted me of guilt.

After incoherently muttering these ideas, I left the garden, and the house, and once more set my horse's head towards the city.

What a state was mine? Sidney's indignation, my cousin's grief, all springing from imputed, but unreal offences of mine, all flowing from the disastrous influence of this stranger! What can I do, said I to shake off this evil?

Clelia is said to be criminally connected with another. This assuredly is false. By what illusions could the caution, the discernment, the benevolent reluctance to condemn, of Sidney, have been thus grossly abused? Why did he charge me with deceit and treachery? I merely asserted that I passed last evening in her company, and this assertion he stigmatized as false!

Does a traitor lurk in Miss Neville's family? It is composed merely of a female negro, who once belonged to Calverton, whom I freed and recommended to my friend, and her servant Margarette, an Irish woman, whom her aunt met with here and took into her family, and whose good sense, modesty, and discretion, her young mistress had warmly commended. Peggy, alone, is capable or willing to disclose domestic secrets, and betray her lady.

I proceeded to recollect and revolve all that I had heard of Peggy. I had never directly talked with her. I had merely marked the circumspection, and propriety of her silent demeanour. I had questioned Clelia, more than once, as to her character and history, and had been told that she had been sometime in America before she had entered Mrs. Keith's service. That her parents, herself, and one brother, had been Irish emigrants, that the parents were dead, but that the brothers dwelt in this city, and pursued the trade of a carpenter.

This brother, whose name was Murphy, and who was a thrifty and honest young man, I was further told, was accustomed to spend his Sunday evenings with his sister in Miss Neville's kitchen, and this was the only associate or acquaintance which Peggy was known to have. Was it possible for surmises and for calumnies to find their way to Sidney's ear through this channel?

No conjecture had more plausibility than this. This man and woman were reported to be honest, but, in this respect, Miss Neville might mistake.

Besides, what reason had my heart to rely upon any evidences of Clelia's honesty. I knew my temper to be sanguine, my ignorance and inexperience, to be great. How should I dissipate this ignorance and restore myself to certainty?

No better scheme occurred to me, none which might be immediately adopted, and my temper could not brook delays, than to seek out Murphy, and, by open or indirect means, endeavour to extort from him the truth. I was personally unknown to him, and might therefore find him unware and unsuspicious. I might easily so adjust the topics of our discourse as to discover whether he and Sidney were known to, and had any communication with each other. I knew where he lived, and, putting up my horse, hastened towards his work-shop.

Scarcely had I got within sight of it, when I saw at a considerable distance, a person come forth from his house, in whom I instantly recognized Sidney himself. Ah, ha! said I, is not the author of the calumny now discovered? Is not this the channel through which Sidney has obtained his intelligence?

Sidney did not perceive me, and walked away in a different direction. I proceeded, but, on inquiring for Murphy, was informed that he spent the day some miles from town, having a job to execute for Mr. Somebody, who was building a countryhouse on Delaware. With great reluctance I prepared to defer this desired interview till the evening.

Meanwhile, the impatience of my thoughts was somewhat lightened by indispensable attention to concerns of a general and indifferent nature. I could not but notice the salutary effects of occupation. A vacant mind, a mind that has nothing to divert it from the phantoms of hope and chimeras of fear, connected with the future, experiences a kind of insanity. The impulses of love, and freaks of jealousy, are the torments of idleness. They are dreams that affect us like realities, merely because realities are absent, and we are not able, by comparison, to estimate their shadowy nature.

My business being despatched before the decline of the sun, my impatience to clear up this mystery revived. Gradually it occurred to me, as the most feasible expedient, to visit Clelia. Was not Sidney right, said I, in thinking that the truth would be unavoidably extorted from Miss Neville by abrupt and unexpected questions? Should I lay before her, without preface or circuity, my knowledge, my doubts, and suspicions? Will she not be surprised into a disclosure of the truth?

This is earlier than I am accustomed to visit her. Should I go thus early, and enter her apartment unannounced and unbetokened? May not discoveries be made which no regular proceeding would reach? This paramour may not be merely idleal, and, at this moment, they may be together.

I was fired into inexpressible eagerness by this

thought. Almost undesignedly I bent my way to the habitation of this girl. I opened the door without warning. As usual, the lower apartments and passages were deserted, and, as usual, I went up the stairs leading to the drawing-room, but, stimulated, almost without regular thought, by suspicion, I moved softly. I wished to enter her room without my approach being perceived.

I reached her door. I paused and listened. How was I confounded by distinctly overhearing two voices within, one of them a female's, doubtless Clelia's, the other wanting in feminine fluidity and sweetness, but not distinct enough for either its peculiar tones or words to be heard.

I shuddered at the inference which I could not but draw from an incident like this! What was to be done? Should I enter, or would not the occasion justify me in hesitating and listening? In this, there was meanness and presumption. Perhaps, had leisure to reflect and compare been enjoyed, I should have seen its meanness and forborne it, but now curiosity and anger were impetuous. The voice of every foreign consideration was stifled. I bent my ear.

The guilt of the intention I was permitted to incur, but not the profit, for I had just time to discover, to my utter confusion, that the voice within was that of Sidney himself, when motion, as of rising from a chair, convinced me that he was preparing to come out. To be found in this situation would be productive of great and mutual embarrassment, from which I involuntarily shrunk. Yet how should I elude this consequence?

By hastening out of the house, I could scarcely elude it, for I could not withdraw with so much speed as not to be overheard, or to attract attention from some one below. At that moment, likewise, I heard footsteps in the passage below, and a voice humming an air. They were those of Peggy.

I hurried to the head of the stair, and, noticing a door a-jar near it, and leading into a room adjoining the drawing-room, I rushed into it. I had no time to look around me, or weigh the dangers that might attend my being found, in a bed-chamber.

The persons within parted, and Sidney left the house, while Miss Neville returned to her drawing-room. Had a glimpse of my person been caught by Sidney as he left the drawing-room, had Peggy been busy in this chamber, or had Clelia entered it on parting with her guest, what misconstructions or embarrassments might not thence have arisen! My good fortune, however, had rescued me from this dilemma. I was now at liberty to pass into the hall, and enter the presence of my friend without the imputation or suspicion of having acted irregularly.

Now, however, new emotions succeeded to those of curiosity or jealousy. Sidney, with his usual unreserve, with his belief of my depravity, with his suspicions of Miss Neville, had sought and obtained a private interview. What effect must such an interview possess upon my happiness, upon her's, upon her good opinion of herself, and her confidence in me? How, in such circumstances, was it my duty, in the approaching interviewwith her, to demean myself?

No hasty reflection could enable me to judge rightly, and I entered her apartment in a mood made up of apprehension, doubt, and perplexity.

My friend was seated, thoughtfully, at a window. On my opening the door, she raised her eyes. They were full of trouble and disquiet. Never, hitherto, had she cast such looks upon me. Familiarity, tenderness, and joy had flown. Solemnity, reserve, fear, were now strangely but significantly blended in her countenance.

I was astonished and chilled by her demeanour. I had not sufficient courage, though it had been my custom, to salute her. I seated myself in silence.

She at length spoke, but her faultering voice evinced how deeply she was agitated. She frequently stopped, looked at me, at one time with earnestness, at another with shuddering and trepidation.

"Unfortunate was the hour that I was born. Disastrous and humiliating has been my life, but I have scarcely known misery till now." There she stopped, and, after an interval of unspeakable distress, resumed:

"Calvert! Felix Calvert! I have questions to ask, to which I conjure you to render me faithful answers. Will you?"

I will.

"My good God! That voice! Those looks! How could it be–yet, surely..." She covered her face and continued.

"When did you–when–did you arrive on these–at this place?"

I mentioned the month and day.

"And whence did you come last?"

From Burlington.

"How long had you resided there?"

Ever since my infancy. All my life, till within the last half year, has been spent here and in Jersey.

Her surprise almost betrayed itself in a shriek. She conjured me to speak true, and repeated the question, to which I made the same answer.

She now, apparently convinced, sunk into silence. She covered her eyes with her hands. Sighs struggled from the bottom of her heart. I was utterly unable to account for these appearances. I partook of her confusion and sorrow.

At length she recovered sufficient composure to request me to withdraw. She wished to be alone. My presence gave her pain.

I was resolute. I was motionless. She repeated, with augmented vehemence, her request that I would leave her. I ventured, at length, to solicit an explanation of this scene, to ask, whither her inquiries teuded, in what I had offended her?

She answered me by repeating her injunctions to leave her. I had offended in nothing. *She* only was to blame. She had been guilty of negligence, and folly, and rashness, never to be forgiven. From that moment, compassion to herself, justice to me demanded our eternal separation. Never more must she see my face.

Still I lingered in her presence, and renewed my intreaties to know the cause of this deportment. Still she declined any explanation, renewed, with augmented vehemence, her assertions of the necessity of my leaving her, of my leaving her forever.

At length, in the midst of my interrogations and my disclaimings of any intentions to injure or displease her, she burst from me and shut herself up in her chamber.

I was astonished! Thunderstruck! Petrified! I had no power, for a time, to leave the room or the house. I strove to awake from what I fondly deemed a fit of madness or an agonizing dream. Thus was I repulsed, cast off, banished, by two beings on whose good opinion my whole happiness reposed, whom I had, indeed, unknown to themselves, treated with meanness, rashness, and duplicity, but who had punished me, if for these offences, with far more severity than they deserved. But not for these offences had they punished me, but for guilt unreasonably imputed, for crimes which I never had committed.

And whence had Miss Neville's newly born antipathy flowed but from the presumptuous and detestable interference of Sidney? Had he not laid open to her the calumnies poured out against her? Had he not informed her of the existence, the excellencies, the expectations, and the rights of my cousin, and thus raised an insuperable impediment between us? Was not this the source of her alarm and her grief.

To wait for, or solicit an interview with, Clelia was in vain. She had seen me for the last time. My presence was an insupportable evil. It wounded more deeply than adder's tongue or the point of a sword. It became me, it was my indispensable duty to withdraw, and whither should I withdraw but to Sidney's, to wrest from him an explanation of this scene, and to avenge or upbraid him for his perfidy and inhumanity.

Sidney was at home, and readily admitted me. As I approached him, my eyes flashed indignation, but his sedateness and tranquility were invincible. I spoke in rage, and incoherently, but he readily comprehended the purpose of my coming and, seizing a pause afforded him by my exhausted breath, rather than by my abated anger, he said:

"I am glad you are come, Felix. So far from acting in fear of your knowledge, I would gladly, had I known where to meet with you, have disclosed to you my purpose of visiting this lady, and have gotten you to go along with me. I sought you at your lodgings and elsewhere, and found you not, but now permit me to tell you what has passed between us. Your approbation of my conduct, I fervently desire, but do not expect. I will be contented with my own, in which, when reflection and experience have opened your eyes, I doubt not of obtaining your concurrence.

"When admitted to her presence, I made my apology, and effected my introduction by simply stating the motives of my visit. These were to know and to communicate the truth. I painted your situation and your character, and those of your cousin. I recounted the intelligence gained from Mr. L___ and from other quarters respecting herself, and endeavoured by being thoroughly in earnest, and by boundless sincerity, to convince her of the rectitude of my motives in acting thus, and of the interest which I felt in her welfare, in your cousin's welfare, and in yours. I have reason to believe that she was convinced of my integrity, for she listened to me patiently. She upbraided me not. She flew not into anger. She was, indeed, deeply, variously, and, in some respects, mysteriously affected. She was visibly shocked by the imputations contained in the Irish letter."

Eagerly, I said, did she deny their truth?

"No. It was the emotion of surprise and horror,

but I cannot say of conscious guilt, yet not of conscious innocence. It was, indeed, inexplicable. It left me power to infer nothing. I put no direct questions. I left her at liberty, by expressing my wishes that the charge should prove false, and by pausing to vindicate herself, but she did not speak. She trembled and wept, but said nothing to confirm or confute the story. Finding her in this mood, I rose to leave her, but first repeated what my compassion dictated. 'I know not,' said I, 'how my conduct on this occasion may appear to you. Your silence and distress do not inform me whether I have been deceived or not, with respect to you. Of that, I must go away ignorant, but, on every supposition, I wish to be your friend, I wish to serve you. Is there no way in which I can serve you?' 'Yes,' said she, with vehemence, 'You can serve me, but only in one way, by finding out Mr. Calvert, and acquainting him with my resolution never to see him more. By prevailing with him to desist from attempting, to desist from even wishing ever to see me again. That is the only good that you can render me, the only good that I can receive at your hands.' 'And that,' said I, 'I will endeavour to do.' Saying this, I left her, and have since been looking for you, though in vain.

"I see, by your manners, that you have had an interview with her, and that her behaviour at this interview has been such as she gave me reason to expect. For her sake, for both your sakes, I rejoice at it. You are angry with me for marring your visionary scheme of happiness. This happiness you have endeavoured to build upon falsehood and deception. So short-sighted were you, as not to see the incurable frailty, the tottering structure of such schemes. Whence you contracted this vice, this stupidity, is inconceivable to me. How could you derive content from being esteemed more highly than you were conscious of deserving? How you could acquiesce in being looked upon as something different from yourself, what views could induce you to conceal your history, the existence of your mother and your cousin, and, possibly, impose upon her a tale utterly false, is a subject of the most painful astonishment.

"To imagine that the time and the course of events would not betray you how could you imagine it? How could you desire to postpone the discovery?

"Did I not know your past life, your education, and your friends, the character of your tutor and your mother, my surprise would be less. But the world is eternally producing what, to our precipitate judgment, are prodigies, anomalies, monsters. Innate, dastardly, sordid wickedness frequently springs up where genial temperature and wise culture had promised us the most heavenly products. The ruffian and sensualist are fashioned by the discipline intended, and, as the fond preceptor dreams, adapted to produce nothing but generous magnanimityand heroism."

These accents, solemnly and calmly uttered, chilled me to the soul. They carried instantaneous and humiliating conviction to my heart. The virtuous upbraiding of this man had a sympathetic influence. It changed me into as profound a wonderer, as immeasurable a contemner of my conduct, as himself. My anger melted into contrition. My confidence was changed to dismay. I hung my head and listened to his rebukes in silence.

He perceived these appearances, and went on in a tone of somewhat less severity. "Perhaps I have been too hasty and censorious. I know not all your motives. I can judge very superficially concerning you. I have made myself the arbiter of your conduct, not from insolence or envy, but because I love your cousin, and am anxious for your happiness, but, in exercising this office, I may, in my turn, and in consequence of erroneous observation, have judged wrong. Will you trust me with your thoughts? Will you relate to me the motives of your conduct towards this woman? No crime has been commited, I persuade myself, which cannot be atoned for. No evil is incurred which cannot be removed."

I had no power to confess my misdeeds. I merely acknowledged the truth of his suspicions in general, and admitted that I had been very faulty, faulty to degree, for which, inexperience, and youth, and a sanguine temper, afforded no apology. Yet I averred the innocence, in one respect, of my intercourse with

Miss Neville. I had entertained no infamous views. I had never sought to obtain favours which her matrimonial obligations forbade. I had no reason to imagine from any particulars in our exclusive intercourse, that insinuation or artifice, had they been exerted for this end, would have ever been crowned with success.

I had, indeed, deceived both her and my cousin. I had studiously misled them as to my actual situation and the motives of my conduct. Not by silence and concealment merely, but by positive untruths had I misled them. My remorse extorted from me thus much, but I meant not to claim his forgiveness. I had deeply offended my cousin, as well as my friend, and neither expected nor sought my restoration to their good opinion. I would instantly retire to the country, to my mother, and prevail upon her to consent to my going to Europe. My conduct hitherto had been base and inglorious, indolent and visionary. Henceforth, I would play a different part, and shaking off these sordid fetters, be active, independent, and wise. I would leave these shores, and they shall never hear from me. I would never return till till my virtue was established on the basis of knowledge and experience.

Sidney now assumed an air of sprightliness and benignity, and, taking my hand, said, "I partly commend your scheme, Felix, but you need not over-rate your offence. You have done nothing for which you may not be forgiven. To see the impropriety of your conduct in its true light, is a sufficient title to my esteem. It will be a valid claim to your cousin's. I highly approve of your design to go to Burlington, for your mother and your mother's affairs have wanted you too long, and retirement and reflection I hope will be of service to you, but, meanwhile, you must go with me to my sister Wallace's. We must see Louisa together, and if possible, establish affairs upon their old footing."

He quickly convinced me that he was thoroughly in earnest in this generous proposal, and I accompanied him with a strange revolution and turbulence of feelings. So much unexpectedness, such total novelty in my new circumstances, such quick transitions from one state of mind to another the most opposite, from fear to courage, from despondency to hope, from self-upbraiding to the whispering of applause, made me, in my own eyes, a paradox, a miracle, a subject of incessant curiosity and speculation. The present condition of my thoughts and feelings was not merely a variation or succession, but the utter reverse of the last. In the short minute I had passed in Sidney's company, I had emerged from agony to joy, from despair to exultation.

"I bring you," said Sidney to my cousin, as he approached her in a lonely spot in the garden, "a penitent, a youth, erring through precipitation and passion, and deserving to be pitied and pardoned.

He promises to be cautious for the future, and I have no doubt of his amendment. Come, give him your hand to kiss, and make him once more your own."

She looked at each of us wistfully, by turns, and, at length, exclaimed, "And do *you* forgive him? Has he justified himself to *you*?"

"He has condemned himself to me. He has acknowledged his error, and that is sufficient. At present, we can ask no more. His conduct must confirm or confute his promises, and, on his sincerity, meanwhile, we must be contented to rely."

"That is, indeed, sufficient. If you think him deserving, joyfully shall I again admit him to my heart." Stretching her arms towards me, she allowed me to salute her with my former tenderness. She admitted the propriety of my returning to Burlington, and, on that very day I set out, my cousin readily assenting to hold a correspondence with me.

In this tumult of passions and rapid succession of events, my mind knew no pause, my feelings no permanence. It was not till I passed the bounds of the city, and once more beheld the tranquil scenery and verdure, and noted the general repose of nature, that I was able to survey the late transactions with unmisty sight.

I was now going to the quiet mansion of my mother, with the feverish and motley images produced by the experience of the last three months, during which I had lived longer, if I may so speak, had admitted more ideas and more emotions, than during the whole period of my preceding life.

The theatre on which I had entered of a noisy and busy city was as opposite as possible to the little circuit of my juvenile existence, the grass-plot, and the tulip- bed. The condition of proprietor of spacious fields, and the master of a numerous household at Calverton, was equally new, but the new impulses of the heart, the new exertions of the intellect, and the new gratifications of curiosity, which my late situation had produced, were perplexing by their number and variety, and astoundingby their magnitude.

The character and demeanour of Sidney, and my cousin, of the Wallaces, and particularly of Miss Neville, passed in review before me. I distributed them in my memory as if they had been arranged in a book, and turned to this or that leaf, pondered on this adventure or that dialogue, and caused, with additional hues and adjuncts, all my recent ideas to pass, and all my emotions to be felt again.

Fortunately, perhaps, for me, or at least as I then considered it, my mother had gone to pass a fortnight or more, at the residence of one of her friends, ten or twelve miles distant from Burlington. No one was at home but a female servant, and an old negro, who was family property, and who assisted me in the court and garden!

My mother's curiosity would have occasioned

much embarrassment. She would have justly deemed herself entitled to know more of my transactions during my absence, than I should have been willing to disclose. My behaviour would have been the subject of her anxious and constant scrutiny. A thousand misgivings and perpetual consciousness would have betrayed themselves to her vigilant eye. I was pleased that her absence took place at this time, and looked forward to my solitude, my woodland walks, and my unfrequented garden, as particularly propitious to that intense musing to which I determined to devote myself.

Having returned home, and resumed my ordinary habits, I began, as I have just described, to ruminate on the past. In this employment, I found a plenteous source of humiliation and perplexity. Two incidents, particularly, at this time, arrested my attention. The first was the charge urged, with so much confidence against Miss Neville, by Sidney of nightly admitting the visits of a paramour, with whom she had intercourse in her native country. The next was the imputation of lying, which he had fixed upon me, in relation to the manner in which I had spent a certain evening.

I now remembered very mysterious words, which he had used on that occasion, and of which, in the hurry of my thoughts at the time, I had neglected to ask for further explanation. "Had you," said he, "been at her door, instead of pushing pieces of wood over a checquered table—" Then, on my affirming that I was, in reality, seated, at that very time, near her, he started, refused credit to my declaration, called me villain and deceiver! What was meant by this?

Sidney is not easy of faith, especially when the tale is injurious to the fame of another. His information, whether true or false, could not but have flowed from specious sources. Had I not nearly lighted on the source, and why did my infatuation forbear to prosecute the search still farther? I was within sight of the goal, when I allowed my attention to be drawn aside.

I was no player at chess. At draughts I had some skill, but had never played, nor even seen the game played by others during my absence from Burlington. My company had always been the Wallaces, Clelia, and my cousin, and my mind had always been too full of occupation, too busy in suspense, too engrossed by passion, to endure the tameness and monotony ofthe draught-board.

Rage at my own negligence, and impatience to repair its effects, began to grow in my bosom. "Shall I not," said I," return this hour to the city, seek out Sidney, and obtain from him a full disclosure? Louisa, and extort from her the cause of her indignation and aversion, so disproportioned, as it now seems, to my offence, so abrupt, so enigmatical, and rush into the presence of Clelia, lay before her the aspersions of her enemies, and wrest from her, by impetuosity irresistible, the cause of her deportment to me at our last meeting? A few hours will bear me thither, and a few hours restore me again to my home."

This impatience was counteracted by other thoughts. At parting from my cousin, I had solemnly avowed my resolution to absent myself from the city during the ensuing month. Would not my return so abruptly and so adversely to expectation, give weight to the charge of fickleness or dissimulation, of disregard to promises, and trampling on my honour?

May not this end be partly accomplished by a letter in which my perplexities respecting the mysterious expressions of Sidney may be mentioned, and a solution of the enigma demanded? Pleased with this scheme, I wrote forthwith. Having taken up the pen, I did not feel disposed to be brief. My heart was pierced by remorse, by newborn sensibility of my cousin's excellencies, by gratitude for her affection. My pen was pregnant with the emotions of my heart, and a thousand things did I say, a thousand incidents relate in this letter, which, before I began it, I was far from designing or expecting to disclose.

I felt a sort of generous pride in self-censure, in even painting my behaviour in darker colours than it merited, in assigning worse motives than truth required, and omitting alleviating circumstances. I seemed to be fated never to hit the just mean, and to carry generosity to as culpable and mischievous an excess now, as vanity had ever been carried before.

The letter was sent. I could not sleep till the answer arrived. I had besought her to inform herself on the points in which I wished for information, and to forward her reply with speed. At any rate, to reply without delay, since many topics of my letter required no deliberation, and no time but that which pen work required.

No answer came. The sun arose and went down, my customary avocations were neglected, my impatience threw me into tremors. I inquired at the usual despository for letters in vain. Four days passed and no letter had been sent, or what was sent had miscarried or been intercepted.

I wrote again, and importuned with new vehemence and much upbraiding, for an answer. In reply to this, after the tormenting delay of five days, the following letter was delivered:

To FELIX CALVERT.

I did not expect, Felix, to write to you. Your two letters I received in due time, and merely write, at present, to prevent you from sending a third. If you do, I shall tear it into pieces, or throw it into the fire unread.

Unhappy Calvert! What smiling prospects were thine! How eager was I once to link mine with thy destiny! Yet, if my precipitation had not been benevolently thwarted and restrained, what misery for my future years should I have laid up in store!

Write to me not, talk to me not, lay aside even the wish to see me again, it cannot be gratified without giving me more anguish than my worst enemy can wish to give me.

While memory, while conscience is with you, you cannot be at a loss why I write thus. You cannot but know your own unworthiness. All this parade of sincerity! All these confessions! So seemingly minute! So apparently dictated by remorse! And yet false, cunning, deceitful! O! How my heart loathes, how it abhors a deceiver!

And stupid as deceitful! Wandering into these crooked paths, when the forthright path is so smooth, conspicuous, and accessible! How deeply rooted must be that wickedness, how near to madness must be that folly, of which thy good name and my peace are the victims! Farewell, Felix.

I take up the pen again to ask–for, possibly–yet, it cannot be. Nothing can I expect but asseverations, which add to thy guilt. Thou wilt not scruple to affirm what is false. Thou wilt not scruple to swear.

O! Wretch! Wretch! But I will not upbraid you. I leave you to the stings of your own conscience. Again, farewell.

L. Calvert.

Wretch! Wretch! Indeed! Here is an entangling net, spread by some secret and flagitious hand for my ruin. To burst its threads is the privilege of that innocence that never stooped from its sunny elevation, that never was enervated by conscious guilt.

What can be meant? Some new offence it must be. It cannot be the mere disclosure of the charge urged against me by Sidney. It cannot be some new aggravation of that charge, for, was not that included in the pardon so generously bestowed on me?

I have it. In my last letter, I pretended to disclose mywhole guilt, and in truth, I did disclose it. Nay, I exaggerated my transgressions, but I said nothing, since nothing could be said, to justify the imputations of Sidney in that mysterious interview. On the contrary, I mentioned them, not merely to express my innocence, but to importune for knowledge of their meaning. Fraught with conviction of my guilt in that instance, this importunity and this inquiry must have looked, to them, like proofs of the last and most profligate degree of impudence.

Shall I be still? Shall I suffer time to disclose their error? Shall I wrap myself up in conscious innocence, and wait till time has rectified their mistake, and they seek my presence to expiate, by prayer and entreaty, the injuries which their easy faith, their precipitate suspicions have done me?

No, I have not intellectual force enough for that. The gratifications of that revenge would be delicious, but I cannot wait for it. I cannot endure to be deemed a guilty wretch by beings like Lousia Calvert and Sidney. That is the worst of evils. I broke from this soliloquy to mount my horse, and set out that very hour for the city.

I first went to Wallace's. I saw Mrs. Wallace. She regarded me with looks in which contempt was mingled with sorrow. I inquired for my cousin. She was gone to Lancaster. She had returned home.

This was an unexpected and stunning blow. I stayed not to parley, but instantly resolved to find out Sidney. I was admitted to his presence. He looked at me with coldness and solemnity.

I threw my cousin's letter before him. I desired him to read it and to explain the contents. He cast his eye on the first line, and then, putting it aside, said, sedately, "I have read it."

You have read it? And know what it means? If you do, I swear by him that made me, that your knowledge exceeds mine.

He started at my emphatic manner, and said, with glances of anger, "Oaths, Felix, are not made to sport with. They areneedless, at least, on this occasion."

Will you explain to me the meaning of this letter? You have read, it seems, and perhaps, dictated it.

He looked at me again, with solemn benignity!

"It stands in no need of explanation."

And you will not give me any.

He paused for some time, and then spoke. "Felix! This demand is strange, but I will comply with it. On the evening of the Saturday before you left town, you were seen in a tavern in this city. There it was you spent the evening. Yet you afterwards affirmed upon oath, that you spent it with Miss Neville. You left the city promising an absence of some weeks, yet in a few days, you clandestinely returned, and renewed your commerce with this foreigner. You skulked all day in a sordid inn of the suburbs, and stole to the place of assignation by night in a contemptible but ineffectual disguise. Yet you wrote letters to your cousin, as if from Burlington, pretending the deepest rompunction for past misdeeds, and promising wondrous reformation for the future."

And this, said I, with a contemptuous and bitter smile, is the explanation of this letter. This charge, false in every part, in every word of it, you have whispered to my cousin. Thus you have tainted her heart, and turned her affections away from me. But be it so. If your credulity is so great as to confide in such lame and ambiguous evidence as that on which a falsehood like this must rest, if your regard for me is so small as not to make you seek for my vindication from my own lips, if she is feeble and absurd enough to lend implicit ears to your tale, ye are both worthless. I cast ye off forever. Henceforth, I seek a different society—a new world." In saying this, my eyes, fixed steadfastly on those of my companion, flashed indignation, and my gestures gave force to the accents that fell from my lips.

The countenance of Sidney assumed an expression impossible to be described. He looked at me, but not as before. After a moment's pause he turned from me in silence, and left the room. There was nothing to detain me in it.

My resolution was now taken. Unhappily for me, external circumstances were favourable to the execution of a scheme dictated by rashness and want of foresight. A ship bound for Ireland, lay at this moment in a cove near the mouth of the Schuylkill. Without preparation, without reflection, without delay, I put myself on board of her. In a few hours she hoisted sail, and in less than two days, left the coast of America. As its sandy heights faintly gleamed in the horizon, I exclaimed "Farewell, my native land, farewell forever!"

Now was I a wanderer on the great deep, unaided by the impulse of courage, and unguided by the rudder of discretion. My voyage was begun in a moment of blind passion, with no suitable provision of any kind, either against the exigencies of my voyage, or against those which could not fail to beset me on my landing on a foreign shore. I had never thought of these. Resentment and despair, the wrongs imagined to be done by Sidney and my cousin, engrossed my thoughts, and excluded all those considerations, that, in any other mind, would have probably obtained the chief place.

These ebulitions, however, subsided in a short time. The novelty and danger of my new situation quickly rushed on my mind. I became timorous, forlorn, and panic-struck. I looked around me on the boundless and turbulent expanse of waters, on the wide interval that severed me from my native country, and which hourly grew wider, on the long, long way that lay before me, with sensations of melancholy not to be expressed.

These were soon changed for worse sensations. I was attacked with sea-sickness, and all its horrors. This completed the conquest of my courage. The breeze with which we left the coast, soon increased to a storm. Dangers of a strange and unforeseen kind encompassed me on all sides, and I began bitterly to lament my undertaking, which now appeared in its true colours to my awakened reason.

What, said I, will the gentle and affectionate Louisa think, when she hears of my sudden flight. Deceived by atrocious, but plausible charges, will she not consider this a confirmation of them all? How will she deplore the fate of the ill-starred Felix, and add those fears for his personal safety, naturally flowing from the knowledge when it reaches her, of my headlong scheme, to those regrets already inspired by my defection from virtue! Was this the conduct which it became me to pursue, either as conscious of my own integrity, and anxious for the purity of my fame, or as grateful for the love which this angel among women bore me, and solicitous to secure her happiness, that happiness which is entangled with mine?

And my mother, who feared nothing more than my voyage to Europe, whose felicity depended, not on my safety merely from perils and temptations, but on my presence. How will she feel when apprised of this rash act? I pictured to myself her surprise, her indignation, and her sorrow. Methought I heard, in my short and unquiet sleep, the voice of her upbraiding, her charge of ingratitude, and when she comes to know the suspicions of my cousin and of Sidney, how will she mourn over the guilt of her idolized child! How will all her hopes with regard to me, expire and become extinct!

These images were excruciating. The sensations they produced were not to be endured. Added to the dangers and horrors of my actual condition, they inspired the most dismal and soul-sickening despondency. I grew impatient of existence, and entreated those near me to drag me from my hammock, and throw me into the sea.

We had now been three weeks at sea. The blustering atmosphere with which we set out, became daily more tempestuous, till, at length, it rose to an hurricane. Our vessel was old, crazy, and in ill condition. The buffeting of the waves quickly produced a leak, which, for a time was not formidable, but grew finally, too much for the strength of an harassed and terrified crew. Incessant pumping did not prevent the slow increase of the water in the hold, and, at length, it was evident that the ship must sink.

In this desperate situation, and before our fate was quite finished, a vessel, which came in sight, generously offered the assistance of which we stood in so much need. They took the crew and passengers on board, and the ship soon after disappeared. I was so reduced by mental distress and sea-sickness, that they were obliged to carry me in their arms from my birth to the boat. This was a large, stout ship, bound from l'Orient to Baltimore.

This transition may be supposed to have had a powerful effect on me. I was now, in spite of contrary expectations and designs, returning to that country which I had abandoned. Heaven had interfered with a benignity to which my merits gave no claim, to obviate the effects of my rashness. The storm speedily abated, and clear skies, smooth seas, a propitious gale, and the prospect of restoration to an home that now was as dear, as it had formerly been hateful to me, dissipated my malady, and gave vigour to my hopes.

On the day that I landed at Baltimore, I hired an horse, and proceeded, with the utmost expedition, to Philadelphia. It was not till my near approach to that city, that I began to ponder on the perplexities of my situation, and revolve the means of escaping them. Sidney and my cousin, it was plain, were strongly prepossessed with the notion of some guilt, which, in truth, I never had committed. This guilt was of no common or excusable kind, and my mother was, probably, ere this, infected with the same suspicions. First, said I, I will go to Sidney. Him I will detain and interrogate, and leave no obscurity unremoved. My mother and my cousin shall be sought for anon, and Sidney's commendations shall attend my appeal to their forgiveness.

I entered the city in the dusk of the evening, and alighting at the inn where my horse used to be kept, proceeded, without delay, to Sidney's lodgings. His mother, sisters, and himself, were abroad, but were expected shortly to return. I resolved to wait his return, and seated myself in the apartment which he used for business and study. My mind was deeply occupied in ruminating on the doubtful prospects before me, when Sidney entered the house. I heard him enquire of the servant if any message had been left for him in his absence, and her answer that Mr. Calvert staid for him in his study.

"Calvert!" said he, "Can that be possible?"

I wondered not at these expressions, nor the tone with which they were accompanied, and yet, methought they denoted not so much surprise as might have been expected from an incident so unlooked for as my return. Of my departure, all my friends could not fail of being apprized, by the measures which I took for that end, in a very short time after it took place. Sidney's tone, however, if it had little surprise in it, had no pleasure, and this I did not expect from his known benevolence of temper.

He entered the room, advanced toward me with a cheerful brow, and offered me his hand, saying, "This return is unexpectedly soon, Calvert. I am pleased that it has happened so, nevertheless I hope you bring good news with you."

This reception was embarrassing, but Sidney's behaviour had ever been too little agreeable to my habits, to warrant me in wondering at any of his actions, and yet, thought I, this is strongly inconsistent with his deportment at our parting interview, but, perhaps, somewhat has happened to clear up the mistakes under which he then laboured.

My embarrassment was increased by his immediately entering into general conversation, as if nothing extraordinary had happened. After a few remarks, he seemed to notice my embarrassment, and asked:

"You are uneasy and reserved, my friend. Surely, it is time to lay aside solicitudes which can answer no useful purpose. I thought you too wise to be in any situation unhappy. Come, what is it you think of? Be it good or ill, it is politic to let it forth."

The surprise which was given me by these words, suggested the thought that possibly my voyage had been hitherto unknown to Sidney.

I now looked wistfully at him and said: Surely, my friend, you cannnt be at a loss as to my cause of uneasiness. You cannot but be aware of the effect which such deportment as yours is likely to have upon me.

"Indeed I am," said he, without any change of his tone. "I cannot conceive why my behaviour should give birth to any uncommon feelings. I thought, when we last saw each other, that a perfect understanding was established between us."

That, interrupted I, is the cause of my present embarrassment. Recollecting your behaviour then, and the conduct which I immediately adopted, and comparing that with present appearances, I confess I am sunk into perplexities.

"What!" said he, with more surprise than he had hitherto disclosed, "I do not comprehend you? Our parting was surely what it ought to have been."

Indeed, said I, discouraged by this assertion. I was persuaded, by your present deportment, to hope that your opinion in that respect was changed.

"More, and more do you surprise me," said he. "I repeat that I do not comprehend you."

Surely, surely, you can be no stranger to the rash, the desperate act to which your treatment and my cousin's urged me.

"Rash and desperate! What do you mean?"

Good Heaven! Then you know not yet. Yet my sudden return may well have contradicted your former intelligence. You knew not of my actual embarcation for Europe.

To describe the changes which now took place, in Sidney's countenance is impossible. He started, and putting his face close to mine, eagerly scrutinized my features. He then withdrew his attention and all his faculties seemed locked up in astonishment and satisfaction.

A pause, on both sides, ensued.

Meanwhile, I, on my part, knew not what to think. His ignorance as to my frustrated voyage was apparent, and yet, why should he be astonished or pleased at my return, and why not manifest this state of mind sooner?

Sidney continued silent. His bosom seemed to labour with some great thought. His eye, fixed on the floor, was void of speculation. A kind of self-debating, a weighing of different measures was apparent in his countenance. Every other emotion gave way in my heart to curiosity.

At length I said: Reflecting on the manner in which we parted, five weeks ago, in this very room, I cannot but be surprised at your present demeanour. Then all was recrimination and anger, now you seem to be my friend. I did not merit any thing but friendship at your hands, and your and my cousin's indignation at imaginary transgressions, awakened the same sentiment in my breast. Hence the sudden adoption of my scheme, which I have been happily prevented from accomplishing by the untowardness of the winds and waves. Has any thing happened, may I ask, in my absence, to change your opinion of me?"

Sidney now looked on me with beaming benignity. "There has," said he, with emphasis. "Appearances deceived me, but such appearances that mere humanity could not fail to be misled by them. I ask not your pardon. I confess not any prejudice or haste in judging. Circumstances being as they then were, I was right in deciding as I did, but these are now past. Sincerely do I rejoice to see you. So saying, he arose and embraced me. "But let me ask," continued he, "Whence came you? I supposed you to be half over the Atlantic by this time."

Indeed! interrupted I. Then you knew that I embarked for Ireland!

"Certainly. It was known to all your friends a few hours after you went on board."

And my mother—

"Will be made happy by the sight of you. But how came this?"

I then gave him a summary account of my disasters. The attempt to do this, and the countenance of Sidney, luminous with pleasure, insensibly opened my heart. I averred to him my innocence of those offences, whatever they were, with which he and my cousin had charged me. I recounted all the rueful thoughts that beset my pillow, during my outward voyage. I concluded with inquiries respecting my mother's and my cousin's welfare.

"They are well," said he. "They have only commiseration and regret on your account, which your return will dissipate. They acquit you of all blame, except on account of the temerity and precipitation of your last scheme, which your juvenile inexperience, the passionate impetuosity of your character, will somewhat palliate. Your mother and cousin will be tomorrow or next day in this city."

I expressed my delight at this news, and my resolution to set out to Burlington immediately.

"No," said he, gravely, "That must not be."

I was somewhat startled, and inquired into the reason of hisprohibition.

"I want to tell you," he replied, "Something of great moment for you to know before your introduction to your friends. Meanwhile, I will ease their cares and suspences by a note." He took up pen, and wrote the following billet to my mother.

Let me make you happy, dear madam, in the information of the safe return of your errant son. The vessel in which he embarked foundered at sea, but the crew and passengers escaped to another, by which they were brought to Baltimore, whence your son has this moment arrived. He longs to pay his duty to you, but as I have much to say to him before your interview, and as you expect so soon to be in town, I have persuaded him to wait your coming.

"This letter with a confirmatory postscript, from yourself if you please, we will send by a special messenger early in the morning. Meanwhile, I must tell you what has happened. Strange incidents they are, and such as, I believe, have now occurred, for the first time, in the history of human beings. But I need not relate them by word of mouth. Your hand rests upon a book, in which the narrative is contained in a more satisfactory form than I can now bestow on it. The book contains transcripts of all the letters that have passed between your cousin and me during your absence. You may read them. You will find laid open in them, all the heart of the writers, and every information respecting what has happened, which you stand in need of.

"I must be gone an hour on some urgent business, and will leave you to this employment." So saying, Sidney left me, and I eagerly opened the manuscript. The letters, for I afterwards read them over so often as at length to have them by rote, were in these words:

LETTER I.

To LOUSIA CALVERT.

Be not too much surprised and grieved, my friend. The event I am going to relate, I own, disconcerted and distressed me for a time, but I now think of it with little discomposure. On the whole, it is, I persuade myself, the best that could have happened.

Hector has just been with me. He brought a letter from Felix for his mother, who, at four o'clock Tuesday evening, went on board the Swiftsure, bound for Cork. She had been wind-bound some time. Hector accompanied his master onboard, and left not the ship till she was under sail, the wind becoming favourable a little before. He was charged to detain this letter till Saturday, and then bring it to me. You see the boy has faithfully adhered to his master's directions. This delay was, no doubt, enjoined, in order to preclude any measures for effecting his return.

Let me repeat to you my counsel, not to be distressed. At least, let not this aggravate the sorrow you already feel. In this act there is no guilt. There is temerity, perhaps, and indiscretion in it, but no more than this inconsiderate and headstrong youth had given us full reason to expect.

No doubt he is at this moment bitterly deploring his ownrashness, and tormenting himself with the thoughts of what misery the tidings of his flight will produce to you and to his mother. But these will be passing evils. Doubtless he has carried money with him, and will easily find out his Lancashire cousin, by whom all deficiencies in purse or in knowledge will be readily supplied. Let not, I once more repeat, let not this incident afflict you too much. I always told you that the youth, in spite of all his faults, will do well at last. I am still as much of this opinion as ever.

I weep to think on his poor mother's astonishment and affliction. That Felix could not paint to himself what that could be, and be inspired, by such images, with a different resolution, is truly wonderful. Tell me, as soon as possible, your thoughts upon this event.

S. C.

LETTER II.
To the same.

Overpowered as I am with surprise and vexation, I know not that I ought to write to you, but the employment is salutary. I have always found that the most efficacious consolation to ourselves, is the attempt to console another, and this letter may afford new proof of my opinion.

I told you, three days ago, that our Felix had embarked for Europe. Such was Hector's testimony, such was the assurance of the letter brought by the servant for his mother. She has written to me since, inclosing her son's epistle in her own. It is an eloquently incoherent composition, dictated, as it seems, by hostile passions and fluctuating purposes. It avers his innocence of what we laid to his charge, declares that his letter to you contains the whole truth of his offences, foresees and deprecates his mother's grief, and defends and accuses himself in the same breath. In short, it is a letter which only Calvert, and, I was going to add, an innocent man could write.

But now, Lucy, what have I to tell you! The lad is not gone. He is still in this city, still harboured in Walden's tavern. I discovered it last night. Thus it was:

I was called to draw up the will of a dying man in Southward. It was eight o'clock in the evening, but the moonlight made every object distinct. I walked pretty fast, the case being desperate, and was accompanied by the messenger. Crossing Pine Street, at its junction with Front Street, I saw before me, crossing Front Street and going down Pine Street towards the water, a figure, whom, to mistake for any other than our Felix was impossible. My way lay down Front Street, but, in spite of that occasion which required my presence elsewhere, I turned and followed him.

He turned Penn Street corner toward the south. I mended my pace so as to come very close to him and take such a survey of his person, as might annihilate all fallacy. He looked not back, but walked as fast as I, and presently turned into Walden's, the very house in which I had before alighted on him.

I now pursued my first purpose, resolving, on my return, to stop at this house, and, if possible, to procure an interview with this mysterious youth. My business was not speedily accomplished with the sick man. I did not leave his house till past ten, but, so much the better, thought I, it is still more likely that I shall meet my fugitive, as he will be returned for the night.

I looked carefully round me in the public room at Walden's, but could not discover Felix among any of the groups. Thus unsuccessful, nothing remained but to make the obvious inquiries of Walden himself. I have long had a slight acquaintance with this man.

By his answers to my inquiries I found the name and situation of his guest were well known to him. Felix, he told me, had lodged at his house during the last fortnight. During this time he spent the day usually abroad, but returned hither in the evening. He had left him the day before, and had come in an hour or two before my visit, and settled his bill. Having done this, he had gone out again, and he had no expectation of again seeing his guest.

"How," I asked the man, "Did he discover

Calvert's name?"

"Why," said he, "One day, a month or two ago, I was dealing with a black fellow in market for some baskets of fruit, when this young man came up, and, speaking to the black, asked him some questions about Calverton, and directed the black to have certain things prepared against such a time, when he expected to bring several friends down who would be likely to spend the night there. I knew what and where Calverton was well enough, for who does not? And I had often had dealings for market stuff with the same dominic. I knew the last owner, and supposed that this might be the young man I heard he left the estate to. I looked at him narrowly, and, when his back was turned, asked the negro who it was. He said it was his master, Felix Calvert. When he first came to my house, I knew him again in a moment, though he was not dressed over and above nice, and I wondered that he should come to such an house as mine for a lodging, but, that you know, was none of my business. I remember when I first called him by his name, he stared at me as if he wondered how I should have found it out."

As to what was Calvert's motive for residing here, how his days were employed, and who were his associates, Walden was totally uninformed, and I left him, plunged in the most painful perplexity.

Clelia has actually left the city three days ago, for I called on her again, resolved to extort from her some explanation of this mystery. I found the doors and window-shutters closed and fastened, and no sign of an inhabitant within.

I am greatly disturbed. I know not whether to mention to you a suggestion that has lately occurred. I would willingly spare you needless inquietudes, but I hope I may rely, in every vicissitude, on your strength of mind. Hitherto I have always had reason to rely upon it.

Calvert's conduct has lately been inexplicable. I cannot account for it on any of the ordinary principles of human action. Misguided passions make many a man a paradox, but the passions, in their wildest energy, produce uniform appearances.

I now look back, with somewhat different eyes, upon my late interview with Calvert. I recollect his visible sincerity in denying my insinuations of falsehood, the tenor of his copious letter to you, and of that to his mother, the suddenness of his resolution to embark for Europe, and this lying incognito in a city where it is impossible that he should not be noticed by some friend or acquaintance.

Putting these things together, I have admitted a suspicion—yet I am loath, while I cannot forbear to admit it. No less averse am I to mention it, plausible as it now appears. But if this suspicion be true, we have hitherto acted most unwisely and unfortunately.

I am now earnestly desirous of meeting this youth, yet know not where to look for him. I have wandered the streets the better part of this day. I have been to all the places where he might possibly be found. I have inquired of the market-coming dominic, and been more than once at Walden's. No tidings of him. Perhaps he has left the city. Perhaps he has gone to Burlington.

I will write again shortly, have I not intelligence.

S. C.

Letter III.

To the same.

I write again, as I promised you, but with intelligence that will call forth all your astonishment, and, I fear, though unreasonably, all your grief.

Last night, after I had written to you, I walked out. That, you know, is my refuge from care. When any thing takes fast hold of my mind, and demands my meditations, I must walk. Since Woodward's garden has been open to all strollers, I usually betake myself to one of its embowered walks.

I had scarcely entered the garden, which, notwithstanding the radiance and mildness of the evening, had only two or three persons in it, when I saw, seated on a bench, in the broadest moon-shine, Felix Calvert! I passed him once, and surveyed him closely, that I might commit no mistake.

He seemed to look at me as I first passed, but spoke not, nor gave any sign of recognizing me. I presently returned, and took my seat close beside him. Still he chose not to recognize or to speak to me. Remembering the manner of our parting, I naturally imagined that he had adopted this mode of showing his resentment. I was at a loss in what manner to begin the conversation with him. At last, I made some trite remark upon the weather. He seconded my observation in the accent and air of one who is addressing an absolute stranger.

I was affected by this coldness, and still imput-ing it to his resentment, and conscious that his indignation was not wholly without foundation, I turned to him, and, pressing his hand in mine, said, in a conciliating tone, "Come, my dear Felix, let me persuade you to forget the harshness and austerity of my behaviour when we last met. I was wrong, and have ever since been anxious to repair the wrong by asking your pardon and promising a different behaviour for the future."

He looked at me with an air of astonishment, but cheerfulness, and said, "Really, I harbour no resent-ment against you, nor, indeed, if I know myself, against any human being. I accept your apology, therefore, though I know not, or have forgotten your offence."

The features of my companion, and the tones of his voice had a significance which I never observed in them before. They used to denote too much of that restless, changeful, and impetuous temper which reigned within, but now, I never saw a more benign complacency. His voice used likewise to be variable, and his utterance sometimes hurried and sometimes tardy, and at no time perfectly and distinctly clear, but now, none of these defects are perceived. I looked at him with great attention, and my former suspicion that all was not well with him, very forcibly recurred. I was at a loss in what manner to renew our discourse, and was silent.

"Pray," said he, "Permit me to ask where and how you and I, sir, were last together. I have really forgotten the event, and cannot outroot the persuasion that this is the first time I ever saw you. Your name, I beseech you, sir, that, perhaps may revive my recollections. My own name is Felix Calvert."

You may easily imagine how low my heart sunk at this address. I looked at him again to dispel the momentary doubt that my eyes had been deceived as to his person, but such deception was impossible. I was still silent, for what could I say?

He continued: "It is strange. This is not the first time, since my arrival in this city, that persons whom I never before saw, have accosted me by my name, and claimed me for an old acquaintance. I have been inexpressibly amazed and confounded, and was determined that I would not part with the next person who should chance to greet me in this style, till the meaning of this conduct was fully explained. You, sir, have chanced to be the next, and, as you seem to be more interested in my fate thanothers have been, I will not part with you till you have perfectly dispelled this mist. Whom do you take me to be, and what wasthe interview to which you have just alluded ?"

All this tended still more strongly to confirm my apprehensions. I could not conceal my distress. He noticed it.

"What a maze is here! You are greatly disturbed, sir. Am I, or is my deportment the cause of it? If we ever met before, it must have been beyond the ocean. So short a time has passed since my arrival, that I could not so soon have forgotten one with whom I have had any transactions in America. Did we ever meet in Europe?"

Judge of the effect which words like these were adapted to produce upon my feelings. At last, my reflections suggested the propriety of humoring this strange perversion, and I said, in a calmer tone, "Perhaps there is some mistake in one or both of us. I will willingly lay before you my reasons for supposing you one with whom I have been long acquainted, if you will favour me with your company to my house."

"With all my heart," said he.

In our way home, neither of us spoke. I was busied in ruminating on an accident so very mournful, for I need not telly ou that these appearances were, in my eyes, sufficient indications of intellects unsound. At length we entered the house and my study, and seated ourselves at opposite sides of a table, with lights between us. I once more fixed my eyes upon his countenance, which was very strongly illuminated. Its expression, so very different from what it used to be, struck me in a very forcible manner. Had I not prepared the means of accounting for this change, I should not have hesitated to pronounce myself mistaken as to his person.

"And now," said he, "Gratify my impatient curiosity. Where was it that you and I were formerly acquainted?"

I paused. What answer could I make?

"Perhaps," said he, "You have mistaken one person for another. Look at me attentively. It cannot be that the faces of different persons are perfectly alike. Some differences must exist to one familiarly acquainted with either. Look at me, sir. Such an error is not impossible nor unexampled."

This intimation now took hold of my belief for the first time. I was willing to suppose myself mistaken. To account for the past conduct of Felix, and for the scene that had just passed, by supposing him insane, was painful and abhorrent to my feelings.

"I complied, therefore, with his request. I perused his features with an eager scrutiny. Strange that I had not noted diversities before, but I had only seen him at a distance or by the dubious light of the moon. The well-known scar upon the left cheek of our friend, his hazel eyes, his dark hair, were utterly wanting in the image now before me.

Twice and thrice, clear and more clearly still, did I examine these features. My whole soul was in a tumult of amazement. These were the lineaments and proportions of Felix, but the eyes were blue, the cheek was smooth, and the hair of the lightest chestnut tint. Were these changes wrought by some omnific spell? And was the man before me absolutely different from your cousin? Yet, his name was Felix Calvert.

He observed my unceasing perplexity.

"What," said he, "have you discovered? Do you not perceive the cause of our mistake? For some mistake it has assuredly been."

"But your name," said I—

"Is Felix Calvert."

Again was I overwhelmed with doubts. How could the names thus exactly agree? "But your age?" said I.

"My birthday was the tenth of August, and I want two months of being nineteen years of age."

I need not tell thee, Lucy, that this was the birthday, and this the age of our Felix.

"Who are your parents?"

"I know them not. I never knew them. I lost them in my infancy. Yet they contrived to secure to me their name, and a knowledge of my age, by engraving them upon a piece of copper."

Thus far I perused, uninterruptedly, Sidney's letter. Here it dropped from my hand. My brain was for a moment clouded by that confusion which Sidney had naturally imagined to account for the contradictions he had witnessed. Thoughts, of such magnitude and number, rushed at once on my mind that they impeded and overturned each other. I held my hand to my forehead. I walked about the room with unequal steps. Surprise, joy, remorse took possession of me. Rapid recollections of my father's history, of his flight from his native country,of my twin-brother, whom my mother was compelled to leave behind her in the care of the faithful Alice, and of whom Alice was robbed by my vindictive grand-father, of the name of Felix, which, in a moment of foreboding, she inscribed upon a piece of worthless copper and fastened round the child's neck, and my change of name, my mother substituting for Stephen, which I first received, that of Felix, which had been conferred upon my brother, supposed by her to be irretrievably lost.

This is that stolen child, that long-lost brother,

whom some freak of nature has impressed with a powerful resemblance of me, and whom some propitious star has thus led to the bosom of his family. Now is the shriek which Clelia uttered in spying her preserver from her window explained, now is that being, for the sake of whom she fled from England, whom she imagined herself to have recognized in me, whose portrait she had, perhaps, clandestinely drawn, now is her mysterious distress, on discovering my real character and history, disrobed of all that created my wonder and anger!

This, then, is he whom Murphy and his sister talked of, *that* Felix Calvert whom they naturally supposed to have reappeared upon this stage, to have renewed his intercourse with Clelia, and this is he whom Sidney discovered at the draught-board? And whose similarity to their Felix, misled him and my cousin into such pernicious errors with regard to me.

But where is this inestimable brother who partakes existence with me in this intimate and wonderful degree? Has he been claimed by my cousin and my mother? Has he gained access to Clelia, and put an end to those doubts and to that distress which were visible at our last interview?

I was still rapidly musing upon these ideas when Sidney entered the room. His eye sparkled with some new and pleasurable meaning. The papers he had given me lay upon the table, and my countenance clearly bespoke the discovery which I had already made by their means.

"I need not ask you," said he, "whether you have read these papers. I see that you have. Have you any inquiries to make which the letter have not solved?"

Ten-thousand, said I, impetuously. Where is this brother? Has he seen your common parent? Does he know of my existence? Has he told you of his adventures?

"Stop," said Sidney, "Not so fast. These questions willmore probably be put to him than me. He is this moment in the outer room, and waits only my signal to enter. Stay a breath, and I will bring him to you." Sidney went out.

The state of my mind, during this interval, would not be easily portrayed. Every fibre in my frame was tremulous. My heart throbbed as if I were on the eve of some fatal revolution. The suddenness of this occurrence, the meeting with a brother so long severed from my side, and whose mode of birth made him, in some sort, an essential part of myself, seemed like passage into a new state of being. My suspenses were quickly at an end, for Sidney returned in a moment, leading in the stranger.

P. S. Calvert's story is a five-act drama. Here ends the first act, and this being in itself complete, the links connecting it with ensuing acts being only afterwards unfolded, it is thought best to stop the piece-meal publication of it here. The reader's fancy has now a clue to all that has heretofore bewildered him, and will easily imagine to itself the consequences of such a meeting as is now about to take place.

The End

www.ingramcontent.com/pod-product-compliance
Lightning Source LLC
Chambersburg PA
CBHW061319190726
48288CB00002B/570